"Guys can be counted on to ride off into the sunset sooner or later.

"Like cowboys," Molly explained.

"Into the sunset, huh? Sounds like you," Jeff observed.

"Yeah, like me," she said slowly. She hadn't thought about it before, but she was the female version of a cowboy. She was the one who would soon ride off into the sunset. So she needn't worry about her attraction to Jeff; the cowboy in her would keep her safe.

"You know, your daughter and I were talking...." Jeff said. "About her father." Warning lights flashed; Molly's heart nearly stopped. "Maybe she'd like some straight facts," he prompted.

Molly clenched her hands. What should she tell Lilly? What could she tell Jeff? "I don't really think it's any of your business," she said.

It was time to circle the wagons.

Dear Reader,

Welcome to Silhouette **Special Edition** . . . welcome to romance.
Each month, Silhouette **Special Edition** publishes six novels
with you in mind—stories of love and life, tales that you can
identify with—romance with that little "something special"
added in.

This month is packed full of goodies in celebration of
Halloween! Don't miss the continuation of Nora Roberts's
magical new series, THE DONOVAN LEGACY. This month
we're proud to present *Entranced*—Sebastian Donovan's story.
And in November, don't miss the third of this enchanting
series—*Charmed*.

October also launches a new series from Sherryl Woods—
VOWS. These warm, tender tales will light up the autumn and
winter nights with love. Don't miss *Love*—Jason Halloran's
story in October, *Honor*—Kevin Halloran's story in November
or *Cherish*—Brandon Halloran's story in December.

We're also pleased to introduce new author Sierra Rydell. Her
first Silhouette **Special Edition** will be published this month as
a PREMIERE title. It's called *On Middle Ground* and is set in
Alaska—the author's home state. This month, watch for the
debut of a new writer in each of Silhouette Books's four
lines: Silhouette **Special Edition**, Silhouette Romance,
Silhouette Desire and Silhouette Intimate Moments. Each
book will have the special PREMIERE banner on it.

Rounding out this exciting month are books from other
favorite writers: Andrea Edwards and Maggi Charles. And
meet Patt Bucheister—her first **Special Edition**, *Tilt at
Windmills*, debuts this month! Her work has been much
celebrated, and we're delighted she's joined us with this
wonderful book.

I hope you enjoy this book and all of the stories to come.

Sincerely,

Tara Gavin
Senior Editor
Silhouette Books

ANDREA EDWARDS
FATHER: UNKNOWN

Silhouette®

SPECIAL EDITION®

Published by Silhouette Books New York
America's Publisher of Contemporary Romance

To the Michiana Fiction Writers—
Sue, Ilse, Terry, Rosemary, Ruth and Frank—
thanks for all the help in keeping the names straight,
the story in line, and our meetings wild fun.

SILHOUETTE BOOKS
300 East 42nd St., New York, N.Y. 10017

FATHER: UNKNOWN

Copyright © 1992 by Ean Inc.

ISBN: 0-373-09770-0

First Silhouette Books printing October 1992

Printed in the U.S.A.

6/1-

Books by Andrea Edwards

Silhouette Special Edition

Rose in Bloom #363
Say It with Flowers #428
Ghost of a Chance #490
Violets Are Blue #550
Places in the Heart #591
Make Room for Daddy #618
Home Court Advantage #706
Sweet Knight Times #740
Father: Unknown #770

Silhouette Intimate Moments

Above Suspicion #291

Silhouette Desire

Starting Over #645

ANDREA EDWARDS

is the pseudonym of Anne and Ed Kolaczyk, a hus-
band-and-wife writing team that concentrates on
women's fiction. "Andrea" is a former elementary
schoolteacher, while "Edwards" is a refugee from
corporate America, having spent almost twenty-five
years selling computers before becoming a full-time
writer. They have four children, two dogs and four
cats, and they live in Indiana.

CERTIFICATE OF LIVE BIRTH

CHILD—NAME: Baby Girl Cahill

DATE OF BIRTH: August 8, 1983

SEX: Female

WEIGHT: 7 lbs. 8 oz.

PLACE OF BIRTH: Denver

MOTHER—MAIDEN NAME: Molly Anne Cahill

BIRTHPLACE: Niles, Michigan

AGE: 17 years

FATHER—NAME: Unknown

BIRTHPLACE: Unknown

Prologue

September 10, 1982

Dear Diary,

Maggie and I hit the big 1-7 at last! Everybody was over for our party. Mrs. Kowalski wanted us all to go into the church so she could play "Happy Birthday" on the organ. Maggie was late because Mom wanted her to take a look at my English Lit essay and Mags got caught up in the excitement of helping me get a B. I wish Mom would lose her guilt and let me take courses that I can handle on my own. Problems can occur in any birth; it doesn't mean she was a lousy mother.

While we waited for Maggie, Gram told us all a story about her mother, who was a twin. Dad got pissed off because I knew all the family relationships. He wanted to know why I could remember all that information but couldn't remember my French vocabulary. Mom had a guilt trip and burst into tears. Gram told Dad I was the family chronicler, so it was my job to know the family history. Geez, the way he acted, you'd think I had touched something in Danny's room!

The new kid Dad hired to clean the church grounds came over to get his work schedule during the party. It turned out to be Niles's own James Dean, Jeff Spencer from my government class! Those moody, broody eyes of his turn my insides to jelly, though I think Dad would like to outlaw his jeans. I said hi, but Jeff acted like he didn't know me. Maggie said not to bother, that he doesn't speak to anybody.

The folks gave me and Mags matching jean skirts and jackets. I got money from the aunts and uncles—my Escape-from-Niles fund is very healthy—and the strangest old pin from Grandma. It was a heart tied with a golden cord. Gram said it meant that the family is only as strong as love that binds it together. Can I be the family chronicler if I'm a thousand miles away? Telling Gram I'm leaving is going to be the hardest thing!

November 28, 1982

Dear Diary,
Champagne corks flew today. Maggie got accepted at Harvard! Dad was so happy, he cried. He's going to get a doctor in the family yet, if they can scrape together the twenty thou a year. When they all started to relive Danny's year at Harvard, I went over to Gram's and put the Christmas lights on the trees out front. Gram said everybody's got to have room to grow on their own—me away from Maggie, Maggie away from Danny's shadow, even Jeff Spencer away from his dad. The rumor his dad ended up in the emergency room after a brawl at O'Day's must be true! Not that I care. I'd still give anything if Jeff would ask me to the Christmas formal.

December 6, 1982

Dear Diary,
The entire universe is at the Niles High Christmas formal tonight, except for me! I'm such a reject. I've got a million boy friends, but can't get a *boyfriend* to save my life. Julie said I should have worked harder on Jeff, but I feel so stupid when I try to flirt. At least, I don't think he's taking anybody else. Staying home with Mom and Dad was pure torture. Mom fussed worse than a mother hen, telling me she just didn't know why the boys in town were so blind. I was pretty and so nice, with the best sense of humor. When she offered to fix me up with Mrs. Kowalski's neighbor, I came down with an acute case of leprosy. A blind date arranged by your mother? Not in my lifetime! I finally escaped to my room to read an article about Niles transplants in L.A. One day, I'm going to be the lead-in to an article like that. *Molly Cahill, international movie star, renovates local theater so fans can enjoy her movies!* Jeff Spencer will be sorry then he didn't date me when he had the chance.

Dad really blew up at Maggie before she left for the dance. Said her dress was cut too low and made her change into the one she wore last year. Okay, so the new one was a little daring. Half his congregation was not going to see her and call her a sleaze. Maggie was really pissed by the time Tim got here!

January 22, 1983

Dear Diary,
Well, Molly the Moron got rescued once again by Maggie the Magnificent. I only asked for some help studying, but she said it was easier just to take the test for me. I know I should be grateful, but I'm so tired of always looking to

Maggie for help. Before she was taking my semester tests, it was book reports and chapter outlines. One summer, Mom even made her share her book list for the library's summer reading program, so that I wouldn't be the only Winnie-the-Pooh that hadn't reached the Honey Pot. Julie says I'm crazy to mind, that she wishes she had a sister like Maggie so she could pass Physics.

I am not wasting another minute of my life on Jeff the Jerk! All I did was offer to help him shovel the sidewalk and he bit my head off, asking me why I was suddenly talking to him. As if I never tried to talk to him before! I hope he collapses in a snowbank and freezes to death. See if I come to his rescue!

April 10, 1983

Dear Diary,
Maggie decided this semester would be trouble the minute she saw her schedule.

What if I can't pass English Lit on my own? Maybe Mom shouldn't have made me take it. And what'll happen if I don't pass? Mom will cry and Dad will disown me. This way, they'll be glad to see the end of me.

Dad fired Jeff yesterday for coming to work "smelling like a brewery." I thought Dad was awful, even if I have crossed Jeff off my list. Dad didn't even give Jeff a chance to explain. When I told Dad this later, he bit my head off. He said he had an example to set, he couldn't condone teenage drinking, Jeff needed to learn the hard truths of life. Nice talk for a minister! I'm grounded for the next month.

April 12, 1983

Dear Diary,
Mags got out of French class for a "doctor's" appointment and took my Lit midterm. I had to vanish, of course,

and went down to River Park. Two more months, I told myself, and I'd be gone. Free to be me. No excuses or apologies. I owe Maggie about half my soul, but maybe getting her freedom from me will be gift enough. She's got to be tired of me hanging on her, too.

It was a beautiful afternoon. I had about half the acceptance speech for my Oscar written when I was interrupted by Jeff. He was surly as ever and demanding to know who I was this time. Good question, since I was supposed to be Maggie. But then, I was also supposed to be at the doctor. I tried to tell him I was sorry about the way Dad acted and that he should have been given a chance to defend himself. Geez, he could be taking some lifesaving medicine that happened to smell like beer and be innocent of Dad's accusations! Jeff just laughed. I mean, really laughed. He told me it was nothing so dramatic. His dad had spilled a six-pack in the car and the smell was still stinking up everything. I thought he should tell Dad and get his job back, but he said he didn't want it. The pay was lousy, the work was boring and the people patronizing. Real nice guy! I did a great Greta Garbo imitation and left. Don't know why I try to talk to him.

April 29, 1983

Dear Diary,

Papers came from Harvard today. Maggie's not getting all the scholarship help she was hoping for. Gloomsville all around! I suggested that she should go to a state school and live her own life instead of Danny's, and got grounded again.

Jeff left town. What a dummy! A month until graduation and he throws it all away. Even I know a high school diploma's better than nothing.

May 15, 1983

Dear Diary,
Maggie won the Niles Ladies Club scholarship and is going to Harvard after all. She cried when she got the news, but her tears seemed too real. About 2:00 a.m., I found out why. She's pregnant! Whoa! Perfect Maggie pregnant? I had to promise on a stack of my movie magazines that I wouldn't tell, and then all she told me was to go to sleep.

I don't think she's told Tim. When I asked her, she told me she didn't want to talk about it. I've never seen him without his grungy old Cubs hat. I wonder if he wore it when they were doing *it*.

May 16, 1983

Dear Diary,
It was building fund meeting night, so I had Maggie all to myself and made her talk. She's six months pregnant already! She's known for two months, but hasn't known how to tell anybody. Everyone's counting on her. She didn't say I wasn't going to do anything to make them all proud, but we both thought it. Well, maybe I wasn't going to be the doctor Dad wanted but did that make me a black sheep?

May 19, 1983

Dear Diary,
Maggie rewrote my term paper—Mom calls it helping—then backed me into a corner. She couldn't let anyone know she was pregnant, she told me. She would lose the Ladies Club scholarship and the chance to go to Harvard. That would kill the folks. Since our brother, Danny, died, they were pinning all their hopes and dreams on her and

she couldn't let them down. They did have another child, I wanted to point out, but didn't. What she was saying was right. I'm just an embarrassment to Dad and source of guilt to Mom. Anyway, Maggie had it all thought out so that she wouldn't lose that Ladies Club scholarship. I was to tell the folks I was pregnant! And that I would go out to Denver to stay with Aunt Agnes. Maggie, being a kind and perfect sister, would go with me, except that we'd switch identities. She'd be pregnant Molly, have her baby and give it up for adoption, then come back home in time to leave for Harvard where she would achieve the family dreams. I could move on, just as I planned. It was all perfect. I guess I am stupid because it didn't seem so perfect to me!

May 20, 1983

Dear Diary,
Maggie said we could tell them Jeff Spencer was the baby's father since he was gone and therefore un-shotgunable. As if they'd buy that! The guy wouldn't have noticed me if I was lying naked on the hood of his car and Mags thinks they'll believe we were lovers! I said she and Tim should own up to their mistake, that Mom and Dad and the McGinns could take it. At dinner, she hinted at not attending Harvard and Dad swore. A first for him, at least in our hearing. Mom cried. I excused myself.

Everything Maggie says is right! They've pinned all their happiness on her, not me. I was planning on leaving anyway, and God knows I owe her. So why am I up here in our room stewing? Because I wanted to be able to return in triumph someday, not sneak out in disgrace.

May 21, 1983

Dear Diary,
Today was six years since Danny's accident. It felt like it was just yesterday. People came over all day to offer their

condolences and the only thing that brought a smile to Mom or Dad's face was talking about Maggie and Harvard. Being able to return in triumph seems so juvenile.

May 22, 1983

Dear Diary,
I told Maggie I'd do it. I already regret it and am more than a little ticked off at her, but I'll keep my word. Having the folks mad at me for a while to protect their dreams is a small price to pay.

Why does Tim get off scot-free? Maggie says she can't stand him anymore, that she never liked him all that much. She liked him well enough at least once, I pointed out, but she ignored me.

June 3, 1983

Dear Diary,
Graduation day. Hardly the celebration anybody envisioned. Mom's spent the past week crying, while Dad's done nothing but yell about disgrace and shame and my lack of morals, especially since I said I had no intention of marrying the baby's father. Mags and I leave for Denver tomorrow and it'll be a relief to go. It's pure hell here. Julie keeps asking me why I'm leaving so fast. She'd thought we'd have the whole summer together. Gram must have hugged me ten million times. She slipped me ten dollars for snacks on the trip, and a family photo album she'd put together for me. She told me to live my own life, something I plan on doing just as soon as possible!

June 4, 1983

Dear Diary,
Well, we're here in Denver. I am now Maggie, college-bound and overachiever. Agnes is great. She runs a bar and has a big, airy apartment on the second floor. Turns out

she left Niles about twenty-five years ago with the rodeo and hasn't looked back since. I've already looked back about six hundred times, but the door's always been closed. I wish we hadn't hurt Mom so much.

June 15, 1983

Dear Diary,
Maggie's really started to show since we came out here. We went down to a rummage sale and got her a load of freaky maternity clothes. I wanted to take her picture, but she practically chewed my head off when I suggested it.

Agnes has a million stories about cowboys, her fatal weakness as she calls them. Don't matter if they wear a suit and tie or jeans, if they are ready to ride out into the sunset rather than make a commitment, they're a cowboy. She says her bar is full of them, so we shouldn't take any of them seriously.

June 30, 1983

Dear Diary,
Agnes and Maggie haven't been getting along too well. Agnes says a woman pays, no matter what decisions she makes about her baby, but keeping it, at least she knows it's safe. Maggie turned on a soap opera.

July 4, 1983

Dear Diary,
While Agnes was busy in her bar, Mom called to see how we all were. Dad was "too busy" to come to the phone. I know what that means. Mom talked to Maggie mostly. She's been sewing up a storm of clothes for the great one to take to Harvard. I felt like telling her that none of them

would fit Maggie now, but went out for a long walk instead. It's confusing having one identity here and jumping back to the real me when Mom calls. L.A. doesn't seem so alluring anymore, not since this drama I've been living. Maybe I'll get an apartment here in Denver and take some classes at night. Agnes was waiting up for me when I got back and we looked at Gram's photo album together. Agnes had the goods on everybody! Dad got caught smoking behind the fire station when he was eight and their father made him smoke a cigar until he threw up. Aunt Flo ran down a guy who tried to get into her car without permission, putting him in the hospital. Mom never dated anyone until Dad, then always wanted Aunt Flo to go with them because she was so shy. I said I was like Mom, hardly dating, but Agnes said she thinks I'm strong like Flo, that I just haven't noticed yet.

July 24, 1983

Dear Diary,

I called Gram today. It was good to hear her voice! She was so concerned about me, wanting to know how I was feeling and everything. She said I should have stayed in Niles to have the baby, that even if Dad didn't realize it, the days of hiding girls away were gone. I didn't say much since we could never have pulled this off in Niles, but I do wish I hadn't left the way I did. Too many doors seem closed now. To give Maggie credit, I don't think she expected Dad's reaction. Not that she's suggested telling the truth. We don't talk much anymore, sort of like we've agreed that we'll abide by this little pretense and then go our own ways. It's kind of sad, but then I wonder if we ever were really that close. Maybe I just assumed that we must be because we were twins.

August 8, 1983

Dear Diary,
Maggie had her baby today! It's a little girl. All Maggie talked about was how much it hurt and how she couldn't wait to get home and put all of this behind her. They brought the baby in while I was there and let me hold her. She's so tiny, all red and wrinkles! I told her all about me and Mags (much to Maggie's disapproval, as if the kid will remember it all and spill the beans in the future), about Mom and Dad and Danny. I felt bad that she'd never get to know any of us, and we'd never get to watch her play soccer or dance in ballet recitals. She's a part of us, of all those people Gram told me about, but she'll never know who she got her eyes from or whose genes help her make that hook shot.

I thought it was the mother that went through postpartum blues!

August 9, 1983

Dear Diary,
Slept lousy last night and finally gave up trying. I went through my album again, and again. I don't know what Maggie's feeling, but I feel awful! Agnes got up to sit with me. She doesn't think most teenage mothers realize the lasting consequences of their decisions. A baby isn't something you can have and then forget about once it's no longer there in front of you. She knows because she was pregnant when she came out here. She gave up her son and never saw him again. She said she offered to help if my sister wanted to keep the baby, but no dice.

August 10, 1983

Dear Diary,
Went to see Maggie and Little Wrinkles today. Maggie pored over the latest issue of *Seventeen* while I held the baby. My mind got made up. I want to keep her. I want us to be her past. I want her to be our future. Maggie had a fit, like everything was going to come out if I did. What's to come out? The birth certificate says the mother is Molly Cahill and that's me. I can choose to keep my own baby, can't I? Maggie refused to even consider it, so I pulled a trick from her book—I keep the baby or I tell the truth! Guess who's a mother now?

August 11, 1983

Dear Diary,
We switched identities again and I'm back to publicly being me. Agnes was so excited that "I" had changed my mind about keeping the baby that she didn't notice that Maggie was the one moving stiffly. Mags leaves tomorrow and it'll be a relief. There's just too many ways she could slip up and let the cat out of the bag.

September 10, 1983

Dear Diary,
Eighteen years old, but the party was a lot smaller this year. Agnes bought a cake from the bakery down the street and got me a catalog from a junior college about a mile away, but was too busy in the bar to spend much time with me. Gram sent money, apologizing for its "lack of originality." Mom called. Dad was "busy." Didn't hear from Maggie. Strangely though, it was the best birthday I could

remember because Lilly (named after Lillian Foster Trundell for Gram) was quite happy to spend her whole day with me!

Chapter One

"Okay, Mom. This time you be Willie and I'll be Waylon."

Molly Cahill looked into the rearview mirror and frowned into her daughter's brown eyes. "How about this time we all relax and be quiet?"

"Aw, Mom," Lilly protested, her soft brown curls bouncing as she pouted.

"We'll get Rufus to whining."

Agnes leaned back over the front seat to look at the dog stretched out next to Lilly. "Yep, that sure is one high-strung dog. We best be real still so's we don't get him to fussing."

Molly could feel the older woman wink at Lilly and heard the almost-smothered laughter nine-year-olds were so good at, but couldn't join in their teasing. All right, so she wasn't really worried about Rufus. The big phlegmatic mongrel could sleep through the raising of the dead.

No, she was worried about this stupid trip. It was nine years since she'd been home. Nine years since Lilly had been born and—

"This is like really boring, Mom." Lilly had a definitely grumpy tone in her voice.

"I'll say," Agnes added. "I mean, look at the land. Nothing but green. Can't get more boring than that."

"Maybe we just should have stayed home then," Molly said, more than half-wishing they had. The knots in her stomach had been pulling tighter with each mile they drove. She'd thought they had a stranglehold on her lungs as she'd crossed the Michigan border, but found as she slowed for the Route 12 turnoff, that they could still pull tighter. She took first one hand then the other off the steering wheel to wipe her sweaty palms on her jeans.

Somehow satisfying Lilly's curiosity about the family didn't seem so urgent anymore.

"Was my grandfather the one who used to sneak smokes over back of the fire station?" Lilly asked. "It's hard to remember all the different relatives."

"Don't worry, kid," Agnes said, as she turned to smile at Lilly. "I have a memory like an elephant and I've got the goods on all of them."

As Lilly flashed a quick smile in return, the farm fields began to give way to sturdy frame homes nestled under towering oak trees. Welcome to Niles. Sidewalks and curbs appeared and Molly slowed to the city speed limit. Slowed down to let the past catch up with her. Old men mowed lawns, teenage boys washed cars and a squalling toddler on a molded plastic rocking horse raced away to nowhere. Nothing had changed from nine years ago except that the old men now wore headphones attached to cassette players, too.

They drove past the YMCA, then over the St. Joseph River and into downtown Niles. Broadway was still lined with stores. A bookstore, a bait shop and a sports card store vied for attention from the meager crowd out, but there were more than a few empty storefronts. The bakery where Molly had been sent to buy bread every Saturday morning was gone, replaced by a video rental place. Molly paused at the intersection at the top of the hill, then went straight through.

"I thought the parsonage was south of us," Agnes said.

"I need some gas."

Agnes leaned over to look at the fuel indicator sitting at about three quarters full. Her lips twisted into a knowing smile before she sat back in the seat.

"Some people like to drive around on the fumes," Molly pointed out. "I don't."

"I didn't say anything," Agnes said.

Too bad, Molly thought to herself, a good fight might knock the jitters out of her system. She turned into an anonymous-looking filling station and pulled alongside a bank of self-service pumps. This could be anywhere in the country, not a half mile from her father. She could breathe in the anonymous air and absorb the anonymous decor and regain her equilibrium.

"Stay in the car with Rufus, honey," Molly said as she climbed out. "I won't be long."

And with only a quarter tank to fill, it didn't take long. But those few moments were exactly what she needed. Time to remind herself that she was grown-up, that she had shed her old image and was a responsible, respected adult. Time to steel her soul for that meeting with dear old Dad.

The silence of the gas pump suddenly woke her from her thoughts. She slammed the nozzle back into its receptacle with a reawakened determination and screwed the cover onto the tank. They were going to have a nice visit no matter what. She strode briskly toward the station to pay.

Two weeks, that was as long as they were staying. She was strong enough to take on her father for fourteen days; then if he was being a jerk, they would leave right after the reunion. She was about to reach for the station door when she froze in midstride at the sight of the youngish man leaving.

Jeff was as tall as ever but not as gangly. He'd filled out. In fact, he'd filled out quite nicely but, while his eyes were still shadowed and murky as the river, his mouth looked more used to laughing than she remembered.

She wasn't the only one back home.

"Hey, Maggie," he cried as he burst through the door. "What ya doing? Slumming it?"

Maggie! Whatever spark of pleasure had appeared at seeing him again was stomped out. She was not Maggie! She'd cut her hair, gone to college and become a totally different person since she'd left this little burg. Yet this big lummox still thought she was her twin sister. Obviously, Jeff Spencer hadn't changed a bit. He was still the same jerk he'd been back in high school when he hadn't noticed she was alive.

"Mom," Lilly called from their car. "Rufus wants to go out."

"Just a minute, honey. Let me—"

"Mom?" Jeff stared at her, then turned his piercing gaze toward the Bronco. "You've got Colorado plates."

"That's the way it works," Molly said. "You buy your license plates in the state where you live."

Uncertainty dimmed his smile, but only for a moment. "Good golly," he said with a laugh. "If it ain't Miss Molly."

"Just plain Molly will be fine. If that's too informal for your tastes, Ms. Cahill will do just as well."

The sarcasm seemed to have no effect on Jeff. He pushed his floppy cowboy hat back and let his grin spread out even more. Enough to cover the rest of the state, including the Upper Peninsula.

Molly couldn't remember him ever smiling. It looked as if he were trying to make up for his sullen youth in a two-minute time frame. And her silly soul seemed ready to laugh with him.

"Molly Cahill." Jeff shook his head again. "You and Maggie are still as alike as two peas in a pod."

Just what she wanted to hear. "How nice." Molly forced a smile to her lips. "That means we'll still be able to trade clothes."

"Not for a while," Jeff replied. "She's getting a little big around the middle. She's going to be a momma."

"So I hear." This was just how she'd dreamed her first ten minutes back in town would be spent—discussing Maggie. Next he'd be telling her that Maggie was married to the president of a small college just over the state line in South Bend and was in the final years of her family practice residency. A frantic whining behind Molly signaled the approaching cavalry. She turned as Lilly and Rufus reached her.

"He really had to go, Mom," Lilly assured her as Rufus sat at Molly's feet, looking inordinately proud of himself for finding her. "It's been ages since he got out of the car."

Molly just gave her rescuers a small smile and turned back to Jeff. "Contrary to how it sounds, neither Rufus nor any of us live in the car. This is my daughter, Lilly, who is prone to exaggeration. Lilly, this is Mr. Spencer, someone I knew back in high school."

"Make that Jeff," he said and stuck out his hand for hers.

Lilly stared at it for a moment as if it were an alien species, then carefully shook it. "Did you really know my mom in high school?"

"Sure did. And your Aunt Maggie, too."

Lilly frowned and Molly rushed in. "Mom and Grandma Lillian have come out to visit us in Denver, but Maggie's never made it out there. Lilly hasn't met her yet."

"So is this your first trip to Niles?" Jeff asked Lilly. "Watch out then. Your mom and Maggie like to play tricks on people. You'd better make sure it's really your mom tucking you in each night."

"Hey!"

But Lilly viewed it as a bone to sink her teeth into. "Did you really pretend you were each other?" she asked Molly.

"A few times." Molly swallowed hard. "But that was a long time ago. We're both too old for such games now." Before either could argue the point, Molly gave Jeff a broad smile and took a step closer to the filling station door. "I guess I'll see you around."

"Oh, no doubt about that," Jeff said. "The one thing about Niles that hasn't changed is its size."

Somehow Molly kept her smile in place as she ordered Lilly and Rufus back to the car and herself into the station. She had the world's worst luck. The first person she meets in town accidentally stumbles onto the secret she'd held in her heart for nine years. She handed a twenty-dollar bill to the high-schooler behind the counter.

It was just a joke, she assured herself. No one knew the truth, no one but Maggie, and she sure wasn't telling. This was just a small town where everybody knew everybody and made jokes about your past. She couldn't jump every time someone made a reference to her and Maggie's switcheroos.

She stared at the hand-drawn posters lining the window of the station, willing the peace and serenity of the small town into her soul. Ice cream socials, community plays. And a rummage sale at her father's church next weekend. This was a place where kids could walk to town and back without getting jumped by gangs, where a woman could walk alone at night. This was a safe place; she and Lilly would be safe here.

The teenage attendant returned her change. "Here you go, Mrs. Novak. Boy, looking at you, nobody'd guess you're going to have a baby in December."

Here we go again. Molly just grunted as she slipped her money into her wallet. She was not about to explain her identity to some kid, but something about him nagged at her, kept drawing her eyes back up to him. Was it the freckles smeared so liberally across his face or the strange bend in his right eyebrow? His name tag said Bill Sheehan, but—

"Good Lord," Molly cried. "You're Scooter Sheehan."

He was staring at her as if her elevator had skipped a few floors. "Yeah. Or I used to be. Nobody's called me that for years."

He was Julie's little brother, who used to tag along after Molly and Julie when they were sixteen and he was about six. He'd heard her and Julie moan about their lack of dates often enough and would offer to be her boyfriend when he grew up.

Even he had known she didn't have a boyfriend.

"I didn't recognize you at first," she stammered. She was unable to admit she was Molly, as if just hearing her name would get him started recounting her dateless past and speculating on her lack of chances to get pregnant. She backed toward the door. "See you."

Lord, had she ever been wrong! This wasn't a safe place for her and Lilly; it was about the most dangerous place imaginable. She needed anonymity. She needed to be a faceless cipher in among a crowd of strangers. Here everyone knew her, knew her history. How could they not all discover her secret?

She climbed back into the car, deaf to Agnes and Lilly's chatter, and pulled smartly out into the street.

"That Spencer boy is certainly his father's son."

"What?"

"He's such a handsome hunk. Just like his father was."

"Was he your boyfriend?" Lilly asked Molly.

"My boyfriend!" Molly repeated, concentrating on changing over to the left-turn lane. "Goodness, no. He was just someone I knew a long time ago."

"Geez, Mom, you got to have had a boyfriend sometime. I mean, *everybody* has a boyfriend. Agnes has her cowboys and I've got Rufus."

"Rufus is your boyfriend?" Molly jumped at the change of subject.

"He's my best friend and he's a boy. Is my dad the only guy you ever dated?"

"Of course not." Where were these questions coming from? Was the past bouncing about on invisible rays, waiting for Lilly to come along and decode it? Molly hoped not. "I've gone out with Zack and Mr. Morgan and Mr. Bieschke."

"Cowboys," Lilly scoffed. Her voice was frowning. "Is Jeff a cowboy? He was wearing a cowboy hat."

"I don't know." Molly said. "He might be. He sure liked being unattached when we were in high school." Just like the cowboys she'd known.

First Street came up all too fast and Molly had no excuses this time. She turned left and saw the church looming ahead of them almost immediately. The dark red brick structure looked as if it had stood there forever, its steeple emerging from a froth of trees. The knots of tension returned and Molly looked for a distraction from her worries.

"Jeff thought I was Maggie," she told Agnes.

"You two are identical twins," Agnes said.

"But we've been apart nine years."

"I don't think that matters. I've seen articles about twins separated at birth who still did things the same. Like cutting their hair the same and wearing the same type of clothes."

"Swell," Molly grumbled. "We can just slip back into the way things were in high school. The past nine years will be like some kind of time warp." She would be overshadowed by Maggie and have an unrequited crush on Jeff. She pulled to a stop in front of the church.

"Is this it?" Lilly asked. "Boy, you didn't have much of a yard to play in."

"Didn't have any. The lawn was off-limits."

"Looks the same as always," Agnes muttered.

And it did, from the green wrought-iron handrail on the church steps to the wax begonias along the walk. Would the people inside be the same, too, with the same prejudices and angers?

Molly turned off the engine. The parish offices and meeting hall were in another building, newer than the church but faintly echoing its line. Far back from the street between the two, butted up against a covered walkway, was the parsonage. Home.

Molly's hands trembled slightly as she took Rufus's leash and got out of the car. Things would go right. Her father could be cool with her but he had to be nice to Lilly. No matter what the circumstances of her birth, she was his grandchild. His only grandchild.

"Agnes?" a man's voice called.

They all looked toward the covered walkway. Molly's parents and Grandma Lillian had come out. Molly's father, more gray and frail than she ever expected, came forward.

"Charles," Agnes said with a nod as she put her arm around Lilly's shoulder, pulling the child to her side. "Lilly, say hello to Grandpa Chuckie."

"Hi, Grandpa Chuckie."

Even from where she stood back a few yards, Molly could see her father's cheeks quiver as he looked down at Lilly. He said nothing, and the world seemed to hold its breath. The birds stilled their songs.

Didn't he see how beautiful she was? Couldn't he feel the wealth of love she had to offer?

Lilly just squinted up at him. "Do you still sneak over to the fire station to smoke?" she asked.

Molly's father laughed, and the world came alive again. He bent to hug Lilly to his chest. "No, honey. I don't smoke anymore, but I still play cards with the firemen."

Molly's heart relaxed, softened into a pool of mush at the sight of Lilly's dark brown hair against her father's gray. Lilly would have a good time here. Molly's worst fears were not going to be realized.

But then her father was releasing Lilly, his eyes searching for Molly's and locking into her gaze. He straightened up.

"Molly." His voice was rough and pleading as he stared at her, seeming to want to take those few steps toward her, but not able to. Something in her soul couldn't help him, couldn't make things easy for him.

"It's good to see you again," he finally said.

She only nodded and dragged Rufus along with her as she went to greet her mother and grandmother.

The evening shadows had pushed the summer's heat back and the air near the river stirred slightly. It always was a bit cooler down here, Jeff thought as he climbed out onto the rocks along the river's edge to sit on the farthest one. The good old St. Joe. It had been a refuge for longer than he cared to remember. Something about the way the current sped along, hurrying off to sights unknown, to days that promised to be better than today.

Not that he needed that kind of refuge anymore. No, just a break from the heat was enough.

He remembered being upset once as a kid because the spring floods had left a huge tree jammed up against the bridge pylons, slowing the flow and catching debris. He'd shared the despair of the odd branches caught by the tree and held prisoner while all the others ran free.

Life had been a Shakespearean tragedy back then.

A friendly bark off to his left made him turn. A motley-looking dog was staring at him, wagging its tail. Rufus. Molly joined the dog at the river's edge, seeming slightly startled to see him.

"Hi," she said, then added, "I'm Molly."

"I know."

"Sure."

Her baby blues hardened with skepticism. He remembered her being meeker, less challenging. Looked like she'd buried the little mouse somewhere along the way.

"You've got to be Molly. Maggie wouldn't let a dog within ten feet of her."

Rufus splashed into the water to retrieve a stick, then dropped it at Molly's feet. She picked it up and flung it across the grass.

"Where's your other buddy?" Jeff asked.

"Exploring Grandma Lillian's house."

"That where you're staying?"

"Yup. There's more room there than at the parsonage."

"Your husband have to stay back in Denver?"

Something changed in the air. Molly turned to study Rufus's approach. "Lilly's father has never lived with us," she said.

That's right. She'd introduced herself as Ms. Cahill back at the gas station. He moved over on his rock.

"Got another ringside seat here, if you're interested," he said.

Molly looked at Rufus, who had abandoned his stick in favor of trailing something in the weeds. With a shake of her head that clearly said "What the hell," Molly climbed over to join Jeff.

She was surefooted and agile, but took his proffered hand for help over the last rock. Her touch was solid and strong, surprisingly inviting. He wasn't at all sure he wanted to let go of it, but she made the decision for him by letting go as she sat down.

Up close, she still looked like Maggie, but he could see—rather sense—differences. Her blue eyes seemed less troubled, more prone to happiness. They had a boldness about them, too, that appealed to him. Maggie always seemed so careful, so concerned about appearances, but Molly seemed strong enough to be herself.

She caught him staring at her and, like a kid, he felt the urge to stammer some explanation. Instead he stared out at the water until his voice returned. "Peaceful spot, isn't it?"

Molly laughed. "Depends on who else is around. I met an absolute grump here once."

The day came back to him. It was just after Molly's father had fired him. It had been the final straw; one more person pretending to be kind and understanding but being just as prejudiced as the rest. He had been one of those twigs caught by the tree and unable to break free.

He'd left town the next day. A clean, sudden break before more expectations tied him down.

And here he was back again.

"I guess the river's been my one constant," he said, turning to smile at Molly. "I used to think if I sat here long enough, I'd see some of the early settlers. French fur traders, Spanish missionaries and British soldiers, along with American pioneers."

"I always thought it was unfair to call this place the City of Four Flags," she said. "After all, the Indians were here first. The very least folks could have done was to give them a flag of their own."

"Were you always a champion of the underdog?" he asked. The idea surprised him. He hadn't known her at all, had he. She had been so quiet and meek as a teen, and he'd been so full of his own angers.

"I wasn't able to champion anything back then," she said. "But I guess I could relate to underdogs, feeling like one myself."

"Because of Maggie?"

She nodded and her eyes took on the shadowy depth of the river. "She just did everything better than me. I ran a very distant second in every race."

"Every one?"

Laughter claimed her lips, bringing a sweet light to her face as the past faded. "I wasn't ready to see that I could do anything well back then. I was a bit of a mouse."

"Maggie could be intimidating." And more than that. She made people notice her, knew how to get what she wanted. She had a ruthless streak behind all her polite mannerisms.

"I guess I had to leave to find myself."

"And now you're a teacher, I hear," Jeff said. She would be good at it with her calm, accepting aura.

"Yep," Molly replied, nodding. "Special education."

"Oh, yeah? I've got a summer program started for special-needs kids."

She frowned at him. "What do you do?"

"I'm the program director at the YMCA here in town. Get to play games all day."

The stillness of her eyes said she wasn't fooled by his jokes.

He shrugged. "Hey, if I can help some kid avoid the pitfalls I've fallen into, then I've accomplished something."

"What did you do after you left here?"

It was old news that he didn't particularly want to rehash. "Oh, just roamed around for a while, made some mistakes and got a little smarter."

"And you came back here."

"Yep. Who could pass up the chance to be the one picking the teams for the rest of your life?"

She smiled. "No more being last one chosen."

"Or not chosen at all." He hadn't meant to bring that shadow back on the evening and forced a smile. "So are you going to be able to give me any help with my special-needs program? Even advice would be a start."

She laughed, the soft tinkling of a bell. "We're not going to be here long."

He shrugged. "I'd appreciate your input."

"I don't see how I'll have time."

Rufus's trailing was leading him closer to the parking lot and Molly stood. "Rufus, come." She turned back to Jeff. "I'd better get on back. Lilly can wear out the most energetic person alive."

"We've got a morning sports program at the Y she might enjoy. Sign-ups are on a week-by-week basis."

"We'll look into it."

Before he could think up any way to make her stay, she was climbing over the rocks and jogging back up the path toward the street. Rufus was running a zigzag course ahead of her to clear the path of invisible varmints. In a moment, she was out of sight behind the trees and Jeff was alone with the river again.

The shadows had grown long and the comfort of the place was gone. For the first time since he was a teenager, being alone felt . . . lonely.

Chapter Two

With darkness falling over the city, it was harder to distinguish the past from the present. Rufus seemed Molly's only link with today, and even that seemed tenuous when he would linger in the shadows, sniffing bushes.

Funny, Jeff being back here. She should have asked him why he'd come back, but she'd been afraid of knowing too much, of being caught once again by her foolish heart. She'd built a safe life elsewhere; this foray into dangerous waters was temporary.

"Hey, Mom." Lilly came flying out the front door, her cheeks flushed and her eyes sparkling with excitement. "Guess what me and Grandpa were doing."

"I have no idea," Molly said, glancing up at her father, who had slowly followed Lilly outside.

"We moved you into a different bedroom," Lilly said, the words tumbling out over one another as if she feared that Molly would issue a restraining order. "You were in my grandma's old room and Grandpa said I could have it."

Molly glanced up to find her father looking almost sheepish. "W-we moved your things into the south bedroom," he stammered. "That way you won't get the early-morning sun."

"Yeah, Mom," Lilly added. "You can sleep a whole lot longer."

Lilly was leading Rufus up the steps. Molly followed.

"I'm overwhelmed by all this concern for my beauty rest," Molly said.

"My room is really neat," Lilly went on, ignoring Molly's attempt at sarcasm. "Grandpa showed me where the secret stairway is, so I can climb up into the tower."

Molly slowly nodded. Grandma Lillian's house was an old Victorian with gingerbread, tall windows and several luxurious porches. The tower was on the third floor at the front of the house, and had been Molly's favorite place when she was young. She'd spent many quiet hours up there herself, hiding from the world and dreaming of future triumphs. She, Lilly and her father went into the house, where the wonderful warm scent of freshly made doughnuts greeted them.

"We made doughnuts, too," Lilly said, leading her mother into the kitchen.

Agnes, Molly's mother and Grandma Lillian were at the kitchen table, talking. Coming from the darkness into the warmth of her family brought back all sorts of happy memories. Making her first cake for Gram's birthday. Eating spaghetti here the night her junior high basketball team won the Southwest Michigan district title. Staring out into the darkness and seeing the shadowy people in Gram's family stories.

"Did they tell you you got moved?" Molly's mother asked, getting up to pour Molly a cup of coffee. "I didn't think you'd mind. That south room is really much better. It's more spacious and the closets are larger."

"Doesn't matter to me," Molly said and took a chair next to Agnes.

"And it has other benefits," Gram said, passing the plate of doughnuts over to Molly. "It's the first bedroom over by the back stairs."

Molly took a doughnut, wearing a curious expression.

"You can sneak your beau upstairs," Gram explained. "And none of us will be the wiser."

What is this all about? "I don't have a beau. I mean, here in Niles." She avoided looking at Lilly.

"How about that guy at the gas station, Mom? He looked like a real rad stud."

Five pairs of eyes stared at Molly as she tried to glare Lilly into silence.

"Don't you remember?" Lilly persisted. "A big tall dude in a white cowboy hat."

The eyes continued staring at her. Molly took a bite of her doughnut as she got to her feet. Something in the air awoke a fear in her heart. "It was just somebody from high school," she told everybody.

"Anybody we know, dear?" her mother asked.

"Don't you know everybody in town?" Molly picked up her coffee cup. "Anyway, he thought I was Maggie. I think I'll go check on my new room. Make sure you got all my stuff out of the old one."

No one stopped her as she raced up the stairs, but the silent shadows of the bedroom offered no relief. This was stupid. She wasn't a high-schooler anymore to run off from the hint of romance with Jeff. So why had she?

Although he hadn't known she was alive back then, he'd been her first real love. He'd invaded her dreams as well as her heart, and had not let go easily. She was an adult now, self-sufficient and sensible. Yet in some corner of her heart, she worried that he might still hold that same fascination for her, that there might not be any real escape from her memories. Did she face these fears head-on or did she hide them away?

She busied herself with unpacking her suitcase, and trying not to remember the surprising light of laughter that had lingered in Jeff's eyes.

"So, what do kids do in this joint?" Lilly asked as Molly pulled open the door at the YMCA Monday morning. The faint smell of chlorine greeted them.

"You go swimming," Molly replied. To face her fears head-on, she had decided, not avoid her memories of teenage love. She was strong enough to fight them now. She and Lilly crossed the tiled floor to the reception desk. "Play sports. Stuff like that."

"Cool. I can handle that."

And she could. Lilly's attitude wasn't just bravado. She was a very confident little kid. Molly wondered if she'd ever been that confident. Hell, she still wasn't. She and Lilly reached the reception desk to find a green-eyed teenybopper staring at them.

"Hi, Maggie. What can we do for you?"

Lilly started to giggle, as Molly's heart sank. Not again.

The girl frowned. "Wait a minute. You're Molly," she said, her words coated in excitement. "I'm Sara Toller. You used to baby-sit me."

Molly remembered the Tollers—friends of her parents—and seven-year-old Sara, whose idea of heaven had been hearing tales of teenage social life. Molly had fantasized a lot to satisfy the girl.

"You've grown up," Molly said and realized that the inanity of that remark deserved Lilly's groan. She seemed to have lost a major portion of her brains since returning here to Niles. "I mean, it's good to see you again."

"We're here about your sports camp," Lilly took charge. "We're visiting my grandma and grandpa, and Mom thinks I need something to do before I drive them all nuts."

"Mr. Spencer said that such a thing was available." Molly pushed his name out. No more waltzing away like a timid little wallflower.

A high-wattage smile covered Sara's face. "Then I'll let you talk to him about it."

Whoa! Molly was ready to fly from the dance floor, but before she could decide whether her condition of cold feet was from anticipation or apprehension, Sara was opening a door behind the reception desk.

"Jeff," the girl called. "You have visitors."

"Bring them in." Jeff's voice was filled with welcome and Molly found herself following Lilly around the reception desk and into Jeff's office.

Sara held the door open, the look in her eyes too knowing. Had the whole town, from infants to the elderly, known that teenage Molly Cahill had had a crush on teenage Jeff Spencer? Molly hurried Lilly past the girl then, into the room. Jeff was getting up from his chair.

"Hey, Mom. It's the gas station dude. The one with the cowboy hat." Lilly stared at him a long moment before turning back to Molly. "He looks like a solid dude, Mom. How come you don't like him?"

Molly could feel her cheeks warm. "I never said I didn't like Mr. Spencer."

"Yeah, but you get all frowny around your mouth and eyebrows when you see him or someone talks about him."

Molly's cheeks blazed and her face grew more than frowny.

"Sara," Jeff said, turning to the teenager. "Why don't you take Lilly on a tour of the facilities, the deluxe tour?"

"Gotcha," Sara replied, winking and giving him the thumbs-up sign. Molly searched for a hole to fall into.

"Won't you sit down, please?" Jeff said once they were alone.

She would have preferred hiding behind the chair but she sat down. "I don't know where Lilly got the idea I dislike you," Molly assured him. "I hardly know you."

Jeff laughed, a deep baritone that did the most outrageous things to her insides. "I wouldn't blame you if you didn't like me," he said. "I'm a little more civilized now, but back in high school I was a real James Dean. All sullen looks and monosyllabic vocabulary."

Molly looked up at him, leaning back in his chair, hands behind his head. His smile was gentle and his eyes had a caring light to them. The James Dean he had been had made her heart race and her dreams X-rated. Yet the man he'd become seemed even more dangerous to her peace of mind. There was a potent strength about him that could break down the most solidly built defenses. She looked away.

"High school's not the best time in the world for most people," she said.

"It's a rocky road," he agreed. "More for some than others."

She refused to let her eyes return to him and glanced around his office. It was hardly spacious, with a desk buried under papers, a couple of mismatched chairs and some filing cabinets crammed into a space only slightly larger than a closet. The walls were covered with team photos and framed newspaper articles about happenings at the Y, adding to the sense that she was about to be inundated. Yet it wasn't an uncomfortable room. There was a real sense of caring in the air.

"I was surprised to see you back here," Molly said. "I thought you had left before I did."

He nodded. "Back in my angry days. I decided Niles was one big lie and I was going to find someplace better." He laughed, leaning forward as he did so that the light in his eyes seemed almost close enough to scorch. "I found out that the army was safe but uncaring, that college was stimulating but out of touch with reality, and that Niles wasn't really such a bad place."

"So you ended up back where you started from?"

"I thought maybe if I did the caring this time, it would be different," he said, his eyes shifting away from hers as if some secret spot in his soul might have been exposed. "And it has been."

Yet among all the photos, none seemed personal in nature. Was that because the Y was his life or because she was missing something? She got up to look at the photos more closely.

"So is there a Mrs. Spencer?" she asked.

He laughed. "I grew less angry, not more stupid."

Molly turned. His voice was laughing, but his words weren't. "Boy, there's a ringing endorsement of relationships. You get burned by an ex?"

He shook his head as if trying to shake away cobwebs of the past. "I didn't mean that quite like it sounded. I don't know what's gotten into me." He grinned at her, setting alive a current of desire buried deep in her heart. "Must be that the return of an old friend has loosened my tongue. No, there's no former, current or future Mrs. Spencer.

Let's just say that while marriage might be the chosen path for some, I'm not willing to trust my soul to somebody else's whims."

He pulled out a program brochure that was buried in a pile and visibly shifted into another dance step, which relieved her no end. She'd had only a fleeting urge to point out to him that they'd never really been friends before, even as another urge gloated that perhaps he'd liked her more than she'd known. None of it was going to be explored.

"It looks like we're going to be here for about two weeks or so," Molly said, coming back to her chair. "Lilly needs to have some time with children her own age."

"We can handle that. I think she'd like our sports camp."

"Do we need to become members?"

"Staff, even part-time, get a free membership for one child," he replied. "Have you thought any more about helping us out?"

And spend more time with him? Facing her past feelings head-on was one thing, flirting with danger was another. "We're only going to—"

Jeff raised a hand. "Just chill a while and ponder it. I'm cool."

"Huh?"

"Kid talk," he said, grinning. "Just relax and think about it. We'll see."

She shook her head again. "I know—"

He put a finger to his lips. "Chill."

How did he do it, shift so easily from the murky waters of the past to lightness and laughter?

"Hey, Mom."

The cavalry again to the rescue. Molly turned toward the door. "Yes, honey?"

"There's kids playing dodgeball in the gym and then they're gonna go swimming. Can I stay?"

"You don't have a swimsuit, honey."

"We have extras," Jeff said.

"How about lunch?"

"I have money," Lilly replied. "Grandpa gave me some."

"Sounds like she's all set," Jeff said.

"Okay," Molly said.

"Thanks, Mom." Lilly gave her a quick hug before turning to Jeff. "Thanks, dude."

"His name is Mr. Spencer," Molly said, trying to correct Lilly, but her daughter had raced out of the office before the first word had spilled out across her lips.

"Your daughter's a super kid."

Molly nodded and stood up. "I guess I'll be on my way then. I promised Agnes I'd take her shopping for a new dress."

Jeff stood up also. "Seen Maggie yet?"

"No. She's coming by tonight."

Jeff smiled. "She's really excited about becoming a mother. I guess the first one is always special."

"I guess," Molly replied. It was definitely time to leave.

"You know, I really like that Jeff dude," Lilly said, as she walked around the table putting a fork at each place setting.

Molly got the plates from the breakfront. "He's pretty nice."

"So why don't you go out with him?"

Molly spun to face her daughter. "Go out with him?"

"Yeah. You know, like a date."

Where was this coming from? "We're only going to be here a few weeks. Why would I start dating someone?"

"'Cause he's a cool dude. Geez, Mom, I'm gonna be grown-up one of these days. You got to have somebody to help you with your crossword puzzles."

The doorbell rang, saving Molly from having to reply. But was the toll saving her or throwing her into a deeper pit?

"That must be Aunt Maggie," Lilly cried and ran to the foyer.

Molly trudged after her daughter, her stomach a sudden mass of nerves, her hands sweating. What if Maggie took one look at Lilly and decided that she wanted her back? Molly stopped in the doorway of the foyer, and came face-to-face with her sister.

"Ain't it weird?" Lilly said.

And it was. Nine years, different people, different paths, and here Molly was staring at herself. Nearly a decade of separation and here they were, the two of them together. They were even sporting the exact same hairstyle.

"Hello, Molly."

"Hi, Mags."

They hugged slowly and carefully like porcupines. Maggie was definitely showing. She was much bigger at this time than she'd been when she carried Lilly.

"Good to see you," Molly said.

Maggie nodded. "Right."

Molly pulled Lilly to her side, keeping an arm possessively around the little girl's shoulders. "And this is Lilly. Your niece."

"Hi, Lilly." Maggie's eyes barely darted toward the child before skating across the room. "Hi, Agnes. How's the bar doing?"

Molly felt relief dance across her heart, even as she felt Lilly's shoulders sag with disappointment. Lilly had wanted to get to know this familiar-looking aunt.

"Aunt Maggie, did you and Mom really trade places and play tricks on people?" Lilly asked.

Maggie's glance was skittish, her smile barely there. "Oh, sometimes." She turned back to their parents. "Bill said if his meeting was over early, he'd stop by, but you know how those budget sessions are."

"Everybody's got a way to spend money that isn't there," her father agreed. Then, leading Maggie into the dining room, he placed her on the right of where he sat at the head of the table. "Let's sit down and eat."

"Isn't there something I can do to help?" Maggie asked even as she sat down.

"No, no," her mother replied. "We have everything under control."

"You're doing too much already," her father said. "Whoever heard of a person working around the clock as a doctor while they're with child?"

"A lot of women do it, Dad."

"Well, it's still ridiculous. You should be resting."

Molly told herself not to feel left out. After all, what did they have to talk about after the many years of sporadic letters? She followed her mother into the kitchen while Lilly sank into the chair next to Maggie.

"Do you like crossword puzzles, too? My mom—" Lilly's voice was cut off as the kitchen door swung shut.

"You should tell Maggie about your degree," Molly's mother said. She carried a saucepan over to the sink, then drained water from the beans.

Molly began to dish up the mashed potatoes. "She knows about it. I told her in a letter and I'm sure you mentioned it, too."

"She'd be interested in your work with the Special Olympics."

"Uh-huh."

Agnes came in, and with her help they carried all the food to the dining room. Molly told herself she should be glad that Maggie wasn't overjoyed to see her; that meant she wasn't overjoyed to see Lilly, either.

"—and then he'll paint little roses all along the back," Molly's father was saying.

"Wow, that'll be neat."

Molly glanced over to see what Lilly was purring over and saw a drawing of a wooden cradle.

"Mom, Grandpa's having a friend make Aunt Maggie's baby a special bed. Isn't that neat?"

What? No throne? Molly swallowed her bitter thoughts and smiled as she sat down next to Agnes.

"You have to be careful with those cradles," Molly said. "When the baby gets too active, they can tip over."

Her father smiled at Maggie, patting her hand. "Maggie knows that. She must have read every baby product safety report ever published. She's going to be the best mother possible."

Maggie had the grace to change the subject, only daring a quick scared glance at Molly, but their father's tone had said it all. Welcome home, Molly the Moron.

"What's that, lunch or dinner?"

Jeff looked into his father's scowling countenance, smiled as he popped a French fry into his mouth. "Both."

"Damn." His father shook his head. "Here it is, almost the middle of the night, and you're eating your one meal of the day in a joint like this. You ain't got any more sense now than you did back when you were a punk kid in high school."

Jeff waved his hand around the shadowy recesses of O'Day's. "I thought this was your favorite bar."

"Don't give me no lip," his father snapped. "Or I'll grow yours."

"Besides, this isn't my one meal of the day." Jeff turned his attention back to his food. "I had two candy bars for lunch."

"Goldarn it, boy," his father exploded. "You keep up that kind of a lousy life-style and you'll be a broken-down old man before you're thirty-five."

Jeff looked into his father's seamed and craggy face, bearing the scars of countless brawls and carrying the wear and tear of a lifetime of hard trails.

"You should talk," Jeff said quietly.

"You're damn right I should talk. You want to get the real scivvy on anything, you go to the man with experience. And I got more experience with hard, low-down living than any fifty men."

Ten years ago they would have been arguing at this point. Twelve, fifteen years ago they would have been in a bare-knuckle fight. But things were different now. Jeff had grown up. He had his emotions under control.

"Things are a little hectic right now," he said. "But once I'm over these rough spots I'll be back into practicing good habits."

"Things have been hectic with you ever since you started working at that damn Y."

"There's so much to be done."

"But you can't do it all yourself."

Jeff concentrated on his hamburger. There were so many kids needing a helping hand, and so few people who seemed to care. Somebody had to step in and take charge.

"What you need is a wife."

"Right, Pop."

"Don't patronize me. Most guys your age are married or heading close in that direction."

"When do I have time for dating?"

"That's the point. You keep yourself so busy that no woman in her right mind would start a relationship with you."

"Maybe that's for the best. Quite frankly, I don't see myself getting married."

"Hell, that's—"

Jeff looked up to see what had seized his father's attention and found himself staring at the door. He turned to look and felt his own tiredness slip off like a scarf that wasn't tied. This time he knew it wasn't Maggie.

"Agnes."

He turned to see his father had stood and was smiling at the older woman with Molly.

"Paul," the woman said, as she stepped up to his father, throwing her arms around his neck. They stood there and hugged, apparently oblivious to the world around them.

"I guess they know each other," Molly said.

Jeff shrugged. "Or plan to."

The two older people finally parted, just this side of acute embarrassment.

"Jeff," his father said, his arm still around the woman. "This is Agnes. She's the love of my life."

"Hello, Agnes," Jeff said. "It's always a pleasure to meet a friend of my father's."

"I'm Molly's Aunt Agnes," she said. "You do know Molly?"

"Reasonably well," Jeff said, grinning.

Molly nodded and turned up her lips, but her smile seemed rather tight. And the light in her eyes seemed fueled more by irritation than by joy.

"I missed you, Agnes." Paul bent down and kissed Molly's aunt. "I thought of you every day."

"We haven't seen each other for thirty-five years," Agnes said.

His father shrugged and his smile dimmed slightly. "The years sort of got away from me."

Agnes laughed and put her arm through his father's. "Paul, why don't you buy me a drink and tell me some sweet lies?"

"But then I won't be able to tell you how beautiful you look."

"Good, Paul." Agnes's deep voice drifted back to them. "That's a very good start."

Jeff watched his father lead Agnes to the bar, then turned to Molly, who was staring after them. "Guess you're stuck with me," he said. "Want to sit down?"

"Sure," she said and ordered a glass of lemonade from a passing waitress.

Jeff gave her a minute, but something about the way she kept watching Agnes and his father nagged at him. Not that he was trying to woo her with charm, but she might at least notice he was there.

"I thought tonight was party night," he said.

She turned to him then, her eyes dark with shadows. "Party night?"

"You said Maggie was coming over. I would have thought you two would have a lot of catching up to do."

"Not that much." She looked at the approaching waitress as if she was a long-lost friend. "Sisters, even twins, don't stay close forever."

"Oh." He waited while she sipped at her drink and let its cooling potions work some magic. She was tight, tense. He could see it in the way she held her mouth, in the way her glance kept darting around as if it was doing what her body wanted. "Anything you want to talk about?" he asked gently.

"No." She put down her drink suddenly and he saw a spark deep in those shadows in her eyes. "Oh, why not? It's just that nothing's changed. I've been gone nine years, got not just a bachelor's degree but a master's also, not to mention a great kid, and back home I'm still a distant second to Maggie. Just Molly the Moron."

He frowned and took her hand. She seemed to need an anchor to hold on to. "Who called you that?"

"Me." She shrugged and looked away, but left her hand in his. "It was always Maggie the Magnificent and Molly the Moron back in high school. She would get the A's, and to keep Mom from crying, would take half my tests for me so I could get B's."

"It's funny. I would think you two would be identical in every way. Why was she better than you in school?"

"There was a problem when I was being born," Molly said with a shrug. "Maggie came out quick and easy, but I was turned wrong and almost died before they could get me out. The doctors thought there wasn't any permanent damage, but I always had trouble with visual interpretation. When I was about ten, the school had me tested and found out that I had a mild learning disability. Since Maggie and I are genetically identical, that's the only thing they could think of that could have caused the difference. Anyway, Mom blamed herself, and Maggie became my guardian."

"And resented it?"

"No, seemed to take it as her duty. That was what was so aggravating. If she'd been rotten about it, I wouldn't have felt guilty about hating her for it."

He smiled. "I can't imagine you hating anyone."

She pulled her hand away at that. "You don't know me," she pointed out. "Not now, not before." A wall seemed to have materialized between them.

He thought of the past, of the times she'd tried to befriend him, and he'd rebuffed her. All he saw in his memory was a pleasant, but hesitant, young girl and his own dark anger. She was right, he hadn't known her.

"Hey, I'm sorry. I didn't mean to snap at you." She reached for his hands this time, cupping them in her own. "Let's change the subject. Is this where you normally hang out?"

Her touch was warm and inviting, leaving him longing for more. It was a dangerous feeling, and rather than give in to it, he looked around the bar. The place looked so ordinary suddenly, with its scarred tables and flashing neon beer signs. In some instances, dim lighting might add mystery to a setting, but here it added a weariness. Yet, this was where he usually came at night for dinner. Was his life ordinary and weary?

He shrugged. "Well, the Y and my bedroom see more of me, but I guess this place comes in third." It sounded depressing, even to him.

But Molly's eyes weren't judgmental. "Agnes owns a bar like this in Denver. A lot of our regulars are single guys. Who wants to go home to an empty apartment after a long day?"

"Or a singles bar?"

She grinned. "Don't tell me such things have actually reached Niles?"

"Complete with ferns and ceiling fans."

"Progress. Can't escape it."

"No, but fernicide would keep it under control."

She laughed, lighting the old bar with her freshness and joy. It didn't seem like such a gloomy old place anymore.

Chapter Three

"You're deserting me," Molly said. "I call this treason of the highest quality."

Agnes just laughed and nudged her suitcase back an inch so that she could close the Jeep's door. "That's me. Everything I do is of the highest quality."

"Is your Aunt Bertha really ninety-five years old?" Lilly asked. She stopped her invisible game of hopscotch. "That means she would have been born back in the 1800s."

"Yep, and doesn't get around too good anymore. That's why she can't come down to the reunion."

"We could be going with you," Molly pointed out. "Lilly would have enjoyed seeing the Upper Peninsula."

"She can see it another time. It's not going anywhere." Agnes gave Molly a hug. "You've got a lot of people here wanting to see you. This is where you belong."

Molly wanted to argue, but knew Agnes was right. Besides, her worries about Agnes leaving were far from rational. She'd been a rock that Molly had leaned on during the worst of times and, even though those times were gone, Molly still didn't feel comfortable knowing the older woman was going to be gone three days.

"Take care of your mom," Agnes told Lilly. "Make sure she has some fun."

"I will."

Great. Just what Molly needed. A nine-year-old activities director. She waved goodbye to Agnes and watched until the car had turned onto Broadway and was lost from sight. It wasn't as if she couldn't get along without Agnes here. She was an adult, Molly reminded herself. She'd just miss Agnes.

"So can we go now?" Lilly asked. "I don't want to be late."

Molly glanced at her watch. They had a good half hour before Lilly was due at the Y, but Lilly had never been particularly patient. "Sure, just go tell Gram—"

But the front door opened and Gram was coming down the steps. "I thought I'd walk with you. Too nice a day to be stuck inside." She glanced around. "Agnes go? Seems my company never stays around long enough anymore. You two are going to be here for dinner tonight, aren't you?"

"Sure, Gram." Molly put her arm around the older woman. "How about if I make some dessert? I've got a great strawberry pie recipe."

"You make a decent piecrust?"

"I got the recipe from you."

The three of them walked through town. It was a beautiful warm day, but Molly felt the shadow of grumpiness returning the closer she got to the Y. That was the real root of her discomfort. She'd had a good time last night with

Jeff. Too good a time. And she needed somebody to protect her from herself.

"Now, if you look just down that way," Gram was telling Lilly, "you can see the police station where John Dillinger was imprisoned back in the thirties. He was a famous gangster."

"Wow."

When Molly was a little girl, Gram had told her all kinds of stories, too. How way before Niles was a town or Michigan a state, Broadway Street had been known as the Great Sauk Trail, which had been used by the Indians and trappers to get down to the river. She saw the bridge down the street from them. New name, same purpose.

"That Jeff Spencer is just a wonderful man."

"What?" Molly blinked, rapidly trying to bring her mind back to Gram's words.

"Jeff Spencer." Gram shook her head. "I declare, child. There are times when I still wonder where your mind is at." She turned to Lilly. "Your mother was always one to daydream."

Lilly just looked at Molly and grinned. Molly ignored her. "What made you think of Jeff Spencer?"

"Lilly was telling me at breakfast about all the fun she has at the Y. And I know that's Jeff's doing."

Breakfast had been thirty minutes ago. Why bring up Jeff now? "Jeff's just one employee," Molly said.

"I know that, dear, but he's the one with the push. He's always out hustling money and help for his kids."

"That's his job."

"Don't matter none," Gram said. "Some folks put as little as they can get away with into their work. Not Jeff Spencer. He always gives his all."

Molly was curious what had brought on Gram's sudden desire to canonize Jeff. She doubted if her father, either officially as a minister or unofficially as a town resident, would agree to Jeff's sainthood.

Memory brought back echoes of angry words: Jeff Spencer was nothing but a ruffian, and he would come to no good like his father. Jeff's name hadn't been mentioned since Molly and Lilly had been back home, but Molly doubted that her father had changed his opinions.

"And I'm not the only one who thinks so," Gram was going on. "He's been nominated for the American Corporate Service Award."

"What's that?"

"Some big old award that a group of corporations give out each year. I guess it could mean a lot of money for the Y and Jeff's programs."

Lilly skipped on ahead of them up the steps to the Y and held open the door. Molly followed her grandmother inside, but a sense of unease hung over her. The old Jeff and his wild reputation would be easier to visit. And of course, he was right there in the lobby.

"Hey, little dude," he called out when he saw Lilly.

"Hey, big dude," the girl shouted back.

"Gonna do some splish-splash?"

"Yup," Lilly replied.

"Catch you on the flip side."

"Later, gator," Lilly said over her shoulder as she ran down the hall.

Jeff turned back to them, his broad smile at full wattage. "Nice kid."

"She used to speak standard English," Molly pointed out. She turned to Gram to suggest they be on their way, but the old woman seemed anything but ready to go.

"You folks did a good job fixing this place up." Gram was looking around the room at the walls and the ceiling. "Last time I was in here, it looked a sorry mess. Cracked plaster, chipping paint. Very nice now. You've given the place new life.''

''Thank you.''

Molly took Gram's arm and tugged slightly toward the door, but the old woman seemed not to notice.

''Man does a good job like this, deserves a reward,'' Gram said.

''That's okay, Mrs. Trundell. Just doing my job.''

''Nope. I insist on treating you to a meal,'' Gram said. ''Come over to my house. Get yourself a decent meal for a change. Put a little meat on those bones.''

Molly frowned at Gram. She was willing to bet that the old woman had never before thought of having Jeff over for dinner. That wicked gleam in Gram's eyes meant she was scheming, and Molly was going on full-scale alert.

''I don't want to put you to no trouble,'' Jeff was saying.

''Ain't no trouble at all,'' Gram said sharply. ''I want to see you at my place tonight.''

''Tonight?'' Molly asked. She couldn't believe it. How was she supposed to avoid repeating the mistakes of the past if he was going to be around all the time?

''Okay,'' Jeff said.

''I'll have pot roast, new potatoes and June peas,'' Gram said.

''Sounds great.''

''And Molly will make some dessert.''

Jeff grinned at Molly as if he could read her mind. ''You mean little Miss Smiley?''

''I'll help her,'' Gram said, patting him on the arm.

Gram was already helping enough.

''Mr. Spencer.'' An assistant counselor was helping Lilly Cahill toward the dugout. ''We have an accident victim.''

"What happened?" Jeff asked.

"I was sliding into third base," Lilly replied.

He looked at the blood smearing the side of her arm. "Not a good idea." It didn't look bad, but he needed to get it cleaned.

"Sit down," Jeff said, at the same time giving the high school boy a quick nod to indicate that he could return to the other kids. "I'll fix you up."

He pulled the first-aid kit off the shelf and took out some peroxide and sterile pads. He poured the antiseptic on the wound, then wiped it with sterile gauze. Lilly grimaced a little but made no sound.

"You're a brave little soldier," Jeff said, as he taped clean sterile pads over the abrasion.

"I'm just like my father."

"Oh." He closed up the kit and put it back in its place on the shelf, his curiosity warring briefly with his good manners. Manners lost. "So your father is a soldier."

"Well, he used to be. He's a secret agent now."

"I see. What's he doing?"

"It wouldn't be a secret if everybody knew," she replied.

"Do you know where he is?"

"I told you," she said patiently. "He's a secret agent. Nobody knows where he is."

Jeff just stared a minute at the girl. What kind of guy had Molly gotten involved with? "Have you ever met him?" he asked.

"No." She shook her head. "He was with the marines in the African desert. And he went on his mission right from there."

He looked at her serious little face and felt an ache in his heart. This was pure fantasy.

"I thought you said he was in the army," Jeff said.

"He was. But he was in the marines, too." Lilly nodded a moment. "He was in the air force, too. He can fly all kinds of planes."

"But he was never in the navy?"

"He started out there. Right after high school."

"Really gets around."

"Yep." It was obvious that the smile on her face was forced. "And he went to college and studied a whole bunch of stuff. You know, how to build airplanes and clean up the ocean. That kind of stuff."

"I see." Jeff let himself down into a sitting position on the ground in front of Lilly, deliberately ending up at a lower eye level than hers. "Do you have a picture of him?"

"No, he had plastic surgery before he went on his secret mission. There's only one picture in the world of him and it's locked in a vault in Washington, D.C."

Jeff nodded. "What does your mom say about him?"

"Oh, she can't talk about him," Lilly said. "Because he's a secret agent."

"Right. I forgot for a minute." Molly doesn't talk about him so Lilly makes up her own father. A good one. One to be proud of. Having done the same thing himself, Jeff could relate to that. Of course, his and Lilly's circumstances were different. He'd known his father, just hadn't liked him. Probably Lilly had never even met her father.

"He used to live around here," Lilly added in a whisper. "So maybe you used to know him."

Jeff tried to hide his surprise. "Oh?"

"I figured it out," Lilly went on. "I was born only three months after Mommy came out to Denver, so she knew my dad here."

And Lilly was nine. That meant Molly had gotten pregnant during her senior year. He frowned into the past. He knew he hadn't been that aware of anybody but himself, but he sure would have guessed that Molly wasn't dating anyone too steadily back then. And unlike a few others he could name, she didn't seem the type for a quick, casual roll in the hay.

"We've always lived with Aunt Agnes," Lilly told him.

"Yeah, your mom told me."

"It's a really neat apartment with a bar downstairs for cowboys. They come there after work. And they drink a lot of beer, fight and throw bottles at one another." She wiped her nose with the back of her hand. "You know, stuff like that."

"Oh." Jeff sighed as he stood up. Damn. It sounded like Molly hadn't had any bed of roses. He'd bet that Lilly's father, besides never seeing her, didn't contribute a nickel to her support, either. Molly was lucky she had Agnes to help her out. Jeff was willing to bet Molly's father had been as pigheaded and unbending about her pregnancy as he was about everything. Well, while Molly was in town, maybe he could lighten her load a little bit.

"I'm coming to your house for dinner tonight," Jeff said.

"Oh, yeah?" A broad grin spread across Lilly's face. "Neat."

"Should I bring anything?"

She shrugged her shoulders. "Grandma already has a lot of stuff in her house."

"How about some kind of present?"

"You can bring Mom flowers."

"Okay."

"Roses. She likes roses a whole lot. Yellow ones."

"Yellow roses for Mommy. Gotcha."

"A lot of them."

"A lot of them?"

Lilly frowned at him. "Are they expensive?" She searched in her pocket and pulled out some bills. "I got two dollars."

"That's okay," Jeff replied.

"I can get more from Grandpa."

Jeff wanted to laugh, but paused to swallow the growing lump in his throat. That would be great. Getting Gramps to kick in money so Jeff could buy roses for his daughter. Old Reverend Gramps would probably have himself a stroke if he found out.

"I can handle it," he assured her. "How about your great-grandmother? What can I get for her?"

"Peanut brittle."

"What?" The old woman was in her early eighties. She probably didn't have her own teeth anymore. "Your great-grandmother eats peanut brittle?"

"Nope, I do." Lilly stood up. "But she said it gives her a great pleasure to watch me eat it."

Jeff stared at her. Boy, what a con artist.

"Besides, Gram gets really mad if people bring stuff just for her," Lilly hastened to explain. "She says it's dumb spending money on an old lady who's already got more than she needs."

He chuckled. "All right, flowers for Mom and peanut brittle for Gram."

Lilly stood up and flexed her bandaged arm. "I'm okay now. I'd better get back to the game."

"Yeah, you'd better."

Lilly started back toward the softball diamond. Jeff watched her a moment before going around to the parking lot and his car. He had some serious shopping to do.

* * *

"Mom. Someone's at the door." Lilly's voice came into the kitchen where Molly was putting whipped cream on her pie.

"You're the closest."

"I'm busy," Lilly hollered back. "Rufus has something wrong with his foot."

"But I have to—"

"I'll take care of the pies," Gram said. "Go see who's at the door, dear."

Molly stomped off toward the front door. This match-making was getting just a wee bit obvious. If it wasn't Lilly, it was Gram. Or her own silly heart, a little voice pointed out. After all, it wasn't Gram or Lilly that was making Molly's cheeks flushed or her breath hard to come by.

She pulled open the door. Jeff was on the porch, a couple of boxes in his arms and a smile on his lips. She tried not to let it affect her, a lost cause if there ever was one.

"Come on in," she said. Her voice came out rougher than she intended.

"Certainly can't resist an invitation like that."

Good. There was a lot she was having trouble resisting. "I'll tell Gram you're here."

"Ah, Molly."

She turned.

"These are for you." He thrust a long white box at her.

"What's this, designer spaghetti?" She made a joke but her fingers shook slightly as she undid the ribbon. She couldn't remember the last time anybody had given her flowers.

Jeff hadn't just given her flowers. He'd given her yellow roses. Her eyes grew watery.

"Thank you," she said, sounding all too quivery for her liking.

"My pleasure." His eyes said he meant it, too.

"Hi, Jeff."

Lilly joined them in the foyer, Rufus sitting by her side. She pulled Lilly's box down slightly so she could see inside. "Ooh, pretty," she said.

They were more than pretty. They were spectacular. Molly didn't know what to say to him.

"Hello, Jeff," Gram said, wiping her hands on a dishtowel as she came into the foyer. "Hope you're in the mood for eating. We made enough to feed an army."

"I'm ready to do my best, ma'am. I haven't eaten since you invited me."

Gram kissed him on the cheek. "Good boy," she said.

"I brought you a little something," Jeff said, handing her a small box.

Gram's face wrinkled in a frown. "This better not be some useless doodad," she said.

"No, ma'am."

Her frown quickly turned to a smile once she'd opened the box. "Why it's peanut brittle." She looked at Lilly. "I do believe we can make use of this." She handed the box to her great-granddaughter. "Would you take care of this for me, honey?"

"I surely will, ma'am."

Molly watched Lilly dash out of the room, followed by a now frisky Rufus, apparently cured of any foot problems.

"She's getting to talk like a real native," Jeff said.

But Gram was shooing them into the dining room before Molly needed to reply. Maybe he was ready for canonization. After all, the man had known about the favorite things of two of the females in the house and had known not to get the third a gift because she disliked them for herself. He was either absolutely amazingly intuitive or a little bird had whispered in his ear. Either way, Molly was feeling incredibly vulnerable.

Dinner passed surprisingly quickly with Molly lost in a muddle of confusion. Luckily Gram and Lilly kept Jeff busy with questions about the Y and the programs he'd started, and no one seemed to notice that Molly made only occasional comments.

She was no longer a teenager with a major crush on a convenient fellow student. But maybe a teenage crush would be easier to deal with. The attraction she felt for Jeff seemed anything but adolescent. The strawberry pie went down easily, and then they were left with their after-dinner coffee. Without any food to occupy her, Molly cast about for a safe topic of conversation.

"Lilly was telling me all about Denver," Jeff said, looking over at Molly.

"Yeah, Mom." Lilly scraped the last bit of strawberry from her plate. "I told him about the bar and the cowboys and the fights."

This was not the topic she would have chosen. "They really don't happen all that often," Molly hastened to assure him.

"It's about time you and Lilly lived in a regular house," Gram said.

"It's a big apartment, Gram. And it's close to work and school."

Gram grunted. "A big house with a yard would be better."

"That's a little out of my reach right now," Molly replied.

"This house is ready for the taking," Gram said.

Molly stared at her grandmother, unprepared for this turn of developments.

"I'm getting old, child," Gram went on. "I can't keep this place up anymore."

"Don't Mom and Dad help with—"

"It isn't just the maintenance, honey. It's just too big and quiet. It needs a family to fill it. Fill it full of laughter and tears. Fill it full of life."

Molly didn't know what to say. This old yellow house on the hill was a part of her life. She couldn't imagine her grandmother not being here. Yet Molly wasn't ready to take her place. Her job and her life were in Denver. Lilly had her friends there. They'd just come here for a short visit. She couldn't risk coming back here to stay.

"Lilly, why don't you and I clean up?" Gram said briskly. "And Molly, you can take Rufus and Jeff and go sit out on the back porch. There's a nice breeze coming up off the river."

"That's okay," Molly said. "I can help."

"Go," Gram said, leaving no room for discussion, let alone argument.

So the three of them went outside. The air was thick with the heavy summer scents of hollyhocks and honeysuckle. Back along the fence, Molly could see the movement of honeybees amid the flowers as Rufus wandered out into the yard. She sat down with a sigh on the edge of the steps. It was peaceful here.

"He looks right at home," Jeff said, nodding toward Rufus as he sniffed breezes.

Molly just stared ahead at the row of tomato plants, heavy with fruit. Back in Denver, their garden was two cut-off barrels on the porch off the second floor. They started out the summer chock-full of petunias, geraniums and marigolds—no parsonage wax begonias—but by the end of July, the plants were stunted and half-dead from the baking heat of the porch.

Jeff sat down next to her. "Your grandmother wants you to stay."

"I noticed."

"You don't seem excited about the idea."

She looked at him, seeing in his eyes traces of the rebellious youth he had been. He had come back and done well, but his problems had all been ones forgivable in an adolescent. She carried too many secrets with her, secrets that she wasn't willing to divulge even if others no longer cared. She could never feel totally secure that Lilly was hers.

"When the trees shed their leaves," Jeff said, "you'll be able to see the YMCA building from here."

"I'll be back in Denver by that time," Molly replied.

"You have somebody back there waiting for you?" he asked.

She should say yes, say that the love of her life lived back in Denver and she couldn't wait to get home, but that kind of lie would backfire all too easily.

"No," she said. "I've got friends there certainly, we all do. But no one special. I've gotten choosy. Too choosy, Agnes says."

"Oh?"

Molly stretched out her legs so that her toes just reached the edge of the shade. She should change the subject, find something innocuous to talk about, but for some reason she felt as if she could open up to Jeff. They'd both been misfits of a sort back in their youth, though they hadn't found solace together.

She closed her eyes and drifted back to the past. "In the beginning, I believed the detergent ads. You know, the ones that showed a mother happily taking care of her husband and kids. I had a perfect daughter and together we would find us the perfect husband and father." Molly opened her eyes.

"Was I ever naive! I thought that the guys hanging around found something special in me." She saw herself back then, so stupidly trusting, and the ashes of a long-ago anger toughened her voice. "I learned the hard way that what they saw was somebody 'easy.' To them, Lilly was living proof that I had given in at least once, so why not again with them. Some were even willing to spring for a hamburger first."

"There are jerks all over." His voice was soft. It was as if a blanket of time was smothering her anger.

She shrugged. "There were one or two genuinely nice guys when Lilly was real little. But I could tell one would never accept Lilly as his own, and the other—well, it just didn't work out." No, not once she weighed the need for real and complete truth in a relationship. "It took me a few guys longer than it should have, but I did learn. Lilly and I are better off alone."

"You sound disillusioned."

"Realistic." Agnes was there for support when Molly needed it, but there was no one she owed the whole truth to. "Now, I just go out with friends and have fun. Cowboys, so I have no great expectations."

"Cowboys? You mean like shoot 'em up, round 'em up cowboys?"

Molly laughed. "Nope. Guys who can be counted on to ride off into the sunset sooner or later. Agnes calls them cowboys."

"Ride off into the sunset, eh? Sounds like you."

She turned to look at him, but her eyes really saw inside herself. "Yeah, like me," she said slowly. She hadn't thought about it before, but she was the female version of a cowboy, both back in Denver and here. She dated no one there with a view to the future, and here she was the one who would ride off into the sunset once the reunion was over. There wasn't any reason to worry about her attraction to Jeff, because the cowboy in her would keep her safe. It would make her pull back in time.

"You know," Jeff said, after a long moment. "It's funny you should mention looking for a father for Lilly. She and I were talking today."

Molly didn't like the way that sounded. "Oh?"

"About her father."

Molly stiffened. Warning lights flashed, but she didn't need them to warn her to be wary. Her heart had stopped, her breath was on hold. Why had she let Jeff peek into her life?

"And what did she say?"

"That he was a secret agent."

Molly relaxed just enough to breathe again. "Kids her age tend to make up stories. They like to glamorize everything about life."

"Maybe she'd like some straight facts."

So much for relaxing. Molly clenched her hands in her lap and tried to squeeze her own tensions out. "Maybe you know nothing about the situation."

"I know enough to recognize a kid who's hurting."

Lots of them were hurting. "Did you ever think the truth could hurt more?"

"I don't believe in lies." His voice was cold, judgmental, and it was easy to tell what his verdict was on her.

"I haven't lied to her."

"Silence can be a lie when she needs to know some facts."

Molly got to her feet. She'd lain awake too many nights worrying about this very problem to have some virtual stranger blithely tell her to tell Lilly the truth about her father. Truths about fathers were connected to truths about mothers.

What should she tell Lilly? What could she tell her? That her father was a gangly, pimply-faced kid in a baseball cap who was never really liked by her mother, who, by the way, was really the aunt that never came to see her? Then Molly could continue with the fact that Lilly's mother was really her aunt and that her grandfather still was angry about the shame Lilly's birth brought on the family. All of that would be enough to turn Santa Claus into a kleptomaniac, and the Easter Bunny into a terrorist.

"I don't think any of this is your business," she said, holding on to the porch rail to keep the shaking of her hands from showing. It was time to circle the wagons and fend off the attackers. "Come on, Rufus, time to go in."

Chapter Four

Lilly was at the Y earlier than Jeff expected the next morning. He caught sight of her as she headed into the gym and he grabbed the bag on his desk, racing out the front door. Molly hadn't even made it to the bridge yet.

"Molly," he called.

She turned. The Denver Nuggets T-shirt she wore seemed a mockery. No nugget of gold could vibrate with the radiance and beauty that she had here in the soft summer sunshine. Unfortunately, the temperature of her eyes was definitely on the cool side.

"Hi," he said and held up the bag. "Want some breakfast?"

"Breakfast?" She looked confused, as if she feared she had forgotten something. "I had my coffee already."

"Well, you could have more, couldn't you?"

The confusion faded from those cool green eyes, but she said nothing.

What would it be like to swim in those eyes, to totally lose himself in her warmth? He shook his head and got back on track. "It would be a lot easier to apologize if you'd sit with me a few minutes."

She shrugged, not an enthusiastic response but better than turning on her heel and leaving. He led her down the path to the river. The river walkway was deserted and they sat on the bench just under the willow. A dampness still lingered in the air down here, a reminder of last night's chill.

"I was out of line last night," he said suddenly, hoping to get the bitter medicine over with quickly. "You were right. Lilly and her father are none of my business."

Molly sighed and stared out at the river. He couldn't see her eyes, couldn't tell if she was still angry or weighing his penance.

So take a chance, he told himself. The worst she could do was dump his coffee all over him. He took the covered cups of coffee out of the bag and held one out to her. She sensed his movement, turning to take the cup. Her eyes were shadowed with pain and something else. Fear?

"I guess I overreacted a bit," she said. "Being an only parent makes you protective in strange ways."

The soft tenor of pain in her voice pinched at his heart. Poor Molly. Lilly was nine years old, yet Molly's scars still hadn't healed. When kids carried such a load of pain, Jeff would give them hugs, but he wasn't sure that would be a good idea with Molly. It could just make her angrier and he could wind up with a black eye. He opted for breakfast.

"I've got doughnuts, too," he said and held out a chocolate doughnut and a fruit-filled one. "Shame to let good food go to waste."

That got a smile out of her. "Especially something so nutritious," she replied and took the fruit-filled one.

After a bite or two, she seemed to relax more. And as she relaxed, he grew braver. He watched the water rushing by and thought how lucky he was to have this little pocket of peace in his day...in his life. Yet something nagged at him and he knew he was going to risk it.

"I know I should keep my big mouth shut, but I think you should know something," he said, and saw just what he expected—her shoulders stiffened. "I suspect Lilly's looking for her father while she's here in Niles."

Molly turned slowly to face him and all he saw were her eyes. The devastation in them was immense. It took him by surprise, cutting into his soul with her pain. His first instinct was to take her into his arms and hold her until the pain went away, to tell her that everything would be all right, that whatever she feared so would never happen. But he wanted to stay her friend and could read the clear signs in her every pore that told him not to trespass.

"Why do you think that?" she finally asked, her voice a ragged thread barely audible.

He tried to concentrate on the hand that held his coffee, not on the hand that wanted to hold hers. "Something she said when we were talking yesterday," he said. "Hey, I could be wrong."

Molly looked at him for a quick moment, then turned away as if the river held the answers.

"She told me that her father used to live in Niles," he said.

Molly flinched as if she'd been struck and he hurried on. "She said she figured it out from when you came to Denver and when she was born. That you were pregnant here."

Molly said nothing, but he knew she had heard. Her stillness was proof of that. The silence grew quickly painful, though, and he went on. "She's got the idea he was in the military. I don't know if that's just another story or if it's from something you've told her about him."

What else was there to say then? He stopped his rambling, even if just for a few minutes, and forced himself to finish his coffee. It tasted like river mud.

"I knew she'd start wondering some day," Molly said. "I guess I thought she'd come to me for answers first."

She needed to be held; her quavering voice revealed as much but her rigid and erect posture was evidence that she'd learned not to lean. That she'd willed herself to be strong long ago. This certainly wasn't the little mouse he used to know. He just took the paper cup from her unprotesting hand and poured the coffee onto the fallen leaves and twigs off the path before tossing both their cups into a nearby trash can.

"Well, she didn't exactly come and ask me questions," Jeff told Molly. "I called her a brave little soldier when I bandaged her scraped arm and it just sort of started from there."

"She's never asked me anything." Molly suddenly looked up, her eyes catching his. "When she was little and we'd read a story that would have a daddy in it, she would ask then. And I'd tell her her daddy went away. That he was a good and fine person, but he had to go away. That's all I ever said about him."

"It's a good start."

"I have no idea where he is now."

He took a chance, reaching out for her hand. She let him hold it, as if clinging to a lifeline. "Well, I doubt that she'll find him," Jeff said. Her eyes seemed hungry for his reassurance. "I mean, I remember you being awfully quiet our senior year, so I doubt Niles is teeming with people who know his identity. Now, if it was Maggie—"

Molly was on her feet in an instant. She looked at the half-eaten sweet roll in her hand as if wondering how it got there, then out at the ducks, who were watching them passively from about ten feet out on the river. Breaking off bits, she tossed them into the water. The ducks came swarming over.

She turned once the pastry was gone. "I appreciate your telling me all this," she said. "I'll have a talk with Lilly, try to answer some of her questions the best I can."

"I'm sure it's just a phase."

She nodded and looked around. No evidence of their visit remained, at least not visibly. That look that had come into her eyes before would stay with him a long time, though.

"Well, thanks for the breakfast and all," she said. "If there's anything I can do for you..."

How about a smile? Or even an attempt at one?

She forced a laugh that fell far short of the mark. "Silly me. I know what you want. You want some help with your programs. Okay. Consider me signed on. Can we start next Monday?"

"Great," he said and stepped aside to let her walk back up the path to the road. Somehow getting a smile from her would have seemed a greater victory.

Molly had never been so excited about a rummage sale, but she welcomed the activity with open arms. She'd had enough time to think walking home from the Y, more than enough time. What should she do about Lilly's curiosity about her father? Ignore it? Make up lies? Dredge up what she remembered about Maggie's old boyfriend? What she really felt like doing was crawling into Jeff's arms and hiding until this whole storm passed over.

That wasn't one of the possibilities though, Molly told herself. She'd just have a talk with Lilly when there was a quiet moment and hope that it would satisfy the girl's questions. As for what she would say...well, Molly hoped inspiration would strike between now and then.

She went straight to the church from the Y, joining with her parent's elderly recruits in sorting through the donated clothes and household items. Children's clothes in one corner—winter items to the right, summer to the left. Shoes here, boots there. Look for more rubber bands to keep the pairs of shoes together. Difficult, exacting work that took up her morning.

"Molly. Oh, Molly." Her mother was waving to her from the double-doored entryway. "Could you come here, please?"

Molly left the box of baby clothes she was sorting and followed her mother down into the basement storage area.

"We have a problem," her mother said. "Mr. Chambliss's father had a heart attack. He had to go to Detroit."

"I hope it wasn't a bad one," Molly said. Frank Chambliss had been the church custodian since she had been in grade school. Why all the secrecy about telling her though?

"No, I think not, but we had counted on him being here today."

Molly waited.

Her mother waved her hands around her. "He would have gotten these tables upstairs for us," she said.

Now Molly understood. The heavy-duty folding tables normally used for banquets and other church activities were piled high on two dollies and needed to be upstairs in the hall. How in the world were they going to get them there?

"Maybe if everyone pitched in," her mother said.

The median age of their helpers had to be seventy-five. "No," Molly said firmly. "Somebody could get hurt."

"What can we do then?" her mother asked, a wail floating out around the edge of her words. "We can't just put the sale items on the floor."

"Ask those folks upstairs if their kids and grandkids could come over," Molly suggested. "They have to know of some younger people available."

"I already asked." Her mother's face switched to defeat. "We were counting on Mr. Chambliss."

Molly sighed. She felt backed into a corner. Had her mother always been this indecisive? But Molly was in no mood to dance around. She had enough on her mind without making a major drama out of moving some tables.

"I'll take care of it, Mother."

She turned and went into the church kitchen to use the phone. It probably wasn't wise to keep bringing him into her life, but she knew he would help. About fifteen minutes later, she heard Jeff's voice out in the foyer.

"Hi, Mrs. Cahill."

"May I help you?" Molly's mother's voice was ice-cold.

Molly hurried over to greet him, her eyes on her mother. So her father wasn't the only one with sour feelings toward Jeff.

"Hi, Jeff," Molly said quickly. "Thanks for coming over. We have a lot of help for the rummage sale, but almost no young muscle."

He smiled, flexing his biceps, and Molly found herself laughing. This man could sure put a spin on a slow day.

"We have to move a bunch of tables from the basement," she said. "I think we need a few more people."

"Do not despair. I've brought more than a pair."

Molly found herself laughing again. "I hope you're better at lifting than you are at poetry."

He just gave her a look as he stepped to the door. "Yo, guys. Come on."

Six early-teenage boys tumbled through the doorway, all good-sized and in fit shape. From their rough look, Molly guessed that they came from the northeast side of town.

"These ladies need some muscle," Jeff said.

His words were greeted by the standard boisterous response of teenage males as the youths grunted and flexed their muscles.

"Okay, chill out," Jeff snapped, fully in command. "Listen up." He turned toward Molly.

"There are some big tables downstairs," she said, pointing down the stairs. "Bring up twelve of them and put them in the big room through those doors."

The boys quickly moved downstairs, pushing and shoving as they went.

"I'd better go with them," Jeff said. "I presume you want the tables up here with the building left intact."

Molly nodded, her smile staying on her lips as she listened to the commotion going on downstairs. Jeff had changed since his high school days. Each and every day that she saw him, he proved that point. She turned toward her mother and was surprised to find the older woman frowning. The look of anger in her eyes went beyond annoyance at the boys' youthful high jinks.

Molly's mother seemed startled when she caught Molly's gaze on her and looked the other way. "I'll just go tell your father the tables are being taken care of."

Molly watched as her mother disappeared among the workers. What bee was in her mother's bonnet now? Rather than follow her mother and demand some answers, though, Molly went after Jeff.

"You guys manage these tables all right?" she asked a group she met on her way down.

"Hey, no sweat."

"This little thing? I could carry two by myself."

"I could carry three," a kid farther down the stairs claimed.

"You guys are just too much." Molly laughed and joined Jeff in the basement. "Got everything under control?"

"Sure."

"You're a real lifesaver."

He just laughed. "This was an easy miracle."

They moved to let a group go by and she saw something change in Jeff's eyes as he watched the kids. A real sense of pride.

"These boys are some of my junior leaders," he said. "Fancy title for kids who I keep busy at the Y. They do some chores around the place, play some basketball and swim and hopefully get some self-esteem along the way. We just hope the activity will keep them from joining the gangs. I was glad you called. I wish they had more chances to do something for the community."

She watched a pair racing down the steps to fight with another group over a table. They were a hardworking bunch. "Did you start this program?" she asked Jeff.

He shook his head. "Nah, lots of Ys have it."

"Did they have it here before you?"

"They didn't have the manpower to start a lot of programs."

Or maybe personnel who cared as deeply, she thought, but knew better than to say it.

"So what now, Ms. Cahill?" one of the boys asked. "We got twelve tables up there."

Obviously the boys were willing to stay and work, so Molly led them upstairs where the elderly volunteers quickly commandeered them to move boxes and set up displays. The kids were silly, saluting after getting direction, but they were respectful and, most of all, cheerful. It was like a breath of fresh air having them here.

"So how are you feeling?" Jeff asked.

It took Molly a moment to understand. This morning seemed so long ago. And not nearly so frightening anymore. She wasn't sure why; nothing had changed. Except that Jeff had come to the rescue.

"Better," she said. "You know, I was just counting up all that you've done for me today. Are you sure helping you out with your program will make us even?"

"For the moment," he said. "I was never very good at counting."

"Hey, Mr. Spencer, come look at this lamp," one of the boys called. "Couldn't we fix it?" With an apologetic look at Molly, Jeff joined his boys.

Gram was right; Jeff was a great addition to the Niles community. They were all lucky to have him; the boys who were kept on the straight and narrow certainly, but the rest of the town, too, for the help he was willing to provide. And why are you drawn to him? a little voice asked. Just general civic admiration?

It was a topic she didn't really want to pursue, and she turned to look for her parents. They had to see the good side of Jeff. She saw them in the doorway, wearing sour expressions of dark disapproval.

Molly could stand it no longer. She hurried toward her parents, but her father moved away before she got there. Clenching her jaw, Molly took the bull by the horns. "Is something wrong, Mother?"

Her mother turned away, an expression of pain on her face that brought memories from Molly's youth tumbling about her ears. They weren't good memories. They were memories of misunderstandings and hard feelings. Well, she wasn't about to be pulled into that guilt trap.

"I really don't understand you," Molly said. "Jeff and his boys have been an enormous help, and all you and Father can do is scowl at them. I know these kids are a little rough around the edges but they are helping. I would think a good Christian would appreciate their efforts."

"How dare you!" her mother snapped as she turned toward Molly, eyes bright and burning. "How dare you accuse your father of being less than Christian! He's dedicated his life to helping people in all levels of society. He's worked for the homeless and he's on the board of the YMCA where your wonderful and charming Mr. Spencer works."

Her wonderful and charming Mr. Spencer? "Do you and Dad still have problems accepting Jeff?"

Her mother looked away.

"Mother, I know he was a bit of a hood in high school, but he's changed. He's a totally different man now."

Chin quivering, her mother looked close to tears. "I guess if anyone would know, you would," she said.

"What do you mean by that?" Molly demanded.

Hardness returned to her mother's face as she turned again to face Molly. "We're not stupid, dear. Your father and I are rather reserved but we're not stupid."

Molly hated these arguments. The manipulations, the attempts to fill one with guilt. "I never said you were."

Her mother took a deep breath and looked away. They stood there, almost suffocating in the long silence.

"Gram says Lilly spends a lot of time at the Y," her mother said suddenly.

"Yes, she's a very active child. She enjoys it."

"Good." Her mother nodded, bobbing her head several times. "Every child should know her father."

She hurried away and out of the room, leaving Molly staring after her, mouth hanging open. *Every child should know her father.* What in the world was Mother talking about?

Lilly. Jeff.

Child. Father.

It had to be Maggie's doing. Molly remembered when her sister had first said she was pregnant, how she'd wanted to say that Jeff was the father. She remembered Maggie saying that it wouldn't matter since he was a hood and had left town. Molly also remembered refusing to go along with that scheme, but then, when had Maggie ever done what Molly wanted?

Anger filled Molly's heart and she wanted to go screaming after her mother. She wanted to tell her that it was just Maggie being mean, spreading her little lies. Only they weren't so little anymore. They could ruin a man's life.

But Molly's feet wouldn't move. She just stood there, letting the anger seethe within her. Could she afford to go around rocking boats? How could this affect Lilly? The devils of anger burned in her soul, but maybe she had to approach things another way.

"It's natural that you should start wondering," Molly said. "Especially coming here and meeting so much of your family."

Lilly just squirmed, playing with the chili left in her bowl rather than answer Molly.

A little feedback would be nice, she thought, but pushed on anyway. "So if you have any questions..."

Apparently chili was of the utmost fascination, only to be exceeded by an itchy nose.

"I mean about your father."

More squirming, accompanied by the need for more crackers crushed up in her chili.

"He was a nice guy and all," Molly said, aware that Lilly's silence was making her ramble. "But we were both young. If I knew where he was, I'd tell him all about you."

Lilly looked up. "We could call 'Unsolved Mysteries.'"

And announce her secret to the nation. The very idea turned Molly's hands to ice. "I don't think that's the best way to tell someone they have a child," she said. "The point is—"

Lilly frowned and pushed her bowl away. "Can I go over and play with Brian and Eric?"

Molly sighed. "Sure. Go ahead." She watched as Lilly raced away. So much for inspiration guiding her words.

"Failure to communicate?" Jeff sat down on the edge of the table next to her.

Molly forced a smile to her face. She felt uneasy with him so close, as if bits of her conversation with Lilly might still be hanging in the air for him to overhear and they would somehow make him sense Maggie's accusation.

"I don't think she heard a word I said," she said.

"She probably took in more than you think. Kids that age don't let on what they're feeling."

"I guess."

She watched Lilly join Jeff's boys. She obviously already knew them from the Y. Lilly had settled in quickly here, but then hadn't both of them? Molly'd found a shoulder to lean on awfully quickly. Too quickly, considering her cowboy status. She got to her feet and started to reach for the pot to take it back into the kitchen, but Jeff beat her to it. She picked up the basket of crackers and some empty trays and followed him into the church kitchen.

"It was great of you to invite me and the boys to stay for some supper," Jeff said.

"We owed you after all the work you did this afternoon." And all the other workers had been invited to stay. Her father's silence toward Jeff and his boys had been churlish to say the least. She hoped it hadn't been obvious that Jeff's invitation had come from her rather than her parents.

"Where do you want this?" Jeff asked about the pot of chili.

"Just on the counter is fine," she said.

"Okay." He put it down next to the sink, and turned, leaning his back against the counter edge. "Anything else?"

"I don't think so."

She put the crackers on a counter near the door, but the trays belonged in the cabinet on the far side of Jeff. No problem, except that the kitchen had shrunk over the years. The aisles had grown narrower, so that she wasn't going to get by Jeff without brushing against him. Something she was suddenly shy about doing.

This was crazy; she'd been alone with him several times over the past few days. Why was she suddenly so aware of him?

Boisterous laughter came from the meeting hall, and Molly put down the trays on a table before she went back to the doorway. Lilly was at the other side of the room, throwing water-soaked napkins at Jeff's crew.

"Lilly," Molly called and waited while the girl shuffled over. "Is that really necessary?"

"They started it," Lilly insisted.

She chose to ignore Jeff's snicker off to her side. It was easy enough for him to laugh. It wasn't his daughter that was acting up. Her hands grew cold and she forced her attention on Lilly.

"Remember what Grandpa said in his sermon Sunday?" Molly asked. "Something about turning your other cheek?"

Her daughter frowned and glared at the boys, who were now making faces at Lilly. "Aunt Agnes says all that gets you is hit again."

Molly pretended not to hear Jeff's muted laughter. "Why don't you go help Mrs. Ewald clear tables?" Molly pointed to an older woman at the far side of the room, away from the boys.

Lilly trudged across the floor. "She's usually a nice kid," Molly said. "But there are times when she is just so darn ornery."

"Like mother, like daughter."

Molly swung around to glare at him. He was close, too close for her peace of mind. She stepped around him to go back into the kitchen. "I wasn't like that," she protested. "I was real shy."

"Right."

She didn't like the sound of his laughter. It was as if he knew what had been in her heart. What still lingered there. "I was," she insisted. "I was too scared to do anything wild."

"You mean like ditching school?" he asked.

"Maggie was the wild one," Molly insisted, feeling her cheeks grow warm.

He looked into her eyes as if he could read her soul. She felt naked, as if stripped of her secrets so that he knew all of her. Yet something held her there, kept her from turning away and protecting her life. Were there no secrets deep in his eyes for her to see or was he better at hiding things?

"Why do I get the feeling that there's more to you than people suspect?" he asked, whispered almost.

She tried to laugh it off, but her voice came out shaky, breathless. "Isn't that true of everybody?" she asked.

He shook his head, his eyes still locked with hers. "You're afraid of something, of letting people too close. Did Lilly's father hurt you that badly?"

She looked away and found the trays still awaiting her. She grabbed them up as if they could shield her. "I'm a cowboy, remember?" she said. "I don't get hurt."

"Cowboys are only cowboys because they've been hurt," he said. "You don't run from something if you aren't afraid of it."

She wasn't afraid of anything, she wanted to say, but couldn't. Not truthfully. Luckily, the sound of his boys' laughter resonated into the kitchen quite clearly.

"My crew is getting restless," he said. "I'd better take them on home."

"Yeah." Molly followed him over to the door and looked over toward Lilly. "You'd probably better. Before my little pal gets riled up."

"Thanks again for the dinner," he said.

"Thanks for the help."

He gathered his crew together and herded them out to the van. Molly watched from the doorway for a moment, then turned toward the foyer. It had been some day.

She heard a noise behind her and spun. Jeff was back.

"Forget something?" she asked.

"As a matter of fact, I did."

But he didn't go past her into the meeting hall, and the look in his eyes immobilized her. All she could do was watch as he came closer. It was quiet in the foyer, too quiet. His shoes seemed loud on the tile floor, or was it her heart beating so?

He stopped in front of her and took her hands in his. "If you ever need anything, just call," he said.

The intensity of his eyes scared her, as if he could get too close. "Hey, I did, didn't I?"

"That's not what I mean," he said.

"I know." For a moment, with his eyes promising such strength and stability, being close didn't seem so frightening. For a moment, heaven seemed a place to lean for just a few minutes.

Before she knew what was happening, he was taking her in his arms. They closed around her, bringing her everything his gaze had promised and more. Peace and safety.

Then his lips came down to claim hers and all that was shattered. Peace was left in ashes as a long-buried spark ignited her soul. Safety was forgotten. The long-ago love she'd felt for him was neither well buried nor too childish to grow again. Her arms wound around him, holding him close to her in what seemed to be the culmination of years of dreaming and longing.

He kissed her, and she kissed him back. She let his lips take her into the clouds, to soar above the shadows and glory in the sun. She felt strong and powerful. His mouth spoke of his hungers, ones that her heart answered in kind. She wanted to press into him, closer and closer.

Then suddenly the present came rushing back. The memory of the here and now was as effective as a cold shower, and she pulled away. Her eyes seemed to hardly know how to face him, yet his look was so gentle, so kind, that her own worries seemed foolish.

"Good golly, Miss Molly," he said softly, his fingers brushing her cheek. "Take care." Then he was gone.

Just as well. She couldn't have spoken to save her life. She closed her eyes and tried to catch her breath.

"Whatcha doing out here?"

Lilly's voice brought Molly tumbling back to earth. She opened her eyes to find her daughter frowning at her. "I was thanking Mr. Spencer for helping us."

Her daughter grunted.

"And we were saying goodbye." Or maybe it was hello.

"Took you a long time," Lilly muttered.

Yes . . . more than nine years.

Chapter Five

"Where're you going with my tools?" Gus asked.

Jeff stopped at the doorway and turned to face the Y's handyman. "I thought I'd work on the roof over the west dugout."

"I'm sorry, Mr. J. I was hoping to get to that early in the week, but those tiles in the weight room were in worse shape than we thought. I had to replace the whole floor."

Jeff shrugged. "It's no big deal, Gus. Roof just needs a few new shingles. Do me good to do some real work for a change." Do him good to be too busy to think.

Gus laughed. "Gonna get your hands dirty."

"That's okay. That way when my father asks what the hell I been doing all day, I can show him."

Whistling tunelessly between his teeth, Jeff climbed up on the dugout roof and began ripping off the worn shingles. Gus had more than enough to do keeping up the facilities. And besides, there were times when Jeff liked being out in the weather, doing something physical, all by his lonesome.

Over the years he'd found that keeping his hands busy cleared his mind. Gave it a chance, as it were, to get the cobwebs blown out.

Deep green eyes, beneath a short, soft mop of light brown hair, floated before his eyes. Of course, some cobwebs were harder than others to be rid of.

Molly's coming back here had really changed life along the old St. Joe. Without her, the Cahills were a pretty boring bunch. Old Reverend Cahill was a mover and shaker in their little community, but not one to warm up to. Molly's mother always looked like she was sipping vinegar when he was around. And all Jeff ever got from Maggie or her husband was a short nod. Oh, well. Old stuffed shirts never were comfortable around him, and the feelings were mutual.

There was no such problem between him and Molly, but then she wasn't an old stuffed shirt. Her shirt, while certainly well filled, was not stuffed.

No, sir. Definitely not. One could easily see that. Especially when she was outside and a light breeze came in off the river and rippled and pulled at the fabric of—

"Damn," he exclaimed and quickly sucked at his finger. Better pay attention to what he was doing. Replacement body parts were hard to come by, even in this day and age.

His hands went back to ripping up old shingles but his mind went back to yesterday. Well, not all of yesterday. Just a little piece. To the moments when he'd held Molly in his arms. He remembered her soft lips, her deep eyes with the yearning lurking in the corners, but most of all, he remembered how well she fit in his embrace.

He stood up and stretched, the memories getting a bit too overpowering. The river was quite a ways down at the bottom of the bluff, and he savored for a moment the queasy little feeling of standing on the edge of the world.

"Hello, up there."

"Ahh!" Molly's voice startled him and he took a deep breath, trying to restart his heart. "What the hell you doing sneaking up on people like that?"

"Well, excuse me," Molly said. Her mouth was teasing but her eyes still held the same old tension. "Next time I'll hire a marching band to announce my arrival."

"I was concentrating on my work."

"You were staring off into space."

"So, I was thinking," he said. "That's a big part of my job."

Her green eyes stared at him. What kept those shadows lurking there? More important, could he get them to disappear? It began to feel like a challenge.

"What do you want?" he asked.

"Someone said you were Superman," she replied. "I came out here to see if you could fly."

Jeff laughed. "Sure. Come up here and I'll take you with me." Somehow with her here, there seemed to be no reason not to think of her, to find her lips all too alluring. "If you come up, I'll let you help me."

"Wow. What an offer. Maybe I should rest awhile until my heart calms down."

"Come on up," Jeff said. "The view's great." With her here, it would be even better.

She hesitated until it became a battlement he had to charge, a mountain he had to scale. If he could convince her to join him up here, maybe he could convince her to—

Maybe he'd better watch where his thoughts were leading him. "There's a nice breeze up here." He held out his hand. "Don't be a chicken."

The look that crossed her face was the same one he'd seen on Lilly's more than once, and he'd known it would work. He held out his hand, but she ignored it, climbing up on the roof herself.

"I imagine a desk jockey like yourself needs a lot of this kind of break," she remarked as she sat down.

"I've always found the river restored me."

For a long moment, they admired the view of the tree-covered slope and the river, winding like a large snake down below.

"I'm sorry about yesterday," Molly said, breaking the silence first.

He knew exactly what she meant—her parents. "Don't worry about it. There's no problem."

"I thought my parents were rude."

"We can't make ourselves responsible for the actions of our parents." He stared at his feet a moment, lightly banging his shoes together, and he could feel the past claim him. "I learned that hard lesson a long time ago."

They held another long silence between themselves. He wished he felt that she was savoring the peace here, healing under it as he did. But somehow, he sensed that she was just hiding behind the silence, that though her body was here, her mind was far away.

"I can start helping you next week," she said.

"That's good." He nodded, switching his mind to the summer program for special children that he'd talked to Molly about. "I have a couple of high school kids who want to help out and some parents who've already been asking about some of the activities we have planned."

"Swimming would be a good thing to start with," Molly said. "Do you have some pool time available?"

"Twelve-thirty to two."

"See you Monday then. I can get together with the counselors. We can start working with the kids on Tuesday."

"Sounds good to me."

"I'm glad I can help."

"I appreciate it," Jeff said. "You ever need any help with anything, you just let me know."

"Anything?"

"Absolutely," he replied. "Anything. No reservations."

"Like helping me make pies? Pulling the weeds from Gram's flower bed?"

"I said anything." Taking the shadows from her eyes, bringing a smile to those luscious lips. Anything.

He turned his attention back to the scene below them, but two well-trimmed ankles kept intruding in his line of vision. "I can use some help with this roof."

Molly looked at his grimy hands, then at her own, already showing dirt just from sitting on the old shingles. "Sorry," she said, smiling. "I don't have a union card."

"I can get you one," Jeff said.

"I have to get back. Rummage sale starts soon and Mom said Maggie's working. I need to talk to her."

"Yeah, but does she want to talk to you?"

Molly gave him a strange look, half-apprehensive, half-startled. "What are you talking about?"

"You're all tense," he said. "I assumed you aren't simply going to ask her for her brownie recipe."

"Nope, angel food cake." She jumped down off the roof, gave him a wave with her fingers and was quickly gone.

Jeff watched her disappear behind the building, then slowly turned back to the river. So much for work that would distract him.

There was something about Molly. She was so nice and fun to be with, but somehow she was like the river. For all the swift, joyful surface of it, he knew there were shadows and secrets buried beneath the surface. And as with the river, he had this hypnotic urge to unearth them.

Just as well she thought of herself as a cowboy, he told himself. He was the one who didn't trust relationships. He got up to return to his shingles.

Molly wandered around the room, staring at the items on display but not really seeing them. So Maggie was working was she? Apparently "this morning" didn't mean the first thing this morning. Maybe Molly should have gone over to Maggie's house last night and demanded some answers. So what if it had been inconvenient? Hadn't she just wimped out by waiting?

Molly sank down at a table in the corner by the children's clothes. Here barely a week and already she was reverting to her old self, worried about causing a stir, afraid to make someone look bad, even if they were doing worse to someone else.

She and Lilly shouldn't have come here; they ought to leave.

She wished Agnes was back, though what good would that do? She wasn't about to go to the older woman, confess the whole story and ask for advice. Neither could she tell Gram the truth. So who did that leave to turn to? Jeff? Molly didn't think so.

She leaned back, putting her feet up on a chair. A grandmotherly type frowned at her in passing, and Molly let her feet slip back to the floor.

Damn. Once a minister's daughter, always a minister's daughter. She and Lilly really ought to leave. Living in a fishbowl at age twenty-six was a bit much.

Molly slouched in her seat and let her eyes roam the hall, daring anybody to respond. If they didn't like the way she was sitting, too bad. She wasn't Molly the minister's daughter anymore. She was Molly the mother, Molly the mature. A smile played on her lips. Molly the best damn bartender in the Rockies.

Just then Maggie walked in the door. It was time. No more Molly the mouse. She swallowed hard and waved her sister over. Maggie came but didn't look too happy about it.

"Have a seat," Molly said.

"I came here to help Mother," Maggie said. "Have you seen her?"

"She's around," Molly said carelessly. "But they don't really need much help right now."

"I really should see Mother first. Let her know I'm here."

Molly frowned at her. "Sit down."

"No, you're slouching. You always slouch when you're in one of your rotten moods."

"Oh, damn it, Maggie. I don't always do anything anymore." Molly straightened up in her chair, then hated herself for it. "I've grown up in the past nine years."

"See. And now you're swearing."

"Maggie," Molly said, taking a deep breath, "if you don't sit down and talk to me, I'm going to strip buff naked, jump up on the table and shout out every swear word I know."

Her sister stared at her.

"And after working all these years in Agnes's bar, I can go thirty or forty minutes without repeating myself."

Maggie sat down across from Molly, holding herself stiff and proper. Her sister's gaze zigzagged around the room while Molly studied her. In some ways, they were so alike it was weird, but in other ways they were very different. In Molly's eyes, Maggie still seemed to care more about appearance than truth.

"Are . . . are you going to be here long?" Maggie asked.

"Maybe." Molly shrugged and hid all her desire to leave under the table. "School doesn't start until the last week of August. That would give us another month here and still leave lots of time for the drive back."

Maggie nodded. Did she also pale slightly, or was that Molly's imagination?

"Getting tired of me already?" Molly asked.

"No. Of course not." Her sister swallowed, as if her throat was sore. "We're sisters. Twin sisters."

Yes, they were, but Molly wondered if that meant anything anymore.

"Why did you tell Mom and Dad that Jeff was Lilly's father?" Molly spoke so quietly that any spirits occupying the empty tables next to them would have been unable to hear.

But Maggie had heard. She turned even farther away from Molly.

"Maggie," Molly prodded when the silence stretched out beyond the horizon.

"You have to understand," Maggie whispered. "It was years ago, when I came back from Denver and told them you were keeping the baby. I was scared. You don't know what it was like."

And Molly didn't know about being scared? Hell. As far as Molly was concerned, she had a lifetime subscription.

"Is that the only time Jeff's paternity was discussed?"

Maggie nodded.

"You haven't talked recently about Lilly and who her father is?"

Suddenly, Maggie's gaze swung full bore onto Molly. Her eyes blazed with all the emotion of the teenage Maggie, the bossy little brat that Molly remembered from high school.

"Of course, I haven't *discussed* such things since," Maggie snapped. "No one talks about such things. All that stuff with Lilly is buried and forgotten, and it would have stayed that way if you hadn't come back."

So it was Molly's fault for coming back. She should have expected that. "Lilly has a right to know her own family," Molly pointed out.

Maggie turned back but her eyes were no longer blazing. Instead, they were overflowing with tears.

"I know," she said hoarsely and stood up. "None of this is her fault. I'm sorry. I'll try to fix it." She hurried out of the room.

Molly stayed at the table, feeling more drained than angry. It was getting to be time for this cowgirl to ride off into the sunset.

Molly stared out at the darkened street, letting the swing's gentle sway match the evening's soft breeze. The crickets were going wild tonight. What did that mean? Rain before morning? A cold spell coming? Living in the city had taken all the country out of her. She glanced down at Rufus, asleep near her feet. Being in the country had taken all the watchdog out of Rufus.

"That does it for me," Gram said, her voice floating out from the living room where she and Lilly had been looking at family albums all evening. "I think it's time we turned in."

"I guess."

Lilly came out on the porch. "G'night, Rufus," she said and gave her dog a hug before turning to Molly. "G'night, Mom."

"Good night, sweetheart." Molly gave Lilly an extra hug before the girl squirmed away.

"Why don't you go out?" Gram said. "It's not even ten yet."

"Go where? This is Niles, remember? The streets roll up here about eight."

"Not all of them."

"Call the dude, Mom," Lilly suggested. "I bet he's still up."

"Good night, you two," Molly said.

Gram turned and pulled the screen door open. "She never did take suggestions well," she told Lilly as they went inside.

Molly watched a car stop down the street. A couple got out and walked into a house, arm in arm. Their house seemed suddenly alight with warmth, the darkness around her more dense. Molly hugged her knees to her chest. Rufus sat up and stared down the street.

Someone was out walking. Her father. He stopped in front of the house, peering up into the darker shadows of the porch as Rufus growled slightly, deep in his throat.

"Hush, Rufus," Molly ordered.

"Molly?" her father said.

"Yeah."

He walked up to join her. "I always walk at this time. Doc says it's good for my heart. I just know it helps me relax."

"That's good." She brushed a mosquito from her arm and stood up. "We were going in. Want to join us?"

"Sure."

He cleared his throat and, from habits ingrained as a child, Molly stiffened up. Her father was about to make a pronouncement. He said nothing, though, as they went inside. He sat on the sofa, picking up Lilly's photo album with *This Is Me* written in her bold hand across the cover. He paged idly through the book, stopping at pictures of birthday parties and Halloweens.

"Lilly's a wonderful child," he said.

"Thank you." Molly felt on edge, wary.

"I've missed a lot of her growing up."

Molly shrugged. It had been his choice, after all.

"I . . . I was wondering if we could have a kind of welcoming ceremony for her the weekend of the reunion," he said. His voice was hesitant, a rarity for him. "It's something we do to welcome older children and adults into the congregation. It's not exactly a christening, but celebrates their oneness with us."

His face reflected such a mixture of hope and yearning that it was almost painful to see. "I think that would be lovely," Molly said. "Assuming Lilly agrees. She's old enough to have a say in it."

He nodded his understanding and started to close Lilly's album. It fell open to the first page. "You know, Molly—" Her father's expression of soft geniality disappeared, replaced by a red look of pure anger. "What is this?" he demanded.

Molly leaned forward. The book was open to the copy of Lilly's birth certificate, his finger was pointing about halfway down the page. *Father: unknown.*

"How could you do this to Lilly?" he cried. "This is an official document. It's used to get in school. To get a driver's license. To get married. She'll be marked by this stigma the rest of her life."

"It's not that big a deal anymore," Molly said.

"A big deal? Not giving your child a father will always be a big deal to me." Her father shut the book, dropping it onto the end table as if it pained him to touch it. "Why isn't Spencer named there?"

"Because he's not the father," Molly replied.

"But Maggie said—"

"How would Maggie know?"

Molly rose along with her voice, and she forced herself to stare at him. She had to run this bluff, had to do it to protect Lilly.

"Your mother and I saw the way you were always mooning around him." Her father's eyes were blazing, his voice dripping with disgust. "The way you followed him around like a sick puppy. He took advantage of your youth and innocence."

"He didn't do anything," Molly said. "He didn't notice I was alive."

"When are you going to stop lying?"

"I'm not lying."

"No? Everyone can see the resemblance." With that he stomped out, letting the screen door slam behind him.

Molly held her breath for a long moment, but she heard no sounds from upstairs. She sank slowly back into the chair, hot tears flowing down her cheeks. *I'm not lying.* What a pompous ass she was. Lying was what she did best. But if she hadn't lied, where would Lilly have been by now?

The emotions, her own and her father's, were suddenly too much for Molly. She had to get out of the house and, putting Rufus on his leash, went out the back door.

She had no idea where they were going, but somehow they ended up at the Y. The building was dark at this hour, but lights and cheers from the park down the street beckoned. An adults' softball game was in progress. Just being around people would help. She walked toward the stands, taking a seat off to the side. Rufus sat at her feet, looking delighted with his unexpected outing.

"Hey, there. Did Lilly say you two could be out this late at night?"

Molly looked up to find Jeff at her side. A sudden rush of new tears threatened and all she wanted to do was hide in his arms. She turned to study the man emerging from the shadows.

"She's in bed," Molly said. "We snuck out."

"You snuck out?" His voice was a great imitation of an indignant parent. "And am I supposed to keep your sordid little secret?"

He was just teasing. She knew that, but her defenses were all too fragile. She blinked rapidly, but to no avail. The tears started down her cheeks.

"Whoops." His arm went around her shoulder, and he was leading her off toward the concession stand. "I know my jokes aren't always great, but I don't usually get this reaction."

"I'm sorry," she mumbled through the deluge, clinging to Rufus's leash. "It's not that."

Jeff got two lemonades and led her around back to an unused, unlit baseball diamond. They sat on the bleachers. She took Rufus's leash off him and he sniffed around under the seats before settling down by her feet.

"Drink up. This stuff is guaranteed to cure the blues."

She doubted that, but sipped at the drink. She suddenly noticed he was in baseball uniform.

"Are you playing tonight?"

"I was going to, but the other team didn't show up with enough guys. So we had to let one more girl play."

"And you were the first one your team wanted to drop?"

"No," he protested. "We drew straws. It was the luck of the draw."

"Sure."

"Hey," he said, putting an arm around her shoulder. "Be nice. I bought you a lemonade."

The tears had stopped, and her heart was feeling stronger. "Maybe I would have preferred popcorn."

"You can't eat popcorn and cry," he said.

"Who said?"

He pulled back slightly, not enough to let go of her shoulder, but enough to feign disbelief. "It's a well-known fact. You eat popcorn during those little hiccupy things you do when you cry, and then you choke."

"This you learned from personal experience or just common knowledge?"

"Not personal experience." His voice was dry and distant. "The last time I cried I was eight and had no popcorn around."

"What had happened?"

He shook his head as if unwilling to dredge up the past, then shrugged. "My father had promised that we'd have a special dinner for my birthday. Instead, he spent the night drinking. I learned then that if you don't trust in the first place, then you don't get hurt." He shook off the past. "No, you pick up certain knowledge working at a Y."

"Valuable knowledge." She hoped it hadn't seemed as if she was prying. She looked around for Rufus. He had moved to the side of the bleachers, not yet asleep but looking close to it.

"I had a discussion with my father," she said.

His arms tightened around her. "Happens to the best of us," he said quietly.

"Seems to happen all the time since I came back here."

"You had a nine-year hole in your relationship. Neither of you are dealing with the present yet. You have to let him come to terms with his anger. He has to let you be an adult."

Molly closed her eyes, leaning closer into Jeff's arms. "How do you know he's angry?"

"Is the sky blue? Will the Cubs lose?"

She laughed and felt his arms tighten around her. "I sure am lucky you're back here. Who else could have given me such sage advice?"

"The Sage Advice 900-number?"

"Is there such a thing?"

"Sure. I work on it in my off hours."

He was so silly, so perfect for her right now. She really was lucky to have him to lean on. "And how do you suggest I convince my father to let me be an adult?"

"Live your own life. Stop trying to please him, and please yourself instead."

"Sounds easy."

"Only because I left out the big one. Let him be angry if he wants, but don't let his anger become yours."

"Sounds impossible."

"No, just really, really hard."

She lay in his arms, listening to the sound of his heartbeat. It was comfortable here, too comfortable. All her problems seemed solvable; she felt infinitely strong.

"So are you sorry you came back?" he asked.

"Sometimes."

"I'm not."

His hand moved over her back—caressing, warming, stirring up fires. She looked up at him. The shadows of the night couldn't hide the fires in his eyes. His lips came down on hers.

It was truly magical this effect he had on her. Just the merest touch of his lips could bring fireworks into the nighttime sky. Or were they just in her heart?

It was too confusing when all she wanted to do was move closer and closer into his embrace, to taste all the sweetness his mouth could give. She turned slightly, sliding her arm around his shoulders. Their mouths met with deeper passion. She felt young and alive, as if she was discovering a splendor that no one had ever found before. Certainly not her, not even in her dreams.

He pulled away slightly to let his lips dance across her forehead and on her hair. Then he sighed as he rested his chin on her head. She just closed her eyes and wished for the night to go on forever.

Chapter Six

"You look like you survived without me," Agnes said.

"Barely. Just barely," Molly said, putting down her crossword puzzle. The rummage sale was about as lively as a convention of hibernating turtles, and through it all she kept daydreaming about Jeff.

Agnes pulled up a chair from a neighboring table and sat down. "You always exaggerate."

Molly closed her eyes. "Let's see now. I always slouch when I'm in a bad mood, I always take suggestions poorly, now I always exaggerate. I must be boringly predictable."

"You are, but we put up with you."

"You're so kind. How was Aunt Bertha?"

"Old. Forgetful. I got some great cherries though in Traverse City. Thought maybe I could talk you into making a pie."

"Gram's got me down to make about ten tomorrow. Said we need to start preparing for the reunion."

Agnes winced and got to her feet. "She's not figuring on me making any, is she?"

"If she is, Lilly and I will disabuse her of the idea. We still haven't recovered from the last one you made."

"Very funny." Her eyes widened as she looked beyond Molly. "My, my. Is this part of your survival kit?"

Molly turned around to see Lilly walking across the room with Jeff. Her breath caught at the sight of them, her father's words echoing in her heart. *Everyone can see the resemblance.*

She looked at them critically, seeking proof to throw in her father's face. They both had dark hair. So did Molly's father. Besides which, lots of people had blue eyes.

She tried to think back to her senior year. Maggie'd had a picture of Tim on her dresser, so Molly had seen it often enough. He'd had dark hair, too, usually hidden under a baseball cap, but the color of his eyes eluded her. Not that it mattered. She could hardly produce Tim as Lilly's father; that would just lead to more problems.

"Did Aunt Maggie really take tests for you in high school?" Lilly demanded as soon as she got close enough to be heard.

Molly gave Jeff a thank-you-very-much smile before turning to her daughter. "Once in a while."

"That's neat. If I had a twin, I'd have her go to the dentist for me." Lilly gave Agnes a hug and plopped herself down on the table next to the older woman. "Guess what, Aunt Agnes? Gram and me were playing poker and I won two of her bedrooms and the basement. She said pretty soon I'm going to own her whole house."

"I don't think it'll fit in the trunk of the car," Molly said.

Lilly just gave her a look and turned back to Agnes. "Want to see a really great bike someone gave to the sale?"

She waited for Agnes to get to her feet before turning to Lilly. "Mom, would you keep Jeff company?"

"I'll try."

He snickered as he took Agnes's vacated seat. "She's quite a little con artist. Told me I had to come help out here. She claimed you were so busy that you were getting slouchy."

"And therefore grumpy."

He eyed her carefully, looking up one side of her and down the other until her cheeks grew red. He finally shook his head. "You don't look slouchy."

"Must be because you came over."

He grinned and did strange things to her heart. "Must be."

Molly just looked out over the sparse crowd, not really avoiding his eyes, but not exactly seeking them out, either. She wasn't sure where this placed her on the bravery scale, but knew she'd rank high on the self-preservation one.

"We're not really all that busy," she said. "You don't need to stay." Though she certainly wouldn't mind if he did.

"Well, I do have a lot of other pressing duties," he said.

Her heart sighed with disappointment, but she told herself it was just as well. No sense either of them getting any more involved than they already were. She was leaning on him too much as it was.

"I had promised my living room rug that I'd vacuum it today," he said. "And then there's the bologna in the refrigerator. It's taking offense at the cheese and I promised to get them all to clean up their act."

She stared at him. The man was truly insane. No wonder he seemed such a relief to be around.

"Are these kids' clothes two for fifty cents?" a woman demanded.

"No, ma'am," Jeff replied. "Four for a dollar."

The woman eyed him strangely, but made a selection and moved on.

"That was terrible," Molly whispered.

"Hey, I wasn't lying."

"Your honesty knows no bounds."

"Nope."

"Hey, dude," Lilly shouted as she raced back, sliding across the floor the last ten feet. She skidded into the table and lay half across it. "So you guys going out tonight?"

"Your honesty is only exceeded by her subtlety," Molly muttered and turned to her daughter. "Lilly, it really isn't any of your business."

"Just checking." She turned her innocent blue eyes on Jeff. "Gram won four tickets to a South Bend White Sox game from a radio station and her and me and Agnes and somebody named Paul are going to go. I just didn't want Mom to be sitting at home all by herself."

"You could have saved a ticket for me."

"You hate baseball. Whatya say, dude? Gonna take pity on Mom?"

Jeff was trying hard not to laugh under Lilly's barrage. "Unfortunately, I've got a swim meet at the Y tonight. I've got to be there."

"So Mom can help."

"Lilly, I know nothing about swim meets."

"What's to know? The people in the pool are the swimmers. Catch you guys later."

Molly glared at her daughter as Lilly sped away. "I think maybe a talk on manners is due next."

"Don't worry. She's just full of energy."

"That's one way to put it," Molly grumbled. The real problem was that she would have liked to do something with him tonight but didn't really appreciate Lilly's throwing them together. "So do you need any help tonight?"

"Won't you be needed here?" he asked.

"Nope." She shook her head. "We close down at five and there are enough volunteers to clean up."

Jeff took a long moment to look around the room. "You're going to be exhausted by tonight."

Didn't he want her around, was that it? Best to find out the truth, even if it wasn't what she wanted to hear. "Are you kidding? You should see a cowboy bar on a Saturday night. Now that's exhausting."

"How about if I stay here and help you out?" he said. "That way it'll be an even trade if you help me tonight."

"We'll run your body ragged," she warned.

His eyes twinkled at her. "A man can always hope." He picked up her crossword puzzle. "Looks like this is the first thing you need help with."

That and keeping her heart under control. Jeff proved as adept with crossword puzzles as he was with carrying out heavy loads for people, and the next few hours were spent basking in the warmth of his laughter. People stopped to talk to both of them about their high school days and earlier. For a time, Molly forgot about the shadows that hung over her and just enjoyed herself.

"Molly," her father said. "May I speak with you a moment, please? Privately."

The angry look he gave Jeff didn't escape Molly, which made her want to strike back. "Of course, Father." She put some sunshine in her smile and molasses in her voice. "Jeff, dear. Would you watch my table for me? Dad wants to talk to me about something."

The elderly ladies around them smiled, while her father's look grew even darker. Molly followed him to a distant corner that was presently empty.

"What is he doing here?" her father asked.

"What 'he' are you talking about?" Molly asked.

"Don't play games with me, young lady."

"There are a lot of men here today, Father." She was just as stubborn as he was and could play his obtuse game just as well.

"You know damn well who I'm talking about. That Spencer person."

"He came by to see if he could be of some assistance."

"We don't need his kind of help," her father snapped.

"Is that right?" Molly snapped back. "Well, for your information, most of the ladies here are elderly. Jeff's been aiding in lifting things. So I say we do need his kind of help."

"I would prefer you ask him to leave."

"He's helping me," Molly said, feeling her jaw tighten in stubbornness. "You tell him to leave. And if you do, you'd better find someone to take my place."

He stared at her, his eyes demanding obedience. Her soul quivered, but Molly had been away from home too long. She had grown up during the past nine years. She was an adult now, giving respect but also demanding it in her own right. Jeff would stay or her father would have to put both of them out.

Her father gave in first. His eyes dropped and he turned to leave, but before he did, he looked back. "You are still my daughter, Molly," he said quietly. "It is wrong to not respect me and my wishes." Then he turned on his heels and stalked away.

Molly had won, yet she felt no joy, just a deep sadness at her father's bullheadedness. It wasn't a matter of defying him. She just wanted to stand up for what was right.

"Are you okay, Molly?"

She hadn't noticed Jeff walk up. There was still a touch of a smile on his lips, but she noticed the gentle concern in his eyes first. She longed to fall into the safe harbor of his arms. He'd make all these problems fade away and leave only what was important in her heart. Yet that was more than she could ask of him. Maybe more than she could ask of herself, to relinquish such power over herself to someone else.

"Do you know how often you ask me that?" She forced a laugh. "Either my life must be a mess or I just look like a sad sack."

"You're gorgeous and you know it." He put his arm around her shoulder. "You didn't answer my question."

He was too perceptive at times. "Everything's fine," she lied. "Nothing to concern my crossword puzzle assistant with."

"Are you sure?"

"Hey, I'm a big girl. I can solve a few of my problems by myself." Just don't take your arm from my shoulders, she pleaded silently.

Every eye in the place was on the row of girls down by the pool. Every eye except Jeff's. No matter how he tried to concentrate on the swim meet, his gaze kept straying to Molly.

He watched her brush at a lock of her hair with the back of her hand. Sweat glistened on her forehead. It was a pleasant night but it was humid here in the pool area.

Every cell in Jeff's body and mind wanted to take Molly outside, out in the cool air and privacy of the night so he could wipe her brow and kiss her sweet lips. Then he would lie back, hold her in his arms and let the cool night breeze wash over them. They would sink into a pleasant cocoon as they counted the stars that filled the sky. He told himself that he ought to stay far away from her, but knew that was impossible.

The whistle blew and the girls dived from the platforms into the water. From benches along the side of the pool, their teammates cheered them on. Red-clad Niles Marlins and blue-clad Dowagiac Dolphins. The winner of this race would win the meet, but the excitement in the air hadn't really touched him. There was a different undercurrent here that overrode all others.

"Come on, come on," Molly muttered under her breath.

Two Niles girls took the lead at the turn and Molly was bouncing on the bench, as if she were rooting for Lilly. Jeff watched her. There was such a vitality about her. She made him feel so alive.

The Niles girls came in first and second, giving Niles the victory. Molly sagged against Jeff as she applauded with the sparse crowd. "Where do they get all that energy?"

"Comes with being young." He got to his feet as the teams were lining up to receive their awards. "We'd better get back to the control desk."

"Seems like more people ought to come to these meets. Not just the parents of the kids involved."

They ducked through the swimming pool offices and into the control desk. "This is a pretty typical turnout," he said. "There's so much going on every place that we're lucky to get this many."

"Still seems a shame. All that work and hardly anyone around to appreciate it." She leaned on the counter and stared off toward the empty hallway. "Lilly plays basketball and soccer in school, but I'd bet she'd love to be on a swim team."

"Move into Gram's house and she can swim here."

He wasn't sure where the words came from, but they took him by surprise as much as they did her. Molly turned to look at him, then grinned, obviously taking them as a joke. "Right."

"Hey, if you're here much longer, Lilly's going to own the house. Where'd she learn how to play poker anyway? From some friend of Agnes?"

"From Gram."

"Ah, that explains her sudden talent for winning."

A few people trickled out of the locker rooms and stopped to turn in keys and wet towels. Molly rehung the keys for the women's locker room while Jeff did the men's. It wasn't exactly a difficult job, but he was still surprised at how nicely they worked together, moving around each other in the small space as if in some well-choreographed dance.

The trickle of people turned into a deluge for a few minutes. People dropping off keys and waiting for their passes to be returned. It was a momentary madhouse.

"Miller? Krecioch? Kelsey?" Molly called out the names and put the passes into eager, outstretched hands. "That our towel?" she called after a departing youngster.

"Oops." He came running back with it, and she tossed it into the bin.

"Once a mother, always a mother?" Jeff teased.

"Or a teacher."

There was such an ease about her. She was a unique combination of relaxing and disturbing. He almost wished she'd stick around for the summer. Almost.

She was the first person he'd met in a long time whom he instinctively trusted. Funny how they'd almost been friends back in high school and had just gravitated together once she came back.

"So now what?" Molly asked.

He glanced over at her key board. All keys were back in place. "We clean out the locker room and pool area, then do a walk-through of the building."

"Aye, aye, sir."

He took her hand as if she might get lost, and they walked into the women's locker room. He liked being with her, liked being close to her. So why were they spending a Saturday evening picking up wet towels? He ought to be able to show her a better time than this.

She let go of his hand to pick up a towel lying on the floor, and he suddenly felt alone, lonely. He stuck his hand into his pocket, then walked over to a row of lockers to check them out. He found two wallets and a bathing suit. Strange the things people left behind.

His eyes strayed over to Molly and he saw the young girl she had been, the hopefulness that had been in her eyes, the need for approval and acceptance. Why hadn't he seen in her then, what he saw in her now? Why had he refused the friendship that she had offered?

Yet someone must have accepted it, or pretended to, since she'd gotten pregnant during their senior year. He felt a strange anger toward Lilly's father. How could he have just used Molly and then pushed her aside, abandoning her and her child?

"Gram said you're up for some big award," Molly said.

"Yeah. It'll mean a lot to the Y if I get it." He tightened the spigots on a sink and stopped a trickle.

"Not to you?"

"The plaque'll look good on the wall, but it's the kids that'll make out like bandits. We'll get enough money over the next five years to hire a part-time counselor and some tutors, and add programs from music lessons to karate.''

"This place is lucky to have you."

He shrugged, not so sure of that. "I'm lucky to be here," he said.

The look she gave him was clearly puzzled, but they were through with the women's locker room and he just moved out into the pool area. He deposited the items he'd collected along the way on a bench.

"We need to move the float back into place around the diving area and take down the strings of flags," he said.

She put her stuff down also, standing next to him as she gazed around the room. "It's so peaceful in here now," she said. "Hard to believe it was the scene of all that excitement just a short time ago."

"We could bring some excitement back," he suggested.

She just laughed. "And would ribbons be awarded for effort?"

"Only for victory."

She turned so that her eyes looked into his. Their green depths seemed to glitter like the surface of the water—beckoning, calling, luring him into their secrets. He took a deep breath, but rather than steady him, inhaling seemed to draw her in completely. She surrounded him, consumed him, drove him to the very edge.

She moved slightly and came into his arms. Their lips met, sending sparks off into the air. A raging hunger engulfed him. Hunger for her lips, her very essence, yet there was a rage too, lurking back in his soul. It was an anger at the man who had used her, then left her, and at himself for not being there for her when she had needed him.

His arms tightened around her, pulling her closer against him. He somehow had to make up for the hurt and mistakes of the past and let his mouth beg for her forgiveness. She deserved cherishing and protection, deserved so much more than life had given her. She moved in his embrace so that her breasts were pressed against his chest, and he felt ready to never let her go.

But she pulled away slowly, reluctantly, taking deep gulps of air. He felt as shaky as she looked.

She laughed and pushed some hair back off her forehead. Her hand was unsteady. "It's warm in here," she said.

"Yep."

She glanced around her. "So what's next?"

All sorts of possibilities raced through his mind. "We could cool off in the pool."

"I don't have a suit with me."

He raised his eyebrows in answer, and she just laughed, giving him a playful push toward the pool.

"Oh, no, we don't. I'm sure skinny-dipping in the Y pool would not help you get your award."

"Boy, you sound so... maternal," he grumped with a smile, then nodded toward the little plastic floats that were threaded onto a rope. "We need to drag that back into the pool and hook it onto the sides."

"Sounds do-able."

"It would be a lot easier if we were in the pool."

She just laughed at him and went over to take one end. He took the other, trying to concentrate on dragging the rope around the lifeguard chair and the top of the pool's ladder, but his eyes kept straying to her.

God, she was so beautiful. Her eyes, her movements, her laughter, all touched him in such unexpected ways. He felt such a hole in his life when she wasn't around, that it scared him. He was happy with his present life, content at least.

They got the float to the water and he hooked his side in place. "Got yours?" he asked. He could go over and help her, but he knew that wasn't all that would happen.

"Yep. No problem. Now how do we get the flags down?"

"Climb up to the top row of the bleachers. I'll use the step stool on my side."

It went all too fast, and in a matter of minutes, he was rolling up the string of colored flags while she was gathering up a few more wet towels.

"Who washes all these towels?" she asked.

"We have a washer-dryer. We go through too many of them to use a laundry service."

With their hands full of towels, flags and wet bathing suits, they went back to the control desk. He would much rather have had his arms full of Molly, but she was intent on cleaning the place up. Maybe he had imagined her answering hunger.

"Where's the washer?" she asked, looking around.

"I'll do them Monday," he said. Maybe if they got away from here, he could coax her back into a tender mood.

"And let them lie here all wet until then? No way." She found the washer herself in the back room and loaded it with wet towels. It was chugging away merrily in a matter of minutes. He felt his grump level on the rise.

"This is just how I've always dreamed of spending my Saturday nights," he said. "A beautiful woman, a starry sky and a washer full of wet towels."

She just laughed, dragging her fingers across his cheek in the gentlest of caresses. "Want to buy me a soda and then take me outside so we can cool off?"

Jeff shrugged. "Soda I can do. The cooling off may be a bit harder. I'm not guaranteeing anything." He took two cans of soda from a little refrigerator in the office.

"Don't worry." She linked her arm in his as they walked to a side door. "I won't sue."

The breeze was cooler than he'd expected. Once they'd sat down on the edge of the loading dock, he took his arm out of hers and put it around her shoulders. "Not going to get cold, are you?"

"Nope," she replied.

"I could go back and get you a jacket."

"Nope."

She leaned farther into his arms and he tightened his hold on her shoulder. "Hard to get a word in edgewise with you around."

"Poor baby."

He stopped, putting both arms around her. "I'm neither poor nor a baby."

The damp smell of the river rose, mingling with the clean smell of her hair. Jeff felt his heart quicken. His body warmed even in the cool night breeze. He leaned down and kissed her.

It was such a mingling of their spirits and their needs that the earth seemed to stand still. He felt her move in his arms. His hands slid over her softness and she seemed to come alive beneath the fervor of his caress. The stars crackled in the heavens, the air felt charged with passion and wanting. He could take this night and let it last forever.

But then he felt her stir, and pulled away just a bit. She didn't leave his embrace but snuggled down into his arms to rest her head against his chest. He closed his eyes and let them both be one with the darkness.

"Can I ask you something?" she asked.

"Sure." With her lying here in his arms like this, she could ask anything of him. Slay a dragon. Find the pot at the end of the rainbow. Ford a raging river.

"How did you learn to get along with your father when you came back here?"

Not a task to prove his manhood, but maybe what he expected. "I'm not sure I did," he said, looking back into the past. "I guess I just stopped expecting anything from him. He couldn't break any promises if I didn't let him make any."

"That sounds so unforgiving."

"Forgiving or not forgiving wasn't an issue," he said. "When I came back here, I basically was accepting who my father was, good points and bad points. What he does doesn't affect me."

"Not at all?"

"Nope."

"I don't believe that," she said and pulled away from his arms to look into his face.

Jeff didn't know what she could see there, but turned away. It was instinct, not a rejection of her. He'd spent too many years being alone, leaning on no one. But to let someone peek inside him now...even Molly who stirred him in so many ways. He felt her eyes on him but just stared away at the dark shadows that were the trees along the river.

"Hasn't your father stopped drinking?"

Jeff shrugged. "Yeah."

"Then aren't you proud of him? Doesn't it make you happy when you see how he's turned things around?"

He didn't know how to make her understand. "I have learned my happiness isn't dependent on what he's doing or not doing."

"In other words, you've closed yourself off from him." Her voice clearly said what she thought of that idea.

"Not at all. We have dinner a couple of times a week. We're friends."

"He's your father. You should be more than friends."

This time Jeff moved away. Not far, just back to where it was safe. "Maybe he should have thought of that a few years back when I needed a father."

He got to his feet. He should have been more careful about this developing friendship with Molly. All of a sudden she seemed too close in ways that made him skittish. He'd been letting his memories speak to his hormones, both of which were short-circuiting his brain.

"I'd better check on those towels," he said.

Molly got to her feet also, grabbing his hand so that he couldn't move away. Her touch was warm, inviting, so much so that he had to steel himself against giving in to the hungers it evoked.

"Jeff, I'm sorry. I didn't mean to get you angry. I just seem to keep butting heads with my own father and thought maybe you'd found an answer."

"I'm not angry," he said, and he wasn't. He'd just been trying to explain to Molly what the truth was; he wouldn't allow his happiness to depend on anybody else.

"Are you sure?" she persisted.

"Positive." He added a laugh for good measure, and she seemed to relax.

"And to prove it, you'll come help me bake pies tomorrow?"

He wanted to say no but those words wouldn't come out. "I'm not much of a baker," he said instead. The urge to spend the day with her dangled in front of him, tempting him, luring him away from his dark solitary paths.

"Pitting cherries is pretty easy."

The night sounds were hushed and he felt the moon smiling down on them. What was the big deal? They were friends and enjoyed each other's company in the ways a man enjoys a woman. In a few weeks, she'd be gone, and then he'd either have regrets or some pleasant memories. Why not opt for the memories? He already had his fill of regrets.

Molly awoke with a jolt. Lordy, it was almost noon. She sprang out of bed and grabbed her robe. The last she remembered, it had just been starting to get light and she'd been going over last night's conversation with Jeff for the four-hundredth time. Worried that she'd angered him by questioning his relationship with his father, she'd been unable to sleep. Apparently she had managed to eventually.

After a quick shower, she hurried into the kitchen to find a whole crowd there. Gram was rolling out piecrust, Jeff was doing something at the kitchen sink, while Agnes and Lilly were at the kitchen table.

"Boy, what a sleepyhead," Lilly said. "I thought you were never going to get up."

"Morning, everybody." Molly poured herself a glass of orange juice before she dared look Jeff's way. His eyes didn't look angry; she felt herself relax. "They've got you working already?"

"Not so 'already,'" he said with a laugh. "I've been hard at work for more than an hour."

"Poor baby," she said, then blushed, remembering his reaction to that statement last night. She turned to Gram. "So how was your baseball game last night?"

"Sox won 5-2," Gram said.

"And we met Rob and Emma there," Lilly added.

"Oh." Molly vaguely remembered her cousins. "And how are they?"

"Great. They want me to come to their farm tomorrow. Agnes said it would probably be okay."

Agnes looked slightly apologetic. "I didn't figure you'd care."

"No, it's fine. I just don't remember where they live."

"I thought I'd drive her. Today we're going to the zoo with your parents, remember?" Agnes said. "We were just waiting for you to get up before we left."

"Oh." Before she knew it, Lilly and Agnes were gone. Molly tried not to feel abandoned and looked brightly around her. "So what do you want me to do?"

"You could take over pitting these cherries," Jeff suggested.

"You can put these crusts into the pie tins," Gram said and gave Jeff a scolding look. "Ain't no need for you to get anxious. Cherry-pitting's always been the man's job in this family."

"The man's job?" Jeff turned to Molly. "What kind of family do you have?"

"The kind in which the men can't roll a piecrust." Molly looked over his shoulder. The woodsy scent of his aftershave was a distraction she tried to shake forcing herself to concentrate on the small pile of pits and the bowl of cherries still to go. "Doesn't look like this next pie's going to be cherry."

"So? Take your choice?" He placed a cherry in the pitter and jabbed down on the spoke that poked out the pit. "I can do it fast or I can do it well. I didn't realize you valued speed over proficiency."

He made a face at her that prompted her to throw a scrap of piecrust in his direction.

"Children," Gram scolded. "We aren't ever gonna get done if we don't get to it."

"Yes, ma'am," Jeff said. His voice was virtuous and proper. Molly stuck out her tongue at him.

Gram sent a pointed look at Molly. "Now, you behave yourself, young lady, and stop riling up my workers."

"Me?" Molly tried to sound indignant, but Jeff's look of superiority was too much and she burst out laughing. "Boy, gang up on me, why don't you? Is this all because I slept a little late?"

"Noon is hardy a little late and that was hardly ganging up," Jeff said. "When I gang up on somebody, they know it."

"I see." Her cheeks felt warm, an all too visible sign that she was remembering how her own feelings seemed to gang up on her around Jeff. Suddenly it seemed wisest to concentrate on the piecrusts. She brought a foil pie plate over and carefully placed the crust into it.

"That Lilly's something else," Gram said. "Wants to know everything."

"Oh?"

"Brought your high school yearbooks over from your parents. Asked a million questions about who you were friends with, what clubs you were in." Gram stopped and frowned at the crust she was rolling out. "You'd think that you never mentioned being a kid, the way she was trying to ferret out stuff."

Great. All the sunshine gathering in Molly's heart vanished and the worries pushed in. She felt Jeff's eyes on her and looked up. He seemed to sense her worry, her fears, and his gaze somehow gave her strength.

"She's had a lot of questions since we came back here," Molly admitted. "I talked to her about . . . things, but she didn't say much."

Gram just grunted. "Seems to me she was coming up with her own answers."

What in the world could they be? Not the right one, that was certain. She would never connect Tim with Molly, and neither would anything she'd find in a yearbook. Yet it showed a pain in the girl's heart that hurt Molly, too.

Jeff shoved the bowl of pitted cherries at her, giving her hand a reassuring squeeze as he did so. "These enough for one pie?" he asked. His eyes told her not to jump to frightening conclusions, that everything would be fine.

Her heart chose to believe him. "Thanks," she said as she took the cherries and dumped them into the pie shell.

"You know how to make the filling?" Gram asked.

"Is the sky blue?"

Jeff grinned at her and she felt some of the shadows disappear from her soul. She was so lucky to have a friend like Jeff to lean on. Nothing would happen to her or Lilly with him there for support.

"You know, I find it hard to picture Reverend Cahill doing this 'man's work,'" Jeff said.

"Never said he did it," Gram pointed out. "Said we gave the job to men in the family, not that they all had a turn. Danny's the last one I remember doing it for us."

"Who's Danny!" Jeff asked.

"My brother," Molly said. She sprinkled sugar over the cherries as she explained. "He was seven years older than Maggie and me and died in an automobile when he was a freshman at Harvard. Maggie and I were about ten at the time so that's probably why you never heard of him."

"Strange no one's mentioned him since I've been back," Jeff said.

"Not really," Gram said. She walked over to peek at the pie in the oven, then sank down heavily on a chair at the kitchen table. "Folks around here are pretty protective. They respect a person's privacy."

She looked down at her hands for a moment. "Danny was the light of Molly's parents' life. They'd been married five years and had thought they'd never have any kids. He was their miracle baby."

Molly cut strips for a lattice topping for the pie. It was strange that her parents never mentioned such things, but they'd never talked about those early years, at least not to Molly.

"Even after you girls were born, Danny was still somehow special," Gram went on. "Especially to your dad. He just doted on the boy. When Danny died, it was like that light had gone out and could never be lit again. Charles never talked about him and no one else did, out of respect."

"It might have helped if they had," Jeff said. "Talking is part of the grieving process."

"Maybe." Gram sighed. "Charles had a hard life though. His own father had died when Charles was in high school. His mother went when Charles had just become pastor here, leaving Agnes, who was just about ten. She was supposed to go to some aunt in the Upper Peninsula, but Charles said no, that it was his place to take care of her. And she was such a wild thing. Ran off with some rodeo rider when she was only sixteen, then got hurt real bad in some kind of accident. Molly's mom was due in another month, but she was determined to go out there and take care of Agnes because she knew it would ease Charles's mind. I thought she was a fool, risking the baby that way, but your father was torn. His sense of family has always been real strong. All he's ever done is try to be the best father he could be."

It was a different look at her father than Molly had ever had. It made some things clearer, but others stayed just as muddied.

She glanced over at Jeff. His face was closed. Had he ever had someone tell him about his father, about the lit-

tle things that made him into the man he was when Jeff
was a teenager? Maybe her friendship with Jeff would help
him look at his other relationships differently, to learn to
trust his father a little not to hurt him again. Molly slid the
cherry pie into the oven and took the other pie out.

Gram got to her feet. "You two want to keep an eye on
that one?" she said. "I'm going to take a little break."

"No problem, Gram. We'll start on the peach pies."

"Do I have to pit those things in here, too?" Jeff asked,
staring at the narrow-necked pitter.

Gram just laughed as she went through the door into the
living room. "Girl, take that man in hand and teach him
a thing or two."

Jeff just looked at Molly. The gleam in his eye was an
open invitation. "I'm all yours," he said, holding his arms
out wide. "Where do you want to start?"

Her mind jumped to all sorts of vivid suggestions that
her cheeks reflected. "I'm only going to be here another
week or so," she reminded him as well as herself. "We
have to keep our lessons short-term."

The gleam changed, deepened, and he took a step closer
to her. "And we probably shouldn't waste any time."

"Probably not."

She was in his arms then. Their lips seemed to start from
where they'd left off last time. There was no gentle climb
to hunger, no sweet prelude to passion. The fires burst
alive at the first touch of his mouth to hers.

She needed him with a strength that defined all reason
and logic. She wanted to feel more than his tongue inter-
mingling with hers, or his hands gently kneading her back.
She wanted to revel in the feel of their bodies pressed together, of love that would take them into the heavens and
show her a joy she'd never found before.

"Jeffrey."

Gram was back and they jumped apart.

"Yes, ma'am," Jeff answered.

"Are you sparking my granddaughter?"

Jeff looked at Molly and gave a half roll to his eyes. "Trying to, ma'am."

"Lordy, boy. There ain't no such thing as trying. Just do it."

"Yes, ma'am."

Molly swallowed hard in her attempt to suppress the soft laugh, but was unsuccessful as she slid back down into his embrace.

Chapter Seven

Jeff barely glanced up at Molly when she walked into his office Monday afternoon. Swell, she thought. Now that he's had time to think, he's running from Gram's teasing. Molly dropped into a chair in front of his desk.

"How did things go?" he asked, without looking up.

"Fine."

He glanced up. "Anything wrong?"

"Everything's terrific," she snapped.

"Look, if anything's wrong I should know. I'm responsible for the programs, you know."

"Nothing's wrong." She glared darts and daggers at him. "The kids who will be working with me are mature and enthusiastic. Your facilities are clean. And the water temperature is just right." Finished, she went back to glaring at the floor.

"Gee, I'm sorry to hear that," he said. "Let me extend my apologies for all of us here at the Niles-Buchanan YMCA."

Molly considered throwing something at him, but settled for giving him a dirty look instead.

He returned her look, meeting her glare of anger with a relaxed, caring expression. "Lilly go to the farm?" he asked.

"Yeah. And left a message at Gram's asking me if she could stay overnight." Molly didn't like the petulant tone of her answer, nor did she like this understanding nod.

"She's never been away from home before, has she? Like to some kind of camp? Overnight at a friend's house?"

Feathers fluttered about in Molly's stomach. How did one explain about Lilly? Explain how, way back deep in Molly's psyche, there was this fear that someday the whole truth would come out. And when it did, Lilly would be taken away from her. So Molly had to keep her close and treasure every moment they had together.

"No," Molly murmured. "This will be the first time she's stayed overnight with someone else."

"I'm sure she'll be fine," Jeff said. His voice was soft and soothing. "She'll have a good time."

"She set up this arrangement," Molly said. Then she stopped. Would Jeff laugh at her? But there was no hint of mockery in the softness of his eyes. "I was supposed to call her around lunchtime. Just before I met with my new assistants."

Jeff nodded.

"She wasn't there. She was out picking blueberries."

"Probably getting some fresh berries to go with her ice cream."

Molly glared some more at him as she grumbled. "She'd rather work than talk to her mother."

He shrugged.

"So I called again," Molly said. "Just before I came to your office."

"Out again?"

"Over to some neighbor's farm. To see some newborn lambs."

"Baby lambs are cute."

Molly gave him one of her hardest looks, the one that could stop a barroom brawl right in its tracks.

"Of course, that's a matter of personal opinion," he said.

"Sheep are dumb."

"She's a levelheaded kid," Jeff assured her. "I'm sure she'll consider the source before she accepts any advice they might give her."

She felt the corners of her heart flicker, but fought against it. "I don't like you," she said.

"Not even a little bit?"

Molly could feel that she was losing the battle. She quickly stood up and turned away. "I have to get home. Gram might need me."

Suddenly his arms were around her and there was nothing to do but lean back into his chest. A kiss landed on one of her ears, then on the other. She felt her grumpiness slip away.

"I suppose I have the clutchy-mommy blues," she said.

"A mild case," he agreed as he softly nuzzled her hair.

"Do you know of a cure?"

"I might."

She turned into his arms, surrendering her lips to his. There was a rightness about being here, about finding such peace in his embrace. His mouth was pliant, warm, de-

NO COST! NO OBLIGATION TO BUY! NO PURCHASE NECESSARY!

PLAY "LUCKY 7" AND GET AS MANY AS SIX FREE GIFTS...

HOW TO PLAY:

1. With a coin, carefully scratch off the silver box at the right. This makes you eligible to receive two or more free books, and possibly other gifts, depending on what is revealed beneath the scratch-off area.

2. You'll receive brand-new Silhouette Special Edition® novels. When you return this card, we'll send you the books and gifts you qualify for *absolutely free*!

3. If we don't hear from you, every month, we'll send you 6 additional novels to read and enjoy. You can return them and owe nothing but if you decide to keep them, you'll pay only $2.96* per book, a saving of 43¢ each off the cover price. There is **no** extra charge for postage and handling. There are **no** hidden extras.

4. When you join the Silhouette Reader Service™, you'll get our subscribers'-only newsletter, as well as additional free gifts from time to time just for being a subscriber.

5. You must be completely satisfied. You may cancel at any time simply by sending us a note or a shipping statement marked ''cancel'' or by returning any shipment to us at our cost.

This lovely heart-shaped box is richly detailed with cut-glass decorations, perfect for holding a precious memento or keepsake—and it's yours absolutely free when you accept our no-risk offer.

PLAY "LUCKY 7"

**Just scratch off the silver box with a coin.
Then check below to see which gifts you get.**

YES! I have scratched off the silver box. Please send me all the gifts for which I qualify. I understand I am under no obligation to purchase any books, as explained on the opposite page.

235 CIS AGM5
(U-SIL-SE-10/92)

NAME

ADDRESS   APT

CITY   STATE   ZIP

7	7	7	WORTH FOUR FREE BOOKS, FREE HEART-SHAPED CURIO BOX AND MYSTERY BONUS
🍒	🍒	🍒	WORTH FOUR FREE BOOKS AND MYSTERY BONUS
●	●	●	WORTH THREE FREE BOOKS
🔔	🔔	🍒	WORTH TWO FREE BOOKS

Offer limited to one per household and not valid to current Silhouette Special Edition® subscribers. All orders subject to approval.

PRINTED IN U.S.A.   © 1990 HARLEQUIN ENTERPRISES LIMITED

SILHOUETTE "NO RISK" GUARANTEE

BUSINESS REPLY MAIL

FIRST CLASS MAIL   PERMIT NO. 717   BUFFALO, NY

POSTAGE WILL BE PAID BY ADDRESSEE

SILHOUETTE READER SERVICE
3010 WALDEN AVE
PO BOX 1867
BUFFALO NY 14240-9952

NO POSTAGE
NECESSARY
IF MAILED
IN THE
UNITED STATES

manding. She gave him all that his kiss asked for, and felt
her own heart's commands. Then she pulled away slightly
to rest in his arms.

"What you need is to find some things to do on your
own," he murmured in her ear.

"Hmm."

His lips touched her forehead, raining light little kisses
along her skin. She felt so whole with him, so complete as
a woman. She snuggled closer into his arms.

"Any suggestions, Doctor?"

"Why don't we go canoeing?" he asked.

"You mean float around in one of those round-
bottomed things?"

He nodded.

Canoes were fairly small. They'd be alone. Was that
good or bad? They tipped fairly easily. Definitely a plus.
She had more on her mind than she could handle right
now.

"Sounds good to me."

"Thanks for the ride, Gus," Molly said as she jumped
out of the pickup truck. "I hope your brother gets better."

"Yeah, he'll be fine," the maintenance man assured
them. "Just getting old and worn-out. Needs a little more
maintenance."

"Give him my regards," Jeff said.

They waved as Gus turned toward South Bend's Me-
morial Hospital, then they made their way through Leeper
Park toward the canoe rental stand. They were going to
float downriver and end up back in Niles.

"I thought all rivers in America flowed north to south,"
Molly said.

"I don't know about all the rivers," Jeff said. "But here the St. Joe flows from South Bend on up to Niles. That's south to north."

Jeff paused a moment as he paid the attendant for the canoe. Then he picked up a life jacket and helped her fasten it. He would have liked to do a lot of other things with his hands, but now wasn't the time or place. He put his own life jacket on.

"Actually the St. Joe bends and twists all over the place," he said. "The river flows north here, then it turns west and empties into Lake Michigan."

"Are you some kind of river expert?" she asked as Jeff helped her into the front of the canoe.

He pushed off and jumped in himself. "Only about the St. Joe," he said with a short laugh. "I spent a lot of time along its banks."

"You mean when you should have been in school?"

"Yeah," he replied. "I ditched a lot. Just like you."

"I didn't ditch all that much," she protested. "I only met you once or twice along the river."

She could hear his chuckle behind her, rumbling in the depths of his deep chest. "Right. The only time you ditched school and ran down to the river was when I was there."

Maybe it was. Maybe her crush on him back then had made her all attuned to his comings and goings. Maybe she'd been subconsciously aware of when he was in school and when he wasn't. It sounded like such an adolescent thing to do, yet she wasn't an adolescent now, and seemed to be more than aware when he was around. Was she letting this be more than a summer romance?

"Aren't those old homes just beautiful?" She pointed to the houses lining the bluff high above them.

Jeff laughed. "Did you learn that from Lilly or did she learn it from you?"

Molly chose not to answer. Let him think she'd been changing the subject away from her school attendance records, rather than the worries that had suddenly entered her heart. Worries that she was not going to let darken her afternoon. She splashed some water back at Jeff.

"Careful there," he said, as the canoe swayed slightly. "You're liable to put us in the drink."

"Yuk."

"Hey, nothing wrong with good clean mud," he said.

"Doesn't mean I want to wade in it." She peered down into the water. "Are there fish in here?"

"No, you must have seen a sea monster."

She flashed a grimace over her shoulder.

He took pity on her. "Yes, there's fish here, and there'll be even more soon. They're building fish ladders along the river, and in another year or two we'll have steelheads and coho coming upstream to spawn. Just like they did before the white man came."

"That'll be good."

It was quiet and oh, so peaceful on the river. Even as they slipped under bridges teeming with traffic, the hustle and bustle of the world didn't touch them. The current was steady and strong, pulling them away from the routines and worries of daily life. In ways, she'd felt as if she were caught in a current since she got back here, as if she were being pulled along without any will of her own on paths that she hadn't chosen. It was like that with Jeff. No matter how she tried to tell herself seeing him was foolish—no, more than foolish, dangerous—although, she kept coming back.

They passed through the developed areas of South Bend and headed north of the city. The buildings of St. Mary's

College loomed up on their right. Something else was looming also, she noticed as they came out from under a canopy of trees. Clouds. And they didn't look great.

"Were they predicting rain?" she asked.

"Not as of this morning."

They paddled in silence for a few more minutes. Molly tried to concentrate on the little things: a turtle slipping and sliding down the slope to the river, a mother duck with a line of babies trailing behind her. The only sound was the gentle splashing noise of the paddles in the water.

"Pretty quiet up front," Jeff called out. "Did you fall asleep?"

"I'm still paddling, aren't I?"

"You're very talented."

"Actually, I'm just vegging out."

"That's a healthy thing to do once in a while," Jeff said. "Get's your batteries recharged."

As they drew into St. Patrick's Park, the first drops began to fall. The sound of the rain hitting the leaves was almost hypnotic, but a flash of lightning up ahead made her jump.

"Maybe we'd better pull in here," Jeff said.

Up ahead, Molly saw the county park's launching dock. Jeff steered them over, and got out to steady the canoe as she climbed onto the wooden planks. Together they pulled the canoe from the water and turned it over, then ran along a gravel path to a picnic shelter as the rain began to fall more heavily.

"Gracious," Molly said with a laugh as she nearly collapsed onto a picnic table. "And here I thought canoeing would be relaxing."

"Have to admit you haven't had a lot of time to mope about Lilly," Jeff pointed out.

"No."

She climbed onto the table to sit down. Jeff came to sit next to her, but she continued to stare out at the storm. The rain was becoming relentless. The towering pines, the oaks, the hickories, all the trees that encircled the small brick shelter seemed muted and dreamlike.

In a way, that was how this whole trip had seemed. At times, she was certain she would wake up and find herself back in Denver, and at other times, it felt as though she had never left Michigan, that Denver was the dream.

"Penny for your thoughts," Jeff said.

She started, then smiled at him. "Nothing too dramatic. I was just thinking how it sometimes feels like I've never been gone."

He leaned back on the table, resting on his elbows. "Ever think about moving back?"

And risk her secret? "Not really. Our lives are out in Denver. Agnes nas her bar, Lilly her friends, and me my students."

"Lilly could make friends here. You could teach here."

Molly shook her head. "No, it feels good to come back for a visit, but not to stay."

He reached over to trace her fingers with a light touch. "How are things going with your father?"

"Great." She grinned. "I haven't seen him since Saturday afternoon."

"Is he the reason you've stayed so far away?"

Molly sighed and pulled her hand away. "No. If I wanted to be here, I'd find a way to get along with him. This just isn't the right place for me to bring up Lilly."

He sat up, coming closer and shaking her equilibrium. "Most people would say just the opposite. That a small town like this was where they'd want to bring up their kids."

"Well, I'm not like most people."

"So I've noticed."

His voice had gotten soft and teasing. It coaxed her from gazing at the trees into smiling at him.

"Why didn't I notice how much you weren't like everyone else years ago?" he asked on the whisper of a breath.

He didn't give her time to answer before his lips came down on hers. She melted into his embrace. His lips asked for passion and her heart rejoiced. His mouth spoke of hunger and her hands echoed the thought. His embrace conveyed that he would never let go of her. Her mind wavered, but was ignored.

Time passed as in a dream. All she knew were his lips and his caress. She felt the joy of belonging. Nothing was impossible, nothing could hurt her. Fears were now far away, as were secrets and shadows. When suddenly she and Jeff parted to find the storm had stopped, she felt stunned, as if awakened from an altered state.

"Guess we'd better be going," he said.

"Yeah."

They walked hand in hand back down the path. In silence, they relaunched the canoe and set off for Niles. The storm had passed as quickly as it had blown up, revealing the sun, which was already peeking through the clouds. Yet Molly felt a shadow crossing over her mood.

She breathed in the damp smells of the river and listened to the occasional splash of animal life near the shore, but she couldn't rid herself of the feeling that something was wrong.

"Almost home," Jeff called out soon.

Home. Damn.

She took a deep breath and sighed. That was why she was getting so mopey. This wasn't home anymore. It was only the place where she was born and grew up. She was an adult now. She had made her own way in the world.

They rounded the bend and passed Island Park, where her father used to take her and Maggie to play. The rocks of St. Joseph River Park sprang up ahead of them. The same rocks she used to sit on when she ditched school. The same rocks where she'd come upon Jeff. Those were the days Maggie would be taking some test of hers.

She sighed again. Home was more than buildings you grew up in. It was a whole bunch of damn memories.

"Pull your paddle inside," Jeff said. "I'll bring us in."

Molly put the paddle on the floor and reached out to steady them as Jeff brought them to the dock. When they hit the dock, she hopped out, then turned to steady the boat for Jeff.

"Thanks," he said.

"You're welcome."

They left the canoe with a park attendant, then started walking up the overgrown path to Broadway. No matter what she said, this place still felt like home. There were ties still binding her here, still calling to her. And one of the strongest was at her side.

"Well, did that chase away the blues?" he asked.

"Completely," she lied. "Thank you for the outing, kind sir."

"I enjoyed it," he said quietly.

So had she up to a point. And that point was self-realization. She was letting Jeff get too close to her. He was becoming too important. No matter how tempting it might be to come home, she couldn't, and that was because Jeff was here. A closer, longer relationship would start demanding truths that she wasn't willing to tell. They walked to Gram's house and stopped at the porch steps.

"I promised my parents I'd have dinner with them," she said.

Jeff nodded. "Yeah, I've got some things to finish up at work."

He kissed her quickly, then left. Once he'd turned the corner at the end of the street, Molly went up the steps. She was almost looking forward to dinner with her father. At least, it should keep her mind off Jeff.

"Are you sure you can handle this?" Jeff asked.

Betsy Hooper grinned at him. "Boss, I've been handling the evening desk for almost twenty years now. I don't think I'm going to need backup. Go home early for a change."

Jeff just frowned at the middle-aged woman. Home was an empty apartment and a television set. That didn't sound too appealing. And neither did O'Day's, where he'd sit amid the regulars, guys like himself who had no reason to hurry on home. Laughing green eyes danced in his memory, mocking his efforts to keep them out.

He shoved his hands into his pockets. "Well, if you're sure..."

"Go," she ordered.

So he went. It was still light outside and the air was mild, inviting him to enjoy the evening. Doing what? he asked himself. He stomped down the steps.

He could put in a few hours on the '65 Mustang he was restoring. It had been neglected lately. Yet the idea of cleaning gaskets until dark wasn't too enthralling. Though he loved the car, it came up short on the conversation end.

"Hiya, Jeff. Nice night, ain't it?"

Jeff looked up to see Bill and Sarah Berry walking across the street, still holding hands like newlyweds. He waved back to them and turned the corner, his mood darkening with each step. What was so nice about the night? Mosquitoes were out for blood and a blanket of humidity lay over the town. The rain this afternoon hadn't cooled anything off.

"Look out, Mr. Spencer," a young voice called.

Jeff turned in time to avoid being run over by a bike. Three youngsters rode by. The sidewalk had obviously become a racetrack. Little juvenile delinquents. But even they had someone to spend the evening with.

Hell. He could spend the evening with someone if he wanted. With lots of someones. He just didn't want to. He liked being alone. He liked not having to account for his comings and goings to anyone. There was a crowd outside the ice cream shop and he crossed the street to avoid it.

"Evening, Jeffrey."

He looked up at the old man on the porch, rocking away. "Hi, Mr. Wilson. How you doing?"

The old man snorted. "How *you* doing, is more like it? What happened to your sweetie? She give you the heave-ho?"

"Not exactly." No point in telling him he had no sweetie. That Molly and he were just friends.

He thought of the way she felt in his arms, the way his heart raced, of how his body came alive. All right, so they were a little more than friends. She wasn't his sweetie—not unless that could be a very temporary classification.

A dog came rushing down the sidewalk to half bark, half welcome him, and Jeff stopped in his tracks. It was Rufus. He looked around him. He hadn't walked home. He had walked to Molly's house.

"Hi," she said, coming down the porch steps. "Rufus, hush."

"Uh, hi." What now? How did he explain his sudden appearance here. "I was just out walking."

"That's what I was going to do," she said. "Take a walk, I mean."

"Nice night for it."

"Yeah."

He stood there staring at her, feeling like a twelve-year-old with his first crush. In other words, he felt stupid. "I hadn't planned on walking here," he blurted out. "My feet just seem to take me places these days."

"I don't think that's a defense that will hold up in court."

"Who am I kidding?" He took her hand and started walking along with her. "So where were you headed?"

"Actually, I was going to the Y. We had dinner with my folks and I felt the urge for some exercise."

"I see. A little pumping iron, a few times around the track."

"I was going to talk to you." Her voice was quieter suddenly, the lilting, teasing note was gone.

"Another argument with your father?"

"No. We had a nice dinner. Only minor confrontations."

"Progress."

She nodded. They stopped at the corner, waiting for a car to turn. Rufus had been sniffing some bushes two houses back and raced to catch up with them. Jeff just waited for her to go on.

She did once they started across the street. "I actually wanted to talk about us," she said.

"Oh?" For a moment, he was worried, fearful that she was going to say that she wasn't going to see him anymore. But then, he shook that off. That was to be expected, actually. If not now, they would both have to deal with her going back to Denver.

"It just seems like we're together all the time," she said and smiled at him. "Not that I haven't enjoyed it. It's just that I'm only going to be here for another week or so."

"I know." So she wasn't dumping him. The night grew more pleasant, the fading sunlight more precious.

"A summer romance is fine, as long as we both remember that's all it is."

"I always thought summer romances were the best," he said and held her hand tighter. "The only kind to go for actually."

"You have many of them?"

Her voice was light and teasing, but he took her question seriously. "Not many. There was a girl I met in the army." Angie. Perfect Angie, the first girl he'd really cared about. She dumped him for a sergeant.

"One in college," he went on. Sweet Sue, who agreed to his face with everything he said, then would agree just as fervently with the next person. Anything to avoid a confrontation.

"Before I came here, I sold medical equipment to hospitals. Did a lot of traveling so I didn't do much dating. Just a dinner here, a movie there."

"So you're a cowboy, too," Molly said.

"Guess so."

"Should have known there was a reason we got along so well."

He slipped his arm around her shoulders. "You mean, besides the fact that I'm irresistibly charming?"

Her eyes sparkled with laughter. "Yeah, besides that."

They walked along in comfortable silence for a block or two. The evening didn't seem so dreary or long anymore. "Want to go for ice cream?"

Her eyes lit up. "Cherry fudge double dip?"

He laughed and pulled her closer. "Hey, I thought you were full from your dinner."

"Some things you always want."

He looked into her eyes, so rich and deep with life, and felt the softness of her body against his. How true, how true.

Chapter Eight

An enormous clap of thunder reverberated around them, rattling the walls and ceiling. Molly was sure her heart had stopped. Then the lights flickered, and went out, throwing the pool area into pitch darkness for a moment.

The cries of the children had barely begun when the emergency lights in the corners went on, casting a weak light over the water. Very weak.

"Stay in your places," Molly shouted, grabbing the hands of two children. "Don't move. Not one single inch. We're going to play a game."

Where was the pool mother? Molly glanced around, then remembered the woman had taken Kim to the bathroom. Damn.

Molly rushed to divert the children's sniffling and crying, which was growing louder. "The game is called Come to the Side of the Pool," she said. "Can we do that?"

"Sure, we can," one of her assistants answered. "It'll be fun."

"It's too dark," one child cried.

"I can't see," another said. There was first one wail, then another; the fear was becoming contagious, and spreading quickly.

"There's no reason to cry," Molly said, but her pleas were drowned out by the panic-stricken cries. She raised her voice. "Everybody hold on to your neighbor's hand."

Molly sensed movement, and turned toward the far door. It was Jeff, with a flashlight. Somehow she'd known he would come, not because of her but because of the kids. He'd know that they needed help.

"Look, Mr. Spencer is going to play, too," Molly called out. "He's going to shine the light over the water, and I want you to hold on to the light." The noise lessened as the kids' curiosity was piqued.

"Who's going to play?" one of the counselors called out.

"I'll play," Ryan said. "I can play real good."

Jeff hurried over to the side, pointing the flashlight at the pool, which created the illusion of a line stretching across the water, then reached out a hand for the closest child. Molly let him take George, appreciating the quick squeeze he gave her hand in passing; next he concentrated on getting Aimee over to the side.

"Don't run," Molly warned. Ryan looked too ready to make this a real game. "You have to sneak up on the light."

Slowly, the counselors all got their kids over to the side and, with Jeff's help, out of the pool. All the while he kept talking quietly to the kids, his voice so low and reassuring that it even helped her relax. Jeff had proved again he was someone to lean on.

He and Ray, one of the assistants, took George, John and Ryan into the boys' locker room, while Molly and Marissa herded the girls into their locker room. Emergency lights in the corners threw eerie shadows over the room, but luckily the mothers were there to help dress the children and calm their fears.

"Mr. Spencer's sure good with the kids," Marissa said. "He really came in the nick of time."

"Things can get out of hand real fast with these little ones," Molly pointed out. "They scare easier and get silly easier than the kids in the regular swimming lessons."

"Guess that's why you need so many adults."

Especially ones that related so well to the youngsters, as Jeff did. Seeing that all the children were taken care of, Molly removed her own clothing from her locker.

"My bracelet's gone!" Aimee cried, her voice taking on a squealing tone.

Molly left her clothes on a bench and hurried over to the girl's side. "It's her medical ID bracelet," Aimee's mother explained over Aimee's cries. "It must have fallen off in the water."

"You said I got to wear it always," Aimee wailed. "What if I get hurt now?"

"I'll go look for it," Molly said.

Aimee's mother nodded her gratitude. "Why don't we get dressed, honey? Ms. Cahill will find it and—"

"I don't want to get dressed. I want my bracelet."

Molly hurried back into the pool area. Its silence was unnerving and its darkness was going to make finding the bracelet difficult.

"Problems?" Jeff asked.

How had he known she needed help? But then, how did he ever know what she needed? Somehow they seemed to find each other, to anticipate each other's necessities in ways she'd never expected. If was both frightening and re-assuring.

"Aimee lost her bracelet. It's one of those medical alert ones and she's getting hysterical." Molly got down on her hands and knees to feel under the bleacher seats where they'd left their towels. "Apparently her mother impressed its importance on her and now that's backfiring."

Jeff was chuckling as he got down to help her look. The flashlight's beam showed nothing under the bleachers though.

"Not even a dust bunny," she said. "I'm impressed."

"So where do we look now?"

"In the pool."

Molly walked over to the side of the pool and stared into its murky depths. A whale could be swimming in there and not be seen. It was just too dark. She got down to the edge.

"You're not going in?" Jeff sounded astounded.

"That seems the best way to find it."

"My God, Molly, it's only a bracelet. The kid can live without it for a few hours."

"Not the way she was screaming."

He grabbed her arm just as she was about to slide into the pool. "This is insane." He sounded angry. "We're in the middle of a major electrical storm. The last place you should be is in water."

"I'll only be a few minutes. She didn't go far from this side. It's got to be right around here."

His grip on her arm tightened. "No. I won't let you."

"You won't let me?" What was he talking about?

"I have a responsibility as director here," he said. "The pool is to be emptied during electrical storms. Period. No discussion."

She jerked her arm away from him. "Want me to sign a release, absolving you from responsibility?" She slid into the water before he could stop her.

"Molly!"

So much for his great understanding of her special kids. If that bracelet wasn't found, Aimee would retreat. Besides which, Molly wasn't sure she liked him telling her what to do. Although she rather liked the notion of having someone besides herself feeling responsible for her well-being.

Molly inched across the pool bottom, trying not to generate too many currents. After a moment or two, her foot touched something metal on the pool bottom. She crinkled her toes around it and brought it up to her hand. The bracelet.

"I've got it," she told Jeff.

He said nothing, just watched as she climbed out of the pool. Through the glass window at the far side, she could see Aimee's mother waving. Molly went through the pool offices to the lobby. The air was reverberating with the sound of Aimee's crying. Still dressed in her swimsuit, Aimee was in her mother's arms.

"Here it is, honey," Molly said and slid the bracelet around the girl's wrist. The crying lessened only marginally.

"Thanks so much," Aimee's mother said. "I can't imagine what we'd have done if you hadn't found it. She just doesn't understand it's replaceable."

Molly nodded, conscious of Jeff's angry gaze on her back. She walked to the door with Aimee and her mother, and watched them dash through the rain to their car. By the time Molly turned around, Jeff was gone.

Just as well, she thought. A full-blown argument in front of the children would probably not be the best thing.

She went into the locker room to change, but her clothes were gone. Her purse and shoes were still in her locker, but her shorts and shirt were gone from the bench where she'd left them.

"Where's my stuff?" Molly asked.

Marissa looked up from where she was helping dress Katie. "Oh, Lord, was your stuff there, too? Aimee was screaming so and her mother decided not to dress her here. She just grabbed up all the clothes there and stuffed them into Aimee's bag."

What else would happen? Molly just sank onto the bench. "Well, I hope she's a Denver Nuggets fan."

Marissa smiled. "Hey, ask Mr. Spencer what he's got to wear. He's always got some extra togs in his closet."

Oh, does he? Extra adult female clothes just in case someone loses hers? It would be good fuel for teasing, that is, if they ever spoke again.

"I'll just get a towel from the control desk."

Molly skirted around small groups of girls, sitting in the semi-darkness and talking. That was a silly thought. Of course, she and Jeff would speak again. It was a minor disagreement, a difference of opinion between professionals. By the time she saw him again, it would be forgotten. But should it be? Maybe the little flash of pleasure she'd felt at his concern should be taken as a warning. Maybe things were getting out of hand, as far as her heart was concerned.

She got a towel from the control desk and wrapped it sarong-style around her. Obviously her help was needed, but where? She went into the gym. Jeff was there, supervising a game of "midnight free-throwing." Fighting the urge to turn around, she walked up to him.

"You need help here?" she asked.

Even in the semi-darkness, she could see the ice in his eyes. "No, we're fine. You could try the little kids' group in the activity room."

She felt as though she should salute. Instead, she quietly slipped away. All right, so he saw it as more than a minor disagreement. Fine. Things were getting too steamy between them anyway. She was much happier without him to consider. But it was one thing for her to decide, another for him to tell her so.

Jeff stared out the windows. It was still storming, but the weather had calmed considerably in the past hour. The tornado that had been sighted just west of them must have touched down someplace else or had blown over.

His attention returned to the activity room and the kids filling all its corners. The level of tension had also decreased in here. A few children were still looking outside, but the power was back on and most of the others were watching cartoons on the television.

Molly sat in a far corner, underneath a picture of Sitting Bull, gesturing to a group of preschoolers seated on the floor in front of her. She was barefoot, and clad only in her bathing suit.

He paused to let his eyes feast on the sight. That bathing suit certainly showed Molly's figure off to fine advantage. Of course, with a body like the lady had, anything would do that. Even a gunnysack.

Jeff frowned. What was with him? He wasn't paid to ogle female staffers. He went out into the lobby. Now that things had quieted down it was time to start giving people breaks. Like Molly, for instance. It was definitely time she had a break. She was overdue an explanation of their pool storm policy. He wanted to make sure she understood it was nothing personal.

"Ray." He motioned to the high school kid, sipping a soda at the counter, to follow him. Ray was young but good with the smaller youngsters. "Molly could probably use a break."

"Sure," Ray replied.

They walked back to the activity room, to Molly and her group. "How about a break?" Jeff asked.

"I'm fine," she replied.

"Ray can tell them stories," Jeff said.

"I'm okay," Molly replied.

"Hey, guys," Jeff said, looking at the eager group. "You want Ray to tell you a story?"

"Yeah," they chorused.

"Gee, thanks, guys," Molly said.

"We like you, Molly," a little girl said, sincerity filling her face. "But we just like Ray better."

Molly made a rueful face as she stood up. "Okay."

Jeff took her arm and led her away as Ray started into a story about a ghost, a baby bear and a baby rabbit.

"Boy," Molly muttered. "Tough house."

"That's show biz. Up one minute, down in the dumps the next." He stopped in the hallway, his conscience egging him. "Can we talk?"

She shrugged, which he took for an affirmative and led her into his office. He felt her shiver.

"Hey, you're cold," he said, putting his arm around her shoulders. "Why don't you go put your clothes on?"

"They're gone," she said. "Aimee's mother picked them up by mistake."

"Why didn't you say something?" he said. "I've got lots of stuff here. We'll find something for you."

Molly laughed. "That's what Marissa said. I just wondered if many women have found themselves without clothes at this YMCA."

Her laughter warmed something deep inside him. And the same tingle of fear that had come over him in the pool returned. He reached into a closet, then removed a long-sleeved dress shirt.

"This is an extra shirt of mine that I keep here for board meetings and such. It should help get rid of those shivers."

She slipped into his shirt, laughing as she did. "Look how big it is. I'm going to get lost in here."

"Just fold up your arms." He began rolling up the sleeves. Once he was done with them, he started to button the front of the shirt.

"Ah, I'm a big girl now." She gently pushed his hand back.

"Sorry," he murmured. "Once I start helping, I get carried away."

"Sure."

Her eyes didn't flash with any sort of irritation so he let his eyes drop, taking a moment to savor the sight. She was definitely a big girl, not in the large sense, but in the grown-up sense. Even the loose fabric of his shirt couldn't hide her attributes.

"Yes?" she said.

"I was just checking," he said.

"Checking what?"

"How big a girl you are."

Molly tried to give him a stern look but couldn't control the smile on her lips. He sighed and sank onto the edge of his desk. Where was that quick, cursory explanation he was going to make? The closer he was to her, the greater his realization that there was nothing businesslike behind his actions.

"Look, I wanted to apologize for earlier."

She just shook her head. "Forget it. It was just a difference of opinion between professionals."

"No, it wasn't," he confessed. Suddenly honesty didn't feel like the best policy, but he didn't seem to have a choice. "Yeah, we have the rule to empty the pool when it storms, but I wasn't really thinking about the rules."

She looked confused. Small wonder, so was he.

"Look, I overreacted, okay?" Embarrassment made his voice brusque. "I thought you were putting yourself into a position of danger for a stupid reason. I overreacted."

Something he couldn't interpret passed over her face. "I overreacted, too," she admitted. "I wanted to prove that I could do what I wanted."

He felt a grin creep out. "Well, I'm glad we were both acting maturely."

"Hey, that's the fun of being an adult. You get to be mature."

"I can think of other fun things adults can do."

"Oh?"

She was in his arms then, all woman and all his for the moment. His lips tasted her sweetness, although he wanted more than just her lips, more than just the brief feel of her body pressed against his. He wanted to know her completely, as a man knows a woman.

His arms pulled her in closer. She smelled of the pool and chocolate bars, an intoxicating mixture that was all Molly. He couldn't believe that she was here, waiting to come alive in his arms. He would show her what love was, what ecstasy could be reached between two people. He'd—

A knock at the door separated them.

"Jeff?" Gus poked his head in. "We got a leak in the northwest corner of the gym. Looks like some shingles got ripped off."

"Okay. Be right there." He turned to Molly. His grin was close to a grimace. "What next?"

"That going to last through the night?" Molly asked.

Jeff positioned the five-gallon bucket under the leak, squinting up at the gym roof as if trying to see the hole. "It should. Gus made some temporary repairs and they aren't predicting any more rain."

"They weren't predicting rain the day we went canoeing either. Storms seem to spring up here unannounced."

"Like a brother-in-law wanting to borrow money."

"You don't have any brothers-in-law," she pointed out.

"And I can't imagine yours asking to borrow money."

He put his arm around her shoulder, and together they walked through the deserted gym. It had been a long day. Molly felt as if her legs were made of rubber.

"What now?" she asked as Jeff turned out the lights in the gym.

"We post a sign on the door canceling evening activities for anyone who doesn't hear the announcement on the radio, then we can go."

"Huzzah."

He looked at her, his eyes frowning as much as his lips. "You didn't have to stay," he said. "Why didn't you go earlier when I sent the rest of the staff home?"

She just shrugged. "Too tired to move, I guess."

It was more than that, she knew. With Lilly away, there was no reason to rush on home. Jeff needed her help and needed her company whether he knew it or not, so this was where she'd stayed.

She leaned against the front desk as Jeff took a piece of paper and a colored marker to make his sign. Once it was done and posted on the front door, he came back.

"Hungry?" he asked.

"Starving."

He held out his arm for her. "Then let us make tracks." She slipped her arm through his. "What are you in the mood for? Italian? Chinese? Barbecue?"

She looked down at her attire: bathing suit and dress shirt. "I think it needs to be real informal."

His eyes followed hers, warming even as she watched. His eyes came back to her face and he gently ran his fingers down the side of her cheek. The trail of warmth they left ran straight to her heart. She leaned forward into his arms.

The worries and weariness of the day exploded in their kiss. It was so good to be held, to have his lips speak magic to her. Their mouths joined, and at that moment, so did their souls. A fire raged between them, burning down the walls she'd built around her heart. This was everything she wanted from life, everything she needed. They pulled apart slowly, but she stayed in his arms.

"So you think the Waldorf-Astoria is out?" he whispered into her hair.

"Definitely."

"How about the Spencer-Astoria?"

"Do they allow scantily clothed women?"

"Oh, quite definitely." His voice was a mere breath.

"Let me call Gram to tell her I won't be home for a while."

After a quick call, they left the Y, stopping to pick up a pizza and some wine on the way to Jeff's place. The storm hadn't cooled things off much, or maybe it was just Molly that seemed warm. Jeff pulled into a driveway leading to a small apartment building.

"This looks like a nice place," Molly said, though it was hard to see much in the darkening evening light.

"Yeah." He shrugged. "It's near enough so that most days I walk."

He turned off the ignition, then rubbed the back of his neck with both hands. It had been a hectic day for everyone, but she realized that Jeff looked especially tired, probably from holding the primary responsibility. They were lucky that a leaky roof was the worst of the damage. With only that to worry about, she should be able to get him to relax.

They went inside in silence; the sudden blast of air-conditioning felt wonderful.

"You want to eat in the kitchen?" he asked. "Or would you prefer the dining room?"

"Wherever's easier."

Molly glanced around his apartment. It looked like general-issue quarters for a busy bachelor. Everything was neat and clean. Except for an overstuffed recliner in a far corner, the furniture was ordinary modern. There was little of the personal touch. Even the artwork depicting outdoor scenes could be bought in any department store.

"You don't spend much time here, do you?"

Jeff looked at Molly for a moment. There was a hint of something in his eyes that she couldn't read.

"No, I guess not."

"Your office is a lot messier," Molly said.

"Do more of my living there."

While he set two places on the countertop eating area in the kitchen, she opened the pizza box. She guessed it wasn't strange that Jeff's life should revolve around the Y, but the barrenness of his apartment seemed sad to her. Surely he had something that was important to him.

Jeff popped the cork on the wine bottle and poured out two glasses. "Dinner is served, madam."

"Thank you, Jeeves."

He scowled at her again as he pushed in her stool but his heart didn't appear to be in it. He was rapidly running out of steam.

"Folks who look for trouble usually find it," he murmured, as he kissed the back of her neck.

"One can always hope."

Jeff paused a long moment, his hand on her shoulder, but then he sighed and sat on the other stool. "I'm starved," he said.

Not surprisingly, Molly found that she also was hungry. Breakfast had been ages ago and lunch had been a couple of chocolate bars. Neither said much as they devoured the pizza, washing down their food with the red wine.

In no time at all, the pizza was gone, leaving behind a tomato-stained carton with a few scattered crumbs. The wine bottle was nearly empty.

Whoa, Nelly, Molly thought as she eyed the bottle. She'd been slugging that stuff down as if it were water. Maybe it was time to call it quits. Gram had told Molly to have fun when she had called, but Molly wasn't sure this was what Gram meant.

The scene around her grew fuzzy, and tilted a bit as she stood up. Driving home was out of the question, and Jeff had drunk just as much as she had, plus he was exhausted. Well, she'd just walk when it was time to go.

"Why don't you sit down in the living room?" Jeff said. "I'll clean up first, then join you."

"I can help."

"I know you can, but there's hardly anything here." He emptied the bottle, filling their glasses up equally. "Take the glasses in. I'll be right there."

Molly walked carefully to the living room. After flicking on the television, she placed the glasses on the lowboy and dropped back onto the sofa. A baseball game was on TV, but she couldn't make out the teams. Blue was batting, white was catching. True excitement.

Though she was vaguely aware of sounds in the kitchen, Molly's eyes drifted closed. It had been some day. First the storm, then the argument, then the making up, which had been all too brief.

Suddenly the sofa bounced and Molly's eyes popped open. Jeff was sitting next to her.

"All done in there?"

"Yep. And all done in, I'm afraid."

He slouched down and put his feet up on the coffee table, letting out a mixture of a groan and a sigh. His arms came around her then, pulling her close as if it was the most natural thing in the world to do. Their lips met for a brief kiss, a sealing of some sort of pact, but then she just let her head rest on his chest.

It was good here, comfortable and fine. He needed her with him for a while. She struggled with her eyelids. They were so heavy and everything was so blurry. What little tension was left totally drained away. The even breathing she felt beneath her was hypnotic and she let her eyes close, giving in to the rhythm and falling asleep.

Chapter Nine

"Molly."

Molly stirred slightly, a delicious tension curling in her stomach. There was a feather-light touch by her ear and then another. She turned to move closer to the warmth. Lips brushed her forehead, awakening other senses, other dreams, and she opened her eyes.

She was lying in Jeff's arms, in Jeff's living room. They had fallen asleep, but she had no idea what time it was. The TV had long since abandoned programing, leaving a picture of a flag on the screen. The far window showed the night to be that inky blackness that comes when the lights of cars and porches have retired. It was magic time.

"Hi," he said.

She just smiled at him; her weariness had passed and other emotions were taking hold. Other dreams were waiting to be fulfilled.

"Want me to drive you home?" he asked.

"Not especially."

He picked up her hand and brought each finger to his lips, kissing the tips so that shivers raced along to her heart. "Are you sure?" he whispered.

What was there to be sure of? She leaned forward to meet his lips and found herself swept up by a tidal wave of desire. His arms came around her. They would keep her afloat, keep the passion from drowning her.

His mouth was her world, his arms her universe. Just the touch of his lips filled her heart with flowers and sunshine. Nothing could touch her, nothing could dim the magic that he had brought her. They drew apart, but his mouth still danced on her skin, along her cheek and onto her neck.

"You are so beautiful," Jeff said, whispering the words as his tongue found her ear.

She gasped at the sudden jolt of tension that shot through her. Her body trembled as he licked her ear, let his tongue slide over the curves and into the hollows. She moved into the sensation, feeling suddenly so alive. Jeff had been her fascination years ago, but it was hardly a teenage timidness that she was feeling now.

She had been resting against him, one arm around him, the other lying on his chest. But the onslaught on her senses drove her higher, into a world of hungers and fires that consumed everything. Her hand clenched slightly, trying to hold on to him for dear life as things began to spin out of control.

"Jeff." She gasped out his name.

He stopped. "What's wrong?"

His eyes were so soft, so gentle that she wanted to cry. "Nothing," she said, feeling her eyes get moist. She shook her head and found a quivery smile. "Nothing at all. I guess I was just a little afraid."

"Of me?" He looked worried.

She brushed his cheek with her hand, her touch trying to say what was in her heart. "No, never. Just of feeling so good."

"Ah, but it gets better," he said.

He moved closer, taking her in his arms with such possession, with such surety, she felt the world must be stopping. He pressed his lips to her neck, planting soft kisses everywhere his mouth touched her, lighting fires that she thought would never be able to be doused. His hands slid under the shirt she was wearing, to the skin-hugging bathing suit.

It was as if there were no barrier. Everywhere he touched, she came alive. Her stomach curled with a delicious tension that spread a warmth down to her toes. She wanted both to stretch in her newfound vitality and to climb closer into his arms.

His hands found every sensitive place that would awaken to his touch. Her stomach. Her side. Her breasts. He stopped for a moment, and she just lay against his chest.

"I feel like there's another storm coming," she murmured.

"Storms can be good."

"As long as you don't get hit by lightning."

It was too late to worry about that. Her body was charged, alive and on fire with longing for him. "I used to be afraid of storms," she said.

"And now?"

She shrugged and unfastened the top buttons of his shirt to place a light kiss on his chest. "I feel safe here," she said and undid another button. "I feel alive here."

She undid the rest of the buttons and let her hands take their turn at exploring. The thick mat of hair on his chest was hers to touch, to run her fingers through. The coarse feel was so masculine. She closed her eyes and breathed in his fragrance. There was a woodsy scent of some long-distant after-shave and the faint smell of soap and sweat.

Her fingers ran deeper through his hair until he groaned and spun over on her. She was suddenly lying on her back on the sofa, Jeff pressing her into the surface.

"You are driving me crazy," he gasped, his voice ragged. "Ever since you came back here, you've been haunting me."

He moved his lips onto hers with a roughness, a passion that spoke of needs too urgent to be delayed. Her heart echoed his wants, delighted in the very strength of his touch. This was right. It was now.

He pushed the shirt from her shoulders and slid her bathing suit straps down. She pulled her arms free even as his hands found her breasts. Freed from the suit, they felt so soft and hungry for his touch.

He touched and gently tugged, kissed and suckled until she wanted to cry aloud. She felt her body arch beneath him, felt the wonderful warm, wet need of being a woman.

"Molly, Molly, Molly." He could barely speak, but got up off her.

She felt alone, abandoned, but then he swept her up into his arms and carried her to his bedroom. She was safe here in his strength, in the castle of his heart. It was a vague and half-made thought as he laid her on the bed and took his place next to her. The light from the living room threw long shadows across the bed that promised secrecy.

But even as the wild peaks of their kiss had driven them into the bedroom, a gentleness—almost reverence—took over his movements now. He touched as if he was in awe of her. His hands, his lips, his fingertips explored the soft expanse of skin above her waist. She ached for more, but his hands would not be hurried.

Then slowly, he pushed her swimsuit down so that his hands could further explore. He found the core of her heat, the center of her needs and bent his lips to stoke the fires. She did cry out then, a sound of pure hunger and need. When he lifted his head, she pushed his shirt off him, then his shorts.

Lying together, they each let their bodies feel the other. They let their hands slide over the length of them before they slowly, deliciously, moved together and became one. Just as the shadows and the night were endlessly joined, so were she and Jeff. Not just their bodies, but their hearts, too, their souls. They danced a slow waltz of love and desire, soaring into the heavens together and then softly coming back to earth and a beautiful sleep in each other's arms.

Jeff looked up as Molly stepped into his kitchen, sleep still in her eyes. She was wearing the shirt he'd lent her yesterday, except today it was only partly buttoned and there wasn't a bathing suit underneath it.

She smiled and came toward him, her face a curious mixture of woman and little-girl innocence. His heart felt so confused it surely was going to burst.

"Hi, sleepyhead," he said brusquely.

"Hello."

She stretched up to kiss him, then paused to linger in his embrace. She fit just perfectly within the fold of his arms, as if they were made for each other. The top of her head blurred and he closed his eyes, bending his head forward to rest it on the top of hers. Some things were just too tempting, and too dangerous. He put her gently away and got a cup out of the cupboard.

"Want some coffee?" he asked.

"Okay."

While she sank onto a stool at the counter, he poured her a cup of coffee. "Cream and sugar?"

"Just cream."

He put her cup down before her and sat down himself. She was so beautiful at any time, but even more so after last night's loving. His heart felt so drawn to her, even as his mind shied away.

He pulled his own cup over to him. "Your grandmother called a little while ago."

Molly had been about to take a sip. Her mouth was open and ready but her arms seemed to freeze. Her cheeks radiated pink.

"You're kidding," Molly gasped. She put the cup of coffee down.

"She—" Jeff found it necessary to clear his throat. "She just wanted to know how you were."

"You should have wakened me," Molly said. "I could have explained things to her."

"She didn't seem to be looking for an explanation." He wasn't sure how to explain the call. "She asked me if I was taking care of you."

Disbelieving green eyes peeked out over the edge of the cup at him.

"I told her I'd certainly tried." A warmth filled his own cheeks. "She told me a young, healthy man like myself should do better than try."

He and Molly stared at each other for a long moment before a grin slipped onto her lips. He echoed it, and before he knew it, they were both laughing.

"She is unbelievable," Molly said.

He shook his head. "She had me come get some strawberries and her crepe recipe so you could have strawberries and crepes for breakfast."

"You went and got our breakfast from her?" Molly stared at him.

"Well, she was planning on coming here. That's a long way for an elderly lady to walk."

"She really is something else," Molly said as she padded briskly to the refrigerator and began taking out ingredients for the crepes.

Jeff watched her for a long moment, then began to set the table for breakfast. Gram wasn't the one that was unbelievable; Molly was. She had so much vitality, so much warmth about her. He wished the night could have lasted forever, or at least a few days. It had been so special, a magical moment when time had stopped. No one else had existed.

But like all bits of magic, the spell had been broken. Morning had come and Gram had called. Welcome back to the real world. Where your secrets weren't secret and everyone had a different idea of what you should do next. Although why the town should be any different than his own mind, he didn't know.

Part of him remembered the delirious feel of holding fire in his arms, and another part worried about the burns that he might find later. Part of him said that Molly's smile could change his life, another part said she was leaving soon.

No insights leaped out at him over breakfast or when they were cleaning up afterward. Maybe it was time to stop looking for any. His life was what he wanted. The momentary warmth Molly had given him was a treasure to remember, not expect to be repeated.

"When is Lilly coming home?" he asked.

"I'm picking her up around noon," Molly replied. "If I leave her out on that farm any longer I'm afraid she won't want to come back."

"Oh, I doubt that."

No matter how delightful the trek off the path was, everyone was more comfortable back on the trail they'd chosen. He would be too, just as soon as the memories of last night faded a little. They put the dishes away and he dressed for work.

"Want me to drop you off at home?" he asked as they left his apartment. The air was already stifling and muggy, the sunlight strong and unforgiving.

She shook her head. "No. Just let me off at my car. I'll drive home and change."

They rode the few blocks in silence, his heart growing more and more heavy. The air coming in through the open windows didn't seem to refresh at all. He pulled into the parking lot and, as luck would have it, a number of the staff were there.

He should have checked and then just driven past if anyone was around, but it was too late now. Everyone had seen him; he could tell by their malicious smiles. Damn. He pulled up by Molly's car.

"Hi, Molly, hi, Jeff," a chorus of voices rang out.

Molly waved and, forcing a grin to his face, Jeff waved, too. He would rather have thrown rocks. He waited while Molly got into her car and pulled out, then he made his way to the door, dispensing smiles in return to the crowd's evil grins.

The joys of a small town. Normally when this happened here, a man didn't have to do a thing. His life was totally out of his hands. Others would set the date, hire the caterer and arrange with the minister. All he had to do was show up.

Well, they had a surprise coming. Molly was heading back to Denver and he was quite happy alone, despite the magic they'd shared.

He stepped through the door and wavered just a moment at another sea of smiling faces. This wasn't the City of Four Flags. It was the City of a Million Eyes.

He wondered if Molly'd like some company when she went to get Lilly.

Molly parked her car around back by the garage and sat for a moment in the silence. Last night had been wonderful, too special for words. It was almost a shock to have to get back to the real world.

She closed her eyes and felt again the magic of Jeff's arms. So much for playing it smart and not falling back into the patterns of the past. Yet she just couldn't scold herself. It had been too good to regret. She didn't care that she was leaving in another week, that that meant seven more days of Jeff's company. Seven more days of her family's disapproval.

She sighed and got out of the car, making her way toward the back door. Gram shouldn't make life difficult for her; she seemed to like Jeff. Of course, that was before Molly had spent the night with him.

Gram was usually gardening out back this time of the morning, but the yard was empty. Nobody. Molly breathed a quick sigh of relief. She could just ease on up to the back door and—

No, that was ridiculous. She wasn't a teenager anymore. She was an adult and responsible for her own behavior. If she wanted to stay out all night, she could. If she wanted to sleep with a friend, she could. If she wanted to have a brief affair while she was here, she could. She marched resolutely around to the front of the house, where she found Gram kneeling before a bed of marigolds.

"Hi."

Gram sat back on her heels, her eyes going from Molly's bare feet to the top of her tousled mop. And then back again to take in Jeff's shirt over her bathing suit.

"Something happen to your clothes, girl?" Gram's voice was deceptively gentle, not at all matching the glint in her eyes.

"It's a long story," Molly replied.

"My age, a person's got nothing but time." Her grandmother pushed herself up and went to sit on the front steps.

Sighing, Molly took a seat on the steps herself, then she recounted in detail the story of the storm, leading the kids out of the darkened pool, entertaining them, how Jeff had given her his shirt, and finally the parents rushing in to claim kids and snatching up her clothes.

"It was an accident," Molly said. "The stuff will turn up in the next day or two."

Gram nodded. Molly observed the lazy morning scene herself for a moment, breathing in the humidity that the sun and yesterday's rain joined forces to manufacture. She'd left out quite a bit, she knew. For example, how Jeff had monopolized her thoughts for the past week. How the slightest brush of his hand seemed to start her on fire. And how the future seemed hazy and unimportant when she was in his arms. Molly became aware that Gram was watching her. Waiting for more?

"Jeff and I were the only ones left at the end of the day," Molly said.

Gram did not reply.

"He asked if I was hungry," Molly went on, growing more restless under Gram's unwavering gaze. "I said I was. But rather than go out some place, we just got some pizza and went to his place to eat it."

Gram nodded.

"Then, after dinner, I was all relaxed." Molly took a deep breath and studiously checked out the house across the street. "We talked." She looked down at her toes as they curled under her feet. There was a limit to how much she would tell. "Then I fell asleep."

There was a long silence that stretched out until her grandmother cleared her throat.

"Why don't you go in and shower, dear?" Her grandmother used Molly's shoulder to steady herself as she stood up. "I got me a mess of weeds that need killing."

Molly stood up and climbed the steps. She felt strangely uneasy. Gram was taking this too well. She should have at least frowned a bit more.

"Oh, Molly."

She paused at the door, turning toward Gram. Here it comes, she thought.

"There's a fella looking to talk to you," Gram said. "Says he's with some kind of foundation. Number's on the message pad in the kitchen."

Molly nodded and went into the house. Agnes came out of the kitchen, leaning against the doorway with a cup of coffee in her hand and a knowing grin on her lips.

"Ah, Cinderella returns," Agnes said.

"I'm not Cinderella."

"No, Sleeping Beauty. That fits better."

Molly turned to go up the stairs. "I'm not Sleeping Beauty either."

Agnes followed her on up. "So are we staying here in Niles?"

That stopped Molly in her tracks. She spun around. "No. Why would you ask that?"

"Oh, no reason." Agnes's grin was trying for innocent, and failing.

Molly just gave her a look and went up to her room. "What happened last night has no bearing on anything," Molly said and hoped her heart was listening.

"It was awesome," Lilly said. "You could see it coming across the fields. The lightning would just come streaking down and hit something."

"It got pretty wild down by us, too," Jeff agreed.

Molly felt her cheeks warm slightly as the car approached a crossroads. She opened her window the rest of the way. The air was too hot to cool her, but the action helped. "Pretty wild" was putting it mildly, but then maybe Jeff was just talking about the storm.

"We had a power failure at the Y in the middle of my swim class," she said.

"Wow," Lilly said.

Molly felt Jeff's eyes on her and the flush in her cheeks deepened. Wow, indeed.

"Your Mom did a good job of getting everybody out of the pool in the dark," Jeff said.

"Way to go, Mom!"

Molly flashed a smile at Lilly, letting the edges of it find Jeff. She was glad that he had offered to drive up with her. Every moment they had together was special. Maybe he sensed that, too. Why else would he have given up his lunch hour to ride out to an old farm? Maybe he—

"Did you give him a big hug for me, Mom?"

Molly was lost for a moment. "Hug? For you?"

"Yeah, Mom. Rufus. Did you give him a big hug every day like I asked you to?"

Molly shook off her confusion and gripped the steering wheel tighter. "Sure, honey. Twice a day. Morning and night."

Other hugging came to mind. Hugging that had been returned in kind. Other hugging that could be addictive.

Lilly had gone on to other things.

"Uncle Rob had this great tattoo he got in the army," she told them. "It had an eagle yelling. I want one just like it."

What a way to be awoken from daydreams! "You're not getting a tattoo," Molly said.

Just what Lilly would need, to be marked for life because of her stupidity. Molly's father's words suddenly echoed in the air, how Lilly was marked for life as a bastard because of her birth certificate. That was different, Molly told herself. It hadn't been her decision to omit the father's name and it couldn't be her decision to rectify the matter. She stared at the road ahead.

Jeff seemed to sense her change of mood. She could feel his eyes on her, the questions in his gaze, but kept her eyes ahead. He turned to Lilly.

"I think Rob's tattoo was probably a Screaming Eagle," he said. "It's the symbol for a certain battalion in the army. Same one I was in actually."

"Really? Do you know Uncle Rob?"

"Lilly, Rob fought in World War II," Molly said. "Jeff and I weren't even born then."

"Oh."

They turned onto Route 51, the intersection appearing suddenly amid the cornfields. Molly had forgotten how much green there was around here. Niles wasn't exactly a farming community, but the surrounding area sure was. Funny, how all she'd thought about as a teenager was leaving, when now she treasured the abundance of fresh produce and the wide open spaces.

"Hey, dude. I got an idea for you," Lilly said.

Jeff chuckled. "Oh, yeah? What is it?"

"You need to make a big meal with dessert and wine and stuff, then you ought to sneak into Gram's house when only Mom is home. And when she comes into the room you could jump out and yell, 'Surprise, surprise.'"

"Where did you ever—" Molly demanded.

"I saw it on television. Cousin Emma and me used to watch these shows when we had lunch."

Soap operas.

"And then this weird music came on and the man and the lady grabbed each other and—"

Jeff began to laugh.

"I think we get the idea," Molly said quickly. "But we'll just forget it. Jeff is too busy to make dinner."

"Oh, I could find time," he said.

She sent a quick laugh in his direction. But she didn't need her daughter to plan her seduction. She had done well enough in that area on her own. "I think not."

"Come on, dude," Lilly pleaded.

But Jeff shook his head. "Your mom said no, so I obey."

"You guys are no fun."

Molly couldn't help but look Jeff's way. The smile in his eyes was deeper and filled with memories. So she and Jeff were no fun, were they? Why then did those memories cause her cheeks to flare red and her heart to race.

Lilly leaned back in her seat, apparently no longer interested in such dull folks. Jeff reached over and took Molly's hand.

"Your daughter always take this much interest in your relationships?"

There hadn't been many, but Molly wasn't going to admit that. "Oh, she's always been a bit of a busybody."

"Speaking of busy, want to go to the Firefly Festival on Friday? The Sound Bend Pops is playing."

"I don't know."

"Mom!" Lilly wailed.

The kid could hear a date invitation at a hundred yards, but couldn't hear a call to dinner.

Lilly was leaning over the back seat, pulling at Jeff's sleeve. "She'll go."

"Lilly, that's the day before the reunion. People will be arriving and my help might be needed." It wasn't that Molly didn't want to go; there were others things to consider.

"I can help and so can Agnes."

"The house will be filled with relatives."

"So they can help too." Lilly leaned closer. "Mom, it's a date with a cool dude."

"And I don't have nearly enough of them," Molly added with a laugh. They were passing a farm with a fenced-in pen of pigs. "Oh, look at the little pigs."

But Lilly wasn't so easily distracted. "I think you should take her out to dinner, too," she told Jeff.

"Okay. Fancy or casual?"

"Fancy. She's got this blue dress covered with sparkles. She got it to wear to a party with Wayne, but one of his rats got sick and he couldn't go."

"One of his rats got sick?" Jeff asked.

"He trained them for movie roles," Molly explained. "But I'm afraid the dress is back in Denver."

"So it's casual then," Jeff said. "I know just the place."

Lilly sat back with a sigh, apparently satisfied now that she'd got their date arranged. Molly flashed a smile at Jeff. The one he sent back her way was hot enough to curl her hair.

Why was she thinking she had so little time until she left? She was the one who decided when to pack up and go. She could decide to go tomorrow or stay an extra week. If she was having a good time, why run away?

Chapter Ten

"I'll get it," Molly called, leaving Lilly to her farm stories as Molly hurried toward the front door.

A middle-aged man was standing in the doorway, with his tie loosened and his suit coat hanging over his arm.

"Molly Cahill? I'm Brett Robinson." He held an identification card with his picture up against the screen. "I'm with the American Corporate Service Foundation."

"Oh, yes. Won't you come in?" She held the door for him and then led him into the small parlor. "Would you like something cool to drink? Lemonade? Iced tea?"

"No, thanks." He sat down, taking off his glasses to wipe his face. "The summer heat's intense in your fair city."

"That's what July's for," Molly said. She was glad to get this chance to help Jeff. He had brought so much into her life, it only seemed right to repay him in some way.

The man rummaged in his briefcase, pulling out some forms and a clipboard. "As I indicated in our telephone conversation, Mr. Spencer is in line for a substantial award from the foundation. Of course, the money will not go to Mr. Spencer personally, but he will get a plaque."

"The money goes for programs at the Y," Molly said. It was still for him in a way.

"Yes indeed," Mr. Robinson replied. "A hundred thousand dollars divided equally over five years."

"That sure would help."

"As you can imagine, there is intense competition for these awards, so we conduct thorough interviews with people who know the men or women in question."

Mr. Robinson paused to find a form and Molly's eyes wandered around the small parlor. Her life had been like this before Jeff, a small room filled with nice things, but closed in. Jeff had brought her the sunshine, the laughter, the freedom of the rest of the world.

"What type of a person do you think Mr. Spencer is?" Mr. Robinson asked. "How would you describe him?"

Molly thought for a long moment. How did you describe someone in a few words when he had so many facets? She saw the welcome in his eyes that first night back when she met him at the river. She felt his understanding when Lilly had been away on her overnight visit. She remembered his anger when she'd gone into the pool during the storm, and his passion later that night.

"He's kind. Generous. Really cares about the kids." It sounded so weak.

"Why does he care so much about the kids, do you think?"

Molly stared at the man. What kind of a question was that? "Because of his childhood, I would guess," she said. "He went through some hard times and wants to help troubled kids get through their problems easier than he did.''

"Sounds almost too good to be true," the man noted.

Molly shrugged. "Luckily, he isn't." Luckily for the kids. Luckily for her. He'd helped her feel alive, helped her see a world beyond Lilly and her work.

"What one fault would you say he has?"

"A fault? I don't know." She shook her head and ticked off the nonanswers. "He's so sensitive. He feels for each child, and sees them as individuals. He's patient. He's loyal."

"In other words, he's perfect." Mr. Robinson's voice was flat and neutral, but Molly sensed an undercurrent of disbelief.

"No, he's not," she said. "He's got a lousy diet—candy bars and fast food. He works too hard and is going to burn out if he's not careful. And he doesn't trust easily enough."

The man made a noncommittal noise and Molly turned to stare out the window. Gram's marigolds and petunias looked parched. Waves of heat rose from the street and a hazy glare seemed to cover everything. Yet across the way, two little girls were playing in the spray of a lawn sprinkler. Their happy cries echoed in the air, sending the oppressiveness of the heat away.

That was what Jeff had done for her, Molly realized. He'd brought water into the desert of her life. She wasn't sure what it really was but knew that it made everything more special, everything a bit richer.

Was it friendship? Laughter? Love?

Molly's heart seemed to stop. That was what had changed. She was in love with Jeff. Somewhere along the way she'd blossomed into a woman in love. It had made her deeper and happier, more fulfilled and ready to experience life. It also doomed her to heartbreak. Love demanded truth and her life for the past ten years had been a lie.

"Who are Mr. Spencer's close friends?"

Molly stared, almost having forgotten she wasn't alone. "His father, I think," she said, stumbling over the words.

How could she have been thinking of staying longer? She'd be better off leaving right now.

After parking the car, Molly just sat a long moment with the motor running, staring at Jeff's small apartment building. She was reluctant to kill the air-conditioning and step out into the heat and humidity outside. No, it wasn't the heat and humidity she was trying to avoid. It was facing Jeff.

She turned off the ignition, picked up his shirt from the seat beside her and stepped onto the parking lot. The surface felt warm to her bare feet. Good thing it was evening. Molly didn't think her feet were tough enough anymore to handle asphalt baked by the noonday sun. Maybe all of her had gone weak.

She rang Jeff's doorbell, then stared around at the tiny yard. Maybe she should just leave the shirt here on the doorstep and run. But there was no running from her foolish heart. She spun around as the door opened.

"Hi," Jeff said.

"Hi," she replied, fighting the momentary urge to flee. She held out his shirt. "Here it is."

He took it, but frowned.

"Gram said you wanted it."

He shrugged. "Well, eventually."

"She said you had to have it."

The questioning lines around his face grew deeper. "That's rather strong. I just figured you'd get it to me sometime or other."

"Sometime or other?"

"Yeah, you know. Like when you came in to work tomorrow. Or when you dropped Lilly off. Something like that."

"Something like that?" Molly felt like a fool. A suspicion was growing in her mind. "Gram said you called and you wanted your shirt."

Jeff shook his head. "She called me at the Y. Wanted to know when I'd be home."

Bingo. Good old Grammy. The matchmaker at work again. Molly shuffled her bare feet and looked out over the parking lot before turning back to Jeff.

"Would you like to come in?" he asked.

"Nah, that's okay." It was safer to stay away from him, at least until her heart healed.

But his smile was so welcoming, so tempting. "You did bring my shirt over."

She had no will of her own. "Well, I suppose. As long as I'm here."

She stepped into his apartment and felt as if she were coming home. The sensation scared and delighted her.

"I'll put this in the bedroom," Jeff said. "Have a seat."

Molly went to the sofa, which welcomed her like an old friend. Jeff was out in a split second. He must have thrown the shirt on the bed.

"Want something cool to drink?" he asked, slowly moving toward the kitchen. "Beer? Lemonade?"

"No, thanks. I really shouldn't stay. We're going to Mom and Dad's later tonight after the Bible class is over. Lilly wants to tell them about her visit."

Jeff sat down. Close, too close, to her. "She sounded like she had fun."

"Yeah."

"Did you get used to missing her?"

"Pretty much." There were distractions.

Jeff took her hand, holding it between both of his. "Probably good for you both."

The distractions? Oh, the separation. "Probably." She couldn't think straight with him so close.

He moved closer, letting her hand go to slip an arm around her shoulders. "I had fun while she was gone," he said.

"So did I."

His lips came down on hers and she let her eyes slip closed, let the memories slip around her. The passion came back, the hunger and the sweetness, the desperate need to be held, to belong if only for a while. What did love matter? It was a secret to be held hidden in her heart.

She moved into his arms, coming to him with all the joys and needs of a woman. This was now. This was all she needed. Tomorrow could take care of itself.

Their hungers met and exploded into passion. His hands slid over her body with sure possession. She was in heaven. His kiss, his touch, the urgency of his caress drove her deeper into his arms. A desperateness seemed to fuel her needs, a sense that she needed to have him now, that time was waiting to steal this bit of joy from her.

His hands moved under her T-shirt, unclasping her bra and freeing her breasts for his pleasure, her pleasure. He knew just what to do, just what made her body hungrier. There was no waiting. It had to be now.

As if they were one already, they slipped onto the floor. Molly lay there, Jeff over her, his impatient hands stripping her of her shirt, her shorts. Then she helped him with his so that their needs could be met, so that this song of joy in her heart could explode into wonder with his.

They lay together, entwined and locked together. If only this could last, if this moment in time could spin out into the universe forever. But then, all thought was gone and all Molly could do was hold him, hold him as the only part of the world that was sane and right and necessary. They flew with the stars, then floated slowly down to earth.

For a long moment, Molly lay still, letting the tenderness last. She could feel his heartbeat slowly return to normal, but still she didn't want to move. Jeff slid off her, lying on his side and smiling down at her.

"Stay the night," he said, leaning over to kiss her breast.

It wanted to start the fire all over again. Part of her was tempted, but she sighed and sat up. "I can't." She reached for her clothes.

"Why not? Afraid Gram will bring over breakfast again?"

"Lilly's back home. We're going to my parents soon." She glanced over at the clock on his VCR. "In half an hour actually."

He didn't say anything more and she was glad. She took her clothes into the bathroom and dressed. He was dressed also when she got out, and pulled her into his arms.

His kiss was hot and hungry, his lips singing to her of desire and sweet love, but then he let her go. Regret hung in the air.

"You can come to my parents, too, if you want," she said. What an idea, yet she couldn't bear to leave him.

"I think I'll take a rain check."

She smiled at him, her eyes taking in everything from the fire smoldering in his eyes to the soft moistness of his lips. She touched them briefly with her fingertips. "See you," she said, then ran from the apartment. Or was it from the sudden fear in the air that this would all collapse on her?

"And then the little baby pony came out."

They were at Molly's parents' house, she and Lilly along with Gram and Agnes, and Lilly was recounting the various happenings that had occurred during her visit to the farm. She had been describing the birth of the colt, pausing to stoke her engine with a huge piece of cherry pie with ice cream.

"She was all wobbly but stood up real fast."

Molly listened to the stories with half an ear, her mind more on Jeff and the love they'd shared not that long ago. It was such a delicious secret, yet in ways she wanted to shout out her happiness to the world. She wished Jeff had come with her. That silly sensation of fear she'd felt as she was leaving Jeff's apartment was as irrational as her fear of caterpillars.

Lilly turned to Molly. "Was it all messy when I came out of you?"

The question took Molly by surprise and she stared at the girl.

"I mean, when I was born," Lilly persisted.

"Yes, hon." Molly tried to come back fully to the present. "It was rather messy."

"Yuk," Lilly said. "I'm not going to have any babies." She finished the last morsel of her dessert.

"More pie and ice cream?" Molly's father asked.

"No, thank you," Lilly replied. "A whole bunch of people came over to see the baby horse get born. Neighbors, people from school, just about everybody. Were there many people around when I was born?"

Shadows crept around Molly's heart. She wasn't sure she liked the direction the conversation was going. Maybe she'd better pay closer attention. "Not too many," she said cautiously. "People usually don't have their babies with a crowd around."

"I was there, kid. In Denver, I mean." Agnes's raw voice cut through the fog of tension like a sharp knife. "I wouldn't have missed it for the world."

"Was anybody else there?" Lilly asked.

"We were back here in Niles," Gram replied. "But we were thinking of you the whole time."

"Your Aunt Maggie was there," Molly pointed out, not certain what demon forced the words from her mouth.

"I don't remember Aunt Maggie very much," Lilly said. "She didn't come around a lot, did she, Mom?"

Molly shook her head. "Just when you were born."

"It takes a lot of work to be a doctor," Gram said. "She had to study a lot."

"You come out to Denver a lot, don't you, Gram?"

"Whenever I can, kiddo."

"And you do, too." Lilly had turned to Molly's mother. "Don't you, Grandma?"

"I'd like to see you every day," her mother said. "And I would, if you didn't live so far away."

They looked across the table at each other, but to Molly it was as if they were looking over the years. Suddenly, so many things just fell away. And what she saw was her mother's needs, her mother's hungers, and her mother's love.

The family scene blurred before her. Lilly wanted a father. Her mother wanted her granddaughter close to her. Gram wanted family close in her golden years. Had Molly herself come back looking for love?

Maybe she should never have come home. She felt like Pandora, opening up a box of pain, a whole boxcar full of hungers that could never be satisfied, not the least of which were hers.

"You have to work real hard, too, don't you, Grandpa?" Lilly said. "I mean, just like a doctor. That's why you don't come visit us in Denver."

Molly's father's face reddened as if he was getting angry, but no explosion came. Molly looked closer. There was no anger in her father's eyes. Hurt. Embarrassment maybe. But certainly no anger.

"Yeah, honey," he told Lilly. "That's why. But I'm going to try to change that. Nothing should be more important than seeing you grow up."

His voice was so soft, yet so riddled with pain and regret that it tore at Molly's heart. She blinked back the wetness that came to her eyes. Maybe it was worth it for them to have come here.

"Well, we'll be glad of your company on our trips," her mother said briskly as she stood up. "Let's get the table cleared. It's past this young lady's bedtime."

Agnes stood up also. "I'll help."

"Oh, hey. Wait a minute guys." Lilly was standing and waving her arms. "I got news."

Everyone paused to look at her.

"Get this," she said, gesturing in an exaggerated fashion. "Mom's got a date for Friday night. Jeff's taking her to dinner and then they're going to some park to watch fireflies."

The pain melted away from Molly's father's face, leaving it filled with anger, just like it always was. He stood for a moment, staring at them all. He looked at Lilly, his mouth opening to say words that never came out, then he just turned and stormed out. Molly sighed, her feeling of warmth evaporating. She picked up some dirty dishes and headed for the kitchen.

* * *

Jeff leaned an elbow on the open refrigerator door and grimaced. The only thing that looked edible in the vast expanse of emptiness was some leftover pizza, and that was pushing the definition of edible. Time to throw the remains back in the bushes behind the apartment house. Give some critters a feast.

He slammed the door shut and went over to the window above his kitchen sink. A slow smile played on his lips. He imagined a young bachelor raccoon dragging the leftovers down to the river. He'd wash the food and fuss around, setting it on some stones while a young lady raccoon looked coyly at him.

"Oh, Lordy me."

Wiping his face with his hands, Jeff went into his living room and threw himself onto his sofa. He leaned back and closed his eyes. It was obvious he needed a vacation. Needed to get away. He was getting punchy.

"Nuts."

He opened his eyes and stared at the silent television set. Too bad Molly and Lilly had that family visit tonight. It would have been nice to have dinner with Molly. And Lilly, too. She was a neat kid.

A grin spread across his face. The little twerp was sharp and really creative. The things that popped out of her mouth were just unbelievable. Sometimes it was as if the kid was in contact with some alien life-forms. A surprise dinner. Wayne and his rats.

The doorbell interrupted his reverie. Jeff sat there and glared in the direction of his front door. He didn't want to talk to anyone tonight. If Molly couldn't be here, he just wanted to vegetate.

He closed his eyes and sank farther into the sofa, but the doorbell continued its annoying sound. His eyes flipped to wide open.

That could be Molly. The time was about right for their visit to be over. It wasn't as if she lacked for people to care for Lilly, although it would be fine with him if she'd brought the kid over. Maybe they could pop some popcorn, or play a game or watch TV. Jeff rose and hurried to his door.

But it wasn't Molly at the door. The welcoming smile slid off Jeff's face. "Good evening, Reverend," Jeff said.

Molly's father stood out there and glared, anger filling his eyes and fueling the color to his face. Jeff wondered what was with the old man. Somebody complaining about service at the Y. Must be pretty bad if the Reverend Cahill couldn't let it go through regular channels.

"May I come in?" he asked.

"Sure."

Jeff stood back from the door and let him walk in. The reverend stopped in the middle of the living room and stood there.

"Would you like something cool to drink?" Jeff asked as he followed him in.

"No, thank you."

The words were polite but the voice was stiff and angry. Jeff clenched his teeth a moment. It was best to get things over with.

"Won't you sit down, please?"

"I'll stand, thank you."

"Okay."

Jeff walked over to the sofa and sat on an arm. He looked into Reverend Cahill's red-flecked eyes and waited. The man had called this meeting, so let him run it.

Reverend Cahill took a deep breath, then exhaled. "I'll get to the point. I want you to do the right thing," Reverend Cahill said. "The decent thing." The old man stared at him a long moment, almost as if he were scum. Just as he used to back in Jeff's old rebellious days. "I want you to put your name on the birth certificate."

Jeff blinked. He'd begun with curious, then moved on to bewildered. What the hell was going on here?

"That child has a birth certificate that says Father: unknown," Molly's father said. "Don't you realize that's a legal document? Every place she shows it, everyone will know she's a . . . a bastard."

Jeff blinked again, still bewildered.

"I don't understand the men of today," Reverend Cahill said. "Not being willing to support and care for their children. But at the very least you should give the child a name. I mean, that won't cost you anything."

Slowly the paralysis left Jeff's brain. Life eased from there into his tongue. "I don't have a child."

"Don't lie to me," Reverend Cahill exploded, waving an angry finger in his face. "My daughter told me and she has no reason to lie."

Daughter?

"My daughter told me that you are Lilly's father."

Molly said he was Lilly's father? Bewilderment flooded back into Jeff's mind and his brain was back to near paralysis. "The least you can do for your child is give her your name."

Jeff shook his head in disbelief.

"If you don't—" The reverend's voice was quiet now. The color had drained from his face, leaving a residue of intense hatred in his eyes. "If you don't, I will do everything in my power to see that you are punished. That you are crushed."

Jeff stared, unable to formulate any thoughts, much less words.

"And you could certainly kiss that foundation award goodbye."

"But—"

The word was barely out of Jeff's mouth when the Reverend Cahill turned on his heel and stalked out the door.

Chapter Eleven

Molly sat on the porch step in the dark and breathed in the breeze coming in from the west, soft yet strong enough to blow away the mosquitoes and the heat of the day. Normally she would have enjoyed sitting here in the evening darkness, listening to the sleepy sounds of her little town, but not tonight. Something was in the air tonight.

Jeff had called a little bit ago, saying he had to see her. His words had said little, but his voice had clearly told her something was wrong.

Molly sighed. It was beginning to look as if her premonition was right. A car pulled up to the curb. She could tell it was Jeff's and went down to meet him.

"We need to talk," he said through the open passenger side window, the motor still running.

"Sure," Molly replied. "Want to come sit on the porch?"

He shook his head.

"Okay, let me tell Gram."

She turned and hurried into the house, trying to hide her uneasiness. Gram and Agnes were sitting in the den, Gram knitting and Agnes reading a book. The TV was on with the sound turned low.

"I'm going for a ride with Jeff," Molly announced.

"That's fine, dear," Gram murmured.

"We're not going anywhere," Agnes said. "Take as long as you want."

Why did Molly fear it wasn't going to be long? How long did it take for a heart to break?

The car door was unlocked and Jeff didn't come around to open it for her. Neither did he say anything when she got in. He just put the car in gear and took it on a winding route that brought them to the parking lot of River Park on the east bank of the river.

He got out and walked through the darkness to the big rocks on the shore. The rocks where they met when ditching school. The rocks where she met him again when she returned to Niles.

Molly quietly followed. She sat down on a rock while Jeff stood and stared at the river, slowly flowing north. The water seemed black in the night darkness, yet diamonds of light flickered on the surface, giving her hope. Whatever was wrong, maybe they could handle it. It seemed like ages before Jeff spoke.

"Your father came by my place this evening. He laid a load on me and I'm trying to straighten things out."

Molly's heart froze. Oh Lord, what had her father done?

Jeff paused as if soaking up strength from the river. "I'd like to lead into things gently but, in this case, I don't know how." He turned to face Molly. "Why did you tell your father that I'm Lilly's father?"

Molly just stared at him. She couldn't have heard him right. The moonlight must have distorted his words, the rushing of the river must have drowned them out. It had to be her own fears speaking. But he was just staring at her, waiting.

"I didn't." Her voice sounded hollow and empty.

In the mixture of moon- and streetlight, Molly saw Jeff's pain, saw the anguish fighting for his soul. "Your father said, and I quote, 'My daughter told me that you are Lilly's father.'"

A trapdoor opened before Molly, swallowing up all her silly dreams of happiness. What could she say? What could she tell Jeff and still keep Lilly safe?

"I never, ever told him anything like that," Molly said, almost in a whisper. "It's a misunderstanding."

Jeff shook his head. "I didn't misunderstand. He said, my daughter told—"

"No, it's a misunderstanding between him and me," she said quickly. She couldn't bear the pain in Jeff's voice.

"A misunderstanding?" he cried. "How do you have a misunderstanding about who's the father of your child?"

Molly stared out over the water. The glittering diamonds were only broken glass, ready to cut and slice if you handled them wrong.

She took a deep breath. "Back before Lilly was born, I wouldn't tell him the name of the father," she said. "We had a terrible argument, but I refused. He knew I'd had a crush on you and just jumped to conclusions, I guess."

Jeff's sigh was more than tired, it was exhausted, but the anger was gone. He came to sit next to her. Close but not touching.

"I should have known it was something like that," he said. "I should have known I could trust you. When have you ever lied?"

His words were knives jabbing at her. "I'll get it taken care of," she said slowly. "It'll be right."

He took her hand. Though his touch was gentle, his hold hardly restrictive, Molly felt as if she couldn't breathe.

"It wasn't that I don't like Lilly," he said. "She's a great kid. We just know she's not mine. I mean, I would have remembered making love to you."

He leaned over then, his lips finding hers in the darkness. His touch was as soft and sweet as ever, yet it hurt. The very surge of joy in her heart caused a sharp pain. She wanted to fall into his arms and cry out the truth. She wanted him to tell her that everything would be all right, but she could do nothing but kiss him back, praying that he would never know about her lies.

Molly drove down U.S.31, the main thoroughfare between Niles and South Bend, barely seeing the fast food outlets, car dealerships and motels that filled the space between the homes still left along the four-lane highway.

It was nearly midnight by this time and the roads were almost deserted. Molly was glad of that. She was having a hard enough time keeping her hands from shaking; having to maneuver around another car would have been more than she could handle.

How could her father do this?

Why was she surprised? She ought to be asking herself why she hadn't seen it coming? Why she hadn't made sure Maggie went to him and told him Jeff was innocent? Because she was the same trusting fool she'd been nine years ago. Because she'd believed Maggie would do what was right just because it was right. Hadn't Molly grown up at all?

It had taken Molly several calls and an obnoxious attitude to locate Maggie. Her first call to Maggie's home had gotten an answering machine, her second her sister's answering service. Finally, she'd tried the hospital in South Bend and learned Maggie was on duty. She'd gotten in her car and drove down.

The area around the hospital had a deserted feel. Visiting hours were long since over. Molly pulled around to the emergency room entrance and parked in the visitors' lot there. She marched into the reception area, letting her anger build to a white-hot temperature.

The receptionist looked up, the frown on her face melting into a smile. "Dr. Novak, I thought you were going up to pediatrics."

It took Molly only a split second to adjust, to throw herself into Maggie's persona. "I was," Molly said. "I am."

Not waiting for the woman to have second thoughts, Molly turned down the nearest hallway. She didn't have the faintest idea where pediatrics was. She went down one deserted hallway and found herself in X ray. Another turn and she was at the cafeteria, closed of course, but there was an elevator just down the way and she took it up to the next floor.

The doors opened onto a sitting area, and there, waiting for the elevator, was Maggie.

"Molly?" Lines of weariness zigzagged across Maggie's forehead and wariness lurked in the corners of her eyes. She didn't look any better than Molly felt. "What are you doing here?"

"I want to talk," Molly said.

Her sister didn't skip a beat. She just turned and took them into an empty examination room down the hall.

"Jeff came to see me," Molly said. "Dad went to him tonight, demanding that he admit to being Lilly's father."

"Oh, God." A sob escaped Maggie's throat and her sister buried her face in her hands.

"I thought you were going to tell Dad that Jeff wasn't Lilly's father," Molly said. "We talked just a few days ago. You said you would try to fix things."

Her sister sobbed, still hiding behind her hands, but Molly was unmoved. She wouldn't mind dissolving in tears but she didn't have that luxury. Finally Maggie looked up.

"It's all going to tell all," Maggie cried. "Everyone's going to find out I was the one who was pregnant." She dug around in her pockets until she found a tissue, first wiping her eyes, then blowing her nose in it. She put the crumpled remains back in her pocket. "I knew you should never have come back here."

"I want to keep things secret just as much as you do," Molly pointed out.

"But you don't have as much to lose." Maggie moaned. "This would just kill Bill. He's got his position to think of, you know."

Some things never change, Molly thought. Maggie was still real good at listing all the reasons why she shouldn't take responsibility, why she was the most injured of injured parties.

"We've all got a lot to lose," Molly said. "But most of this could have been avoided. Why didn't you go to Dad and tell him the truth? Or at least, tell him that Jeff isn't the father."

Her sister's chin began quivering and tears flowed again. Maggie looked away toward the far wall. "Because he is the father," she answered in a very small voice.

Molly could only stare. No words formed. No words came out. This had to be another of Maggie's games.

"Jeff was the only one I had sex with in high school," Maggie said.

Molly still couldn't say anything.

"And it was just once." Now her sister's tears were the fruits of bitterness. She dabbed at them with a paper towel. "One stupid time. It wasn't love. It wasn't fun. It wasn't anything. Remember, the Christmas formal our senior year? And you remember how Dad made me change out of the dress I bought just for that dance?"

Molly nodded.

"Well, that really ticked me off. And then Tim was a real jerk. He spent all his time with the guys, drinking beer and laughing like a fool." Maggie crushed the paper towel and threw it into a wastebasket. "Everything was just crowding in on me. So I got drunk, stinking drunk."

Maggie paused for a moment to blink back some tears that wanted to start a new run. "Then I went out into the cold without anything. No coat, no boots. Nothing. I don't know where I was but Jeff came along in his father's car. He offered me a ride." Maggie paused to shrug her shoulders. "I got in."

She let out a deep sigh. "I knew how Dad disliked him and it seemed like the ultimate revenge. So I really came on to him." She shrugged. "And, as they say, the rest is history."

They shared the silence, a deafening silence that pounded on their ears. A few voices outside bounced around the exterior walls. Soft footsteps echoed in the empty hall. Stillness of a small town hospital in the middle of the week.

"So." Words finally came to Molly's tongue, stumbling and bumbling their way to the surface, like early risers in a college dorm. "Jeff is Lilly's father."

Maggie nodded. There was no more pain in her sister's face, just a stone-dead tiredness.

Neither spoke for a while. What was there to say? Of all the men in the world to be Lilly's father, Molly couldn't think of anyone else she would have chosen. Jeff was a wonderful, gentle, caring man. He was the man she loved.

But what difference did it make now? No matter in what form the truth was trotted out, someone would feel an excruciating pain. Molly walked to the door and turned the knob.

"I wish I could go back," Maggie said. "I wish I could go back to that December and undo all this."

That was one thing Molly would never wish. "Then there would be no Lilly," Molly replied.

She opened the door and left.

"Aw, come on, Mom," Lilly whined, following Molly through the kitchen. "Why can't I go?"

"Because I said so."

Molly bit her lip and took a deep breath. She hadn't meant to snap. None of this was Lilly's fault. It was just the long sleepless hours of the night beginning to take their toll.

"Look, honey," she said. "Gram needs help getting ready for the reunion. I'm only staying at the Y for my swimming lesson, then I'll be right back to pitch in, too."

Lilly didn't look pleased, but gave up her battle. Molly felt Lilly's eyes on her as she hurried out to the garage. The five-block walk was beyond her today, but just about everything seemed beyond her.

She'd gotten home from seeing Maggie long after everyone else was asleep. There was no one to notice if she went to bed, so she didn't bother, just curling up on the porch swing in back and letting the night bring answers.

It didn't, though, and neither did the dawn.

What did she do—tell Jeff and risk the whole secret coming out, or deny him the joy of knowing his child?

The morning had been blessedly busy as she, Gram and Agnes aired out rooms and put fresh sheets on beds, but the time for Molly to go to the Y for the swimming lessons had approached with frightening speed. What was she to say to Jeff? She'd promised to make it all right, but how could she?

She parked her car and took a deep breath before going into the Y, her heart in her stomach. Jeff was in the lobby.

"Hi," she said. She wanted so much to see him, to let her eyes feast on him, but her heart just knew fear. She still didn't know what to tell him.

"Hello." He waited.

She swallowed hard and glanced about her. People milled by, but no one was really paying attention to them. "I haven't seen Dad yet," she said slowly. "I tried but there just wasn't time this morning."

"There wasn't time?" His eyes grew hard. That old familiar distrust was there for all to see. "The man's going around town telling everyone I've neglected my child and you don't have time to talk to him?"

Molly clutched her gym bag tighter. "I will, I promise. It's just that . . ." It was just that she didn't know what to do.

"It's just that your father still runs things, and that you're too scared of him to stand up for the truth."

His eyes were unforgiving, and for one long endless moment he stared into her soul. She felt his anger, his distrust and then his shutting her out. Something closed in his eyes, and he turned to walk away.

Molly watched him go, wanting to run after him. But what could she say? The only thing she knew at the moment was that her heart was breaking into a million pieces. She sped into the locker room.

"Why the hell are you eating that in the middle of the night?" Paul Spencer asked. "I thought you were going to straighten out your eating habits."

Jeff twirled a long yellow French fry in his fingers before throwing the grease-laden morsel into his mouth. The damn thing tasted like paper, but eating was something to do.

"I'm still busy," Jeff replied. "And I still get hungry."

"I thought you and your little sweetie were settling into a more normal routine," Paul said.

Jeff didn't even bother looking at his father. He just sat there pushing a French fry back and forth through a blob of catsup.

All he wanted to do was run. Leave this damn town in his dust, just as he had back in high school. But then what would all his kids do? A mocking laugh rang out back in his subconscious. He wasn't going to do them a whole of good staying here. The old reverend was going to see to that. If it wasn't this, it would be something else. Molly wouldn't do anything to stop him. Oh, maybe she'd try to put a crimp in his plans, but she wouldn't really stand up to him.

Jeff felt his teeth clench in anger. The big and powerful always like to stomp on the weak and innocent. That was what made them feel big and powerful. It would take more than an old blowhard like the reverend to run him out of town.

"I don't have a little sweetie," Jeff finally replied. He threw the strip of food onto the plate and looked off toward the bar. "We parted."

"Boy," his father grumbled. "You sure don't keep them long."

"You should talk," Jeff snapped.

They stared at each other for a long moment, flashing twin fires of anger. His father's burned out first but Jeff felt no joy of victory. Just more tired.

"Anything you want to talk about?" Paul asked.

Jeff shook his head. A lump swelled in his throat, radiating waves of pain that reached to the farthest corners of his heart. Why had he thought he could trust her? She was just like everyone else.

"Molly sure seems like a nice kid," his father said. "More so than her sister. Not that I'm saying Maggie is mean. She just has a sharper edge to her."

Molly was a cowboy, said so herself. Liked to travel fast and travel light. That must mean no loyalties, no guts.

"That little kid sure is cute. Although she's sort of spooky to look at."

Jeff frowned at his father. "Spooky?" Lilly was a lot of things, but somehow he'd never thought she was spooky.

"Aw, hell," Paul said. "Forget what I said. I'm just an old man seeing ghosts."

Jeff pushed his plate back. Something froze in his heart, something that made him afraid to push on, but he did anyway. "Whose ghost?"

"There are times, when that kid looks at you out of the side of her eyes, when she reminds me of your mother."

Jeff just stared at his father, his hands turning to ice. He tried to get his mind jump-started, but nothing seemed to make sense.

"Ah, forget it," Paul said. "I'm just an old man whose eyes are playing tricks on him. I mean, how the hell could the granddaughter of the high and mighty Reverend Mr. Cahill look like somebody from our family?"

Jeff sipped at his coffee. It was cold, tasteless but something to hold on to. "The high and mighty Reverend Cahill claims that I'm Lilly's father."

"You're kidding." Paul shook off his shock. "Are you?"

"No." The coffee cup was no help, and Jeff put it down, then ran his fingers through his hair. "It's not like I was a model citizen back then. I was a typical young stud with more urges than sense, but I never touched Molly. She was..." He sought for the right word. "Such an innocent."

"Not with everybody."

The words set off a blinding burst of rage, so strong that Jeff had to fight back the desire to strike his father. He clenched his fists and took a deep breath. The old man was right, he told himself. Molly hadn't been an innocent with everybody. She had gotten pregnant. He took another deep breath to steady himself.

"How'd the reverend pick you as the father?" Paul asked as he waved over a waitress, who refilled their coffee cups.

It gave Jeff a moment to compose himself. What was with him? So he'd had fun the last couple of weeks with an old friend and it was over. Nothing unexpected about any of that. The waitress left and Jeff found the coffee more palatable.

"He says Molly told him," Jeff said.

Paul's eyebrows rose. "She told him? Why would she do that?"

"Damned if I know. She didn't have much of an answer when I confronted her with it." Jeff's anger was back. "Now, if it had been Maggie..."

Paul had been staring into his coffee, but looked up at his son, piercing his gaze with directness. "What about Maggie?"

Jeff shrugged, sorry he'd mentioned it. "There was this one night when we were seniors. She'd dumped her boyfriend at the Christmas formal and was out walking by herself. I picked her up."

"And?" His father's voice was dry, impatient.

Jeff looked away. This wasn't an episode he was particularly proud of. "And we decided to vent our personal frustrations in a mutual way." He looked at his father. "We had sex. Just that once. Then she turned back into Miss Icicle. Acted as if she'd never seen me before. It was okay by me. I hadn't thought we were going to be great chums."

"How'd you know it was Maggie?"

"What?" Jeff just stared at his father. "I knew. She was all dolled up, more brazen. Molly never . . ."

The world seemed to come to a screeching halt. How did he know what Molly did or didn't do? Hadn't she told him a number of times since she'd been back that he hadn't known her?

"Damn."

"I never could tell the two apart," Paul said. "Maybe when they were together, but not separate."

Things started to make sense. "They were always switching places," Jeff said. "For tests, for bets, for fun. They used to laugh about it." He felt again the sting of the laughter, the feeling of being an outsider.

"So this was another—"

"Game," Jeff said, his voice bitter. "Just another game. Just another set of lies." And for nine years, those lies had robbed him of his daughter.

Chapter Twelve

"Molly," Marissa said.

Startled, Molly looked up from her gym bag. The swimming lesson was over and she was anxious to be on her way. She didn't know where she'd go, just as long as it wasn't in the same building with Jeff. A different universe would be best, but one had to make do with whatever was available. He had the right to know he was Lilly's father, but she didn't have the courage to risk the consequences of telling him.

"Aimee wants to give you a hug," Marissa said.

The girl stood before Molly, small for her age, now wearing an expression heavy with concern. Guilt rode in and melted the hardness covering Molly's heart. She reached out and hugged the little girl, receiving a hearty squeeze in return.

"I loves you," the girl said.

"I love you, too, honey," Molly murmured.

Aimee held on to Molly's hands, concern again flooding her eyes. "Don'ts you feels good?"

"I'm fine, honey." Molly forced a heartiness into her voice and lightly mussed the child's black locks. "I'm just a little bit tired."

"Then takes a nap." Aimee nodded wisely. "When I gets tired, Mommy always makes me takes a nap."

"Okay." Molly had to smile in spite of herself. "I'll try that."

Marissa moved in and took the girl's hand. "Come on, Aimee. Your mom's here to get you dressed."

Frowning slightly, Aimee followed the counselor but after a few steps stopped and turned. "And when I wakes up I feels a whole lot better."

The best Molly could do in reply was force a smile to her lips. She waved at Aimee, who having dispensed her advice, was now skipping along after her counselor into the locker room.

Feeling suddenly listless, Molly picked up her towel and slowly shuffled off after them. She wished things were so simple. Just take a nap and let the past nine years just slip away. But then she wouldn't have Lilly. She dressed quickly and hurried out into the lobby.

Lilly was waiting by the door, waving at her. "Gram wants us to stop at the store. She gave me a list and told me to meet you here."

"Okay." Molly took the grocery list and frowned at it while they walked out the door.

"It won't take long, will it?" Lilly asked. "I promised Rufus I'd give him a bath this afternoon so he'd look pretty for the reunion."

"No, it shouldn't." Molly just felt so tired lately. The oppressively hot air didn't help.

"You know, Rufus really loves it here." Lilly skipped along down the stairs to the sidewalk. "Especially the big backyard that Grammy has, but he likes me to play with him, too."

"I'm sure he does, honey."

"He doesn't like Denver anymore," Lilly said. "The yards are too small."

Oh, please, Lilly. Please. Lilly fought back the weariness that wanted to swallow her soul.

"He doesn't like it that every time he wants to do his business or check stuff out, somebody has to take him for a walk."

Molly wrapped her arms around her gym bag, hugging it to her chest as if it were a shield that would keep further hurt away. They should never have come here. There were millions of people who went through a lifetime without knowing any of their extended family. What was Lilly going to get out of this trip, but the pain of dreams that could never be fulfilled?

"Hey, there's Jeff."

Molly tried to grab her daughter's hand so they could hurry along, but the kid was too quick. She was already running across the bridge toward him.

"Hey, big dude," Lilly shouted.

A few days ago, Jeff would have shouted a reply back to Lilly, but today he just stood rooted in place and stared at them. "Hi, little dude," he finally said.

"I'm going home to take care of Rufus," Lilly announced. "He likes Gram's big yard. He didn't have much of a yard in Denver."

"Yeah." Jeff nodded. His eyes seemed to be watching Lilly intently, unable to leave her face. "Dogs like a big yard."

"I like it here, too."

"Yeah, it's a nice place."

He finally glanced up at Molly. The emptiness in his eyes reflected her own soul. She wanted to run away but knew that look would haunt her. She had to find a way to tell him.

"How did the class go today?" he asked. His voice was dead.

Molly nodded. "Fine. Just fine, thank you."

"That's good."

They had shared so much in the past several days. They'd instituted a new program at the Y, worked through a storm and shared each other. And now they stared at each other like strangers. Strangers who feared each other. Strangers who belonged to warring tribes.

"You'll need an adult to supervise the program, of course," Molly said, fighting for words to fill the silence. "But Marissa can run the swimming part. She really understands the kids and their needs."

"That's good," Jeff said. "It might take a bit to find a properly qualified adult."

"Check with the special-ed teachers in the area," Molly said. "With the money from that foundation grant, you should be able to pay them a small salary."

He shrugged. "We don't know who's going to get the grant. I'm sure all the people they're looking at are qualified."

She took a deep breath but that seemed to be all she could accomplish. She knew that she should say goodbye and go, but she was afraid of the words of farewell, afraid that they might really be final. Whom did she protect— Lilly or Jeff?

"How come you guys didn't have lunch together today?" Lilly asked, her bright, piercing eyes going from one to the other.

"We were both busy, dear," Molly said.

"Yeah," Jeff agreed. "We were busy."

"You're coming to the reunion this weekend, aren't you?" Lilly asked. "Lots of people are getting here tonight."

Oh, Lord. Molly held her breath. She'd completely forgotten that they'd talked to him about coming.

He just looked at her and she just looked away.

"We should be going, honey," Molly said. "Rufus will be waiting for us!"

"And then two more pins go here," Aunt Flo said as she stuck two blue-headed pins into the map at Grand Rapids.

They'd put up a big map of the Midwest on a bulletin board in the church activity room and were marking the locations where everyone in the family lived. It was a great way to start off the reunion.

"We sure have a big family, don't we?" Molly said, standing behind Lilly with her arms lightly around the girl.

"But they all live around here," Lilly moaned.

"Not all of them," Flo assured her. She pointed to some pins off to the east of the others. "Your Cousin Patsy's family lives in Pittsburgh and your Uncle Doug lives in Cleveland."

"They're still on the map," Lilly said.

"And we have our own little map," Molly said. Off to the west was tacked a piece of Colorado with three pins stuck in that. "Makes us special for coming so far."

"That's the idea." Flo messed Lilly's hair, then picked up some more pins. "If we marked where everyone was born, then we'd really be spread out. Your grandmother and I were born in St. Louis. Your Aunt Betty was born in New Jersey and the Dinkler kids were born all over the globe, wherever Joe was stationed at the time. Why even your mom's brother Danny was born someplace else.''

"He was?" Molly hadn't known that.

"Yep. He was born while your mom was out in Denver taking care of Agnes after the accident." She turned back to the map. "Now how many names we got for Kalamazoo?"

While Lilly helped Flo fix the map, Molly wandered among the relatives who had been arriving all evening.

"Maggie, it's so good to see you." An elderly woman pulled Molly into a tight hug.

"I'm Molly," she said.

"Really? My goodness, can't tell you two apart yet."

"Molly." Agnes waved her over. "Come take our picture, will you?"

So Molly made the rounds, getting hugs meant for Maggie and snapping pictures for people. Everyone seemed genuinely glad to see her, yet she had a hard time sharing their excitement. She felt like a zombie, going through the motions but without any heart.

No, that was wrong. If she had no heart, what was causing the constant pain?

"We're here!" someone called from the doorway.

Molly turned. The Dinkler clan had arrived, Joe and Clara and their eight kids, who stampeded through the room like a herd of wild horses.

"Oh, dear. We're going to need more cookies." Molly's mother stood in the kitchen door, her hand pressed to her mouth. "I knew I should have brought over more from Gram's."

"Want me to go get them?" Molly offered.

Her mother looked relieved. "If you don't mind, dear."

"No problem." Lilly had stopped helping Flo and was now skidding across the tile floor with some of the middle Dinklers. "You want me to take Lilly?"

"No, of course not. Let the child have some fun."

Molly managed to bite her tongue and say nothing, though sliding on the tile floor had been a capital offense when she was Lilly's age. She would rather leave Lilly here anyway. Molly's mopes were better dealt with alone.

It was still hot outside, but that edge of heat had tapered off now that the sun was getting lower in the sky. She walked along the front of the church property and then down the street, but at the corner, she hesitated. The path down to the river beckoned. It wouldn't take much more time to walk along the river than the street and somehow the idea of the river felt healing.

She turned and walked down the gravel drive to the parking lot. A few cars were there, belonging most likely to the fishermen along the banks. She walked through the parking lot to the path along the river's edge.

It was cooler down here and she felt less pressured. She stopped to stare out at the water. It had the strength to keep moving, keep rushing on. Why couldn't she be more like it, instead of always getting caught by snags and tugged in all directions?

She walked to the end of the dock and slipped off her shoes, sitting on the edge to dangle her feet in the water. Where would she find an answer to this whole mess? Why did it have to seem like a choice between Lilly and Jeff? Why did one's happiness have to be threatened by the other's?

"This is a surprise."

Molly slowly turned around. Jeff was there. Was that why she'd come, because she'd hoped he would be here? His eyes were as cold and distant as they'd been lately.

There was no hint of a thaw coming, no bit of softening in his stance. She got to her feet.

"I guess I'm kind of slow," he said. "But I figured it all out last night."

Molly went dead inside. How could he possibly know? He couldn't know that Maggie had given birth to Lilly, that Molly was an impostor. He couldn't, could he? She wanted to ask him not to tell but fear made her mouth too dry to speak.

"I don't know why it took me so long," he said. "I mean, it was your pattern all through school, wasn't it? When you didn't like what life handed you, you switched places."

"It wasn't quite like that," she said, but her voice was so weak she could barely hear her own words.

"Sure."

He stopped, his eyes wandering over the water. Looking anywhere but at her? The steady rush of the river told her to be strong, to fight for her love.

"You don't understand," she said.

He turned to face her. The burning anger in his eyes said how deeply he'd been hurt. "You're right. I don't understand, but then I've never had the option of being someone else." He made a face. "Gee, I'm tired of being Molly," he said in a fake little voice. "I think I'll be Maggie for a while."

"I never thought that. Whenever we switched it was for a reason."

He snorted. "A reason. Like making a fool of somebody?"

"No."

"No? Then why else were you out the night of the Christmas formal pretending to be Maggie?"

He didn't know. Molly just stared at him. He didn't know the real truth.

"If you wanted to have a little fun, why couldn't you just have done it as yourself? Why pretend to be her?"

"I didn't." There was such pain in his voice, such bitterness, that she couldn't bear it. All she wanted was to take that hurt away. "I wouldn't have tricked you like that. You know me better than that."

"I don't know you at all, but I do know a bunch of lies when I hear them."

"Jeff!"

"Oh, why even talk about it?" He gave her no time to speak. "I don't care what silly little games you two played or play. All I care about is that you kept my daughter from me for nine years."

"It wasn't that way at all," she cried. She couldn't let him think he'd been betrayed again. She couldn't let that fragile growth of trust be trampled. "Jeff, I love you. I think I've always loved you. I would never have knowingly hurt you."

The look he gave her was of pure scorn. "For God's sake, spare me the drama. I didn't get to see my child take her first step because of you. I wasn't there to wish her luck on her first day of school, to cheer her through her softball games or to read her stories when she was sick. All because of you."

"I didn't know," she said, fighting back the tears.

"Cut out the lies," he said. "It's over. Tell your father he won. Not because of his threats, but because I want my daughter to know she's mine." Then he spun on his heel and walked away.

"Jeff." Molly started after him, took a few steps even, but then stopped. She could get him back only one way—

with the truth. And that could endanger Lilly. What was she to do?

"Hi, Mom."

"Hi, honey," Molly said as she wrapped silverware in napkins. She hadn't slept much last night, but luckily, with the reunion in full swing, she could keep busy enough not to think.

Lilly laid out a napkin in front of her. "How come my teeth are so close together?"

Molly stopped, staring at her daughter's straight and strong white teeth. Why was she asking such a question? Because she'd seen pictures of a young Molly and Maggie, both gap-toothed and wearing braces?

Molly swallowed her rising unease and fear and wrapped the silverware she had. "It's something you inherit from your parents," she murmured quietly.

Lilly merely grunted and picked a knife out of the pile. "Can I get them sort of spread apart?"

"You want your teeth spread apart?"

"Yeah, so I can spit farther." Lilly picked out a fork.

Her daughter's earnest face swam before her and Molly had a strong urge to break out into hysterical laughter. Here she was fearing a question about Lilly's father and his teeth, and all Lilly was thinking about was spitting.

Lilly added a spoon to the pile and rolled them all up. "Bobbie Dinkler can spit really far. And he says it's because his teeth don't come together in front."

"Good for him," Molly said. "But you don't really want to be a champion spitter."

"Yeah, I do," Molly insisted. "Bobbie told me all about this cherry pit-spitting contest. They hold it every year in a place called Oh, Clear."

"Eau Claire," Molly said.

"That's what I said." Lilly climbed up to sit on the table. "Anyway, people come from all over the world to spit. It's really neat. Bobbie practices every day. He's gonna try and be the Under-twelve Champ."

"That's nice, honey."

"Can we go watch him, Mom? Bobbie says it's not that far from here. His father says it's a couple hours' drive from Niles."

"We'll see," she said hoarsely.

"Great." Lilly put her rolled napkin on Molly's pile and raced off.

Molly watched her for a moment, which was as long as she had before Lilly disappeared into the crowd. The child was such a joy. Molly loved her with a desperateness, a completeness that sometimes astounded her. She couldn't imagine life without Lilly, couldn't imagine a world without her.

Yet that was what Jeff had had.

Molly turned back to her napkin chores.

"Molly."

She looked up to find Maggie in front of her.

"Need any help?" her sister asked. Maggie's eyes reflected her worries, her voice, uncertainty.

"If you want." Molly just concentrated on her own work.

Maggie took a small stack of napkins and began to roll. "Have you talked to Jeff lately?" she asked with an innocence that didn't fool Molly for a moment.

Molly finished the napkin she was rolling before answering. "I talk to him often."

There was a long silence, then Maggie sighed. "You know what I mean."

"Does he know that Lilly's his child?" Molly said, speaking more briskly than she felt. "He suspects she is.

Does he know you're her biological mother, no. He thinks I pretended to be you that night."

Maggie looked at her, no doubt trying to read something in Molly's eyes. Molly just stared back.

"Does it matter?" Maggie finally asked.

"Matter? Why should it matter?" Molly laughed more harshly than she intended. It only mattered if Molly had loved him and had dared to dream of happily-ever-afters with him. Luckily, she wasn't so foolish. She fought to swallow her anger. "I'm going back to Denver in a few days. No, it doesn't matter."

Maggie took her at her word and worked in silence for a long time. "Bill is so good to me. He comes from a really old family, lots of money and big on civic responsibility. We met at a fund-raiser for the hospital."

"Oh."

She put a napkin on the pile. "He thought I worked too hard, was too focused on medicine and nothing else, and liked to take me out for dinner. No place real special—Mark's, Frank's Place, the Pizza Joint. He's almost twenty years older than me and had been married before. His wife was perfect. You know, good, kind, sat on all the right committees, but she died about five years ago. I couldn't believe it when he wanted to marry me. I mean, I could never live up to her."

"Do you have to?" Molly asked.

Maggie looked surprised Molly'd voiced the words. "Of course. Bill deserves it. He deserves the best." She glanced down at her hands. "He doesn't know anything at all about that time in high school. It would kill him to find out."

Kill him or the marriage? Molly wondered, but didn't ask. This wasn't the type of relationship she'd pictured Maggie in. She'd always viewed her sister as being the strong one in a relationship, or at least an equal partner. Hadn't she been the strong one of the two of them?

It made Molly uneasy, this need to be the leader, to take care of Maggie and not let her applecart be upset. But like it or not, it wasn't a duty she could shirk.

"Well, he won't find out from me." Molly finished up the napkins and patted the pile. "I'm not planning on telling anyone."

Maggie sat down hard and wiped at her face. "I didn't think you would, but I've been so worried."

About whom? But Molly didn't say it. She just grabbed up the tray full of silverware. "Maybe you'd better wipe your eyes then. Dad's coming over."

Maggie made a quick recovery and Molly was going to leave the two of them alone, but her father stopped her.

"I heard about your working at the Y," he said.

Molly braced herself for a battle. "I was just helping out with a new program."

"I know," he said and slipped his arm around her shoulders. "It's been something the board has talked about for years. It was so good of you to help get it started."

"It was Jeff's doing."

"And your expertise. Thank you." He gave her shoulders another squeeze before he turned to leave.

"Dad," she called him back. "About Jeff. Have you been interviewed yet? Because . . ."

Her father's face twisted as if he'd swallowed a bitter pill. "He does a good job," he said. "I have to admit that. I may not personally like the man, but he does a fine job with the young people."

"He didn't know, Dad. Not until you told him."

His eyes clouded and he looked away, fighting visibly for control. When he turned back to her, he seemed himself except for a sadness echoing in his smile. "I sang his praises to Mr. Robinson," he said slowly. "I couldn't really hurt the kids. Danny loved going to the Y. I did it for him, for his memory as much as for anyone else."

"Thank you," she whispered, blinking back the tears. Her father just shrugged and left. She turned slowly and carried the tray of silverware over to the beginning of the buffet.

The afternoon sped by. Everyone ate and told stories. Cheers went up for the oldest and the youngest family members attending. Lilly got to accept the prize for the one coming from farthest away—because her bedroom was farther west than Molly's or Agnes's—then everyone cheered Molly's parents for hosting the event. By the time all that was done, it was time to eat again. Molly manned the kitchens, watching from the kitchen doorway for dishes that needed refilling, content to be on the edge of things.

"How come Jeff didn't come?" Agnes asked.

Molly shrugged her shoulders as if he hadn't been on her mind all day. "Probably too busy."

"Right. Just like he's been too busy to give you the time of day these past two weeks."

Molly's mother waved from the other end of the buffet table. "Molly, can you get some more bread?"

"Sure."

Molly hurried into the kitchen, too busy to talk to Agnes, too busy even to listen. She fixed another tray of bread, then took out some more salads for refilling. All the while Agnes stayed in the doorway.

"Don't you think maybe it's time for some truth?" Agnes said, finally taking a relish tray out of Molly's hands.

Molly just turned to look at her. "What are you talking about?" Her voice sounded braver than her heart felt.

"Truth. You know, as in what really happened."

Molly began to arrange another platter of ham, laying out slices in a precise circular pattern. "There aren't any truths that need telling," she said.

Agnes said nothing for a minute, then sighed. "You know," she said quietly. "No two things in this world are exactly alike."

Molly didn't move, the platter of ham disappeared as her world collapsed. Hell, why had they thought they could get away with it? Agnes was no fool.

"They can be close," Agnes said. "Very close, in fact. But they won't ever be exactly the same."

Molly botched the ham pattern and had to start over. Her hands were shaking so, it was a wonder she didn't break the dish, too. Agnes just watched.

"How long have you known?" Molly asked, each word quivering around the edges as it left her lips.

"Well, when you guys first came out I didn't know who was who, but then the little things came out. One was a little pushier than the other. The other one tended to make fun of herself while the first took herself more seriously." A soft smile came to rest on Agnes's lips. "Just a bunch of little things."

All these years Molly had lived with a lie. She'd thought that there were only two people in the world who knew their little secret. Now she knew there were three. Could there be more?

"I didn't know who was actually who, but I could tell one from the other. And once you brought Lilly home, the cat was out of the bag." A sad grin flickered for a moment on Agnes's lips. "I mean, you were so full of love for that tiny creature, but it was the same caring you'd shown toward the stray cats in the alley and some of my stray customers. You weren't the one that gave birth."

Molly looked at her. "Why didn't you say anything?" Now it was her turn to stare hard. Her turn to ask the tough questions.

Agnes turned her eyes to the far wall. After what seemed like nearly forever, she finally shrugged. "I don't know. It seemed to be what you both wanted." She turned to look at Molly. "Maggie didn't want the baby, you did."

Agnes looked away again. "It wouldn't have been the first baby in this family that got passed around."

Molly suddenly saw things more clearly. "Danny was your son, wasn't he?" she asked.

Agnes, startled, nodded, her eyes flooding with tears that she blinked away.

"You never came to see him," Molly said. "Why? Wouldn't Dad let you?"

Agnes looked shocked. "Your dad? Oh, no. Your dad never knew. He thought your mother was really pregnant and he never knew I was. It was between your mother and me. She was desperate for a child. I never came back because I was afraid, afraid that I'd want him, afraid that the secret would come out somehow." Her face closed and fell. "And then it was too late."

Right before her eyes, Molly's steel-strong aunt faded. "Oh, Agnes." Molly enfolded her aunt in her arms and let the older woman cry. Why was everything so hard?

But Agnes wasn't one to cry for long. She pulled away from Molly. "Don't let it be too late for you," she said, her voice as brusque as ever. "Don't let it be too late for Jeff."

Molly just sighed and watched as Agnes went back to join the others. There were so many people here gathered together. The family, hundreds strong, laughing and talking together. Maggie kept looking up at her husband as if he were a god himself. Molly's father looked so gray and stooped, and her mother, well, she had a sadness about her that never seemed to go away. Molly felt as if they were all hers, and all her responsibility. How easily she could shatter their peace, how easily she could shout out their secrets.

Maggie and their father were together now. Talking but not laughing. Then Maggie's husband moved in to join them. The talking continued, still no laughing but small smiles made an appearance.

A family was like a pond. Ripples traveled its surface, reaching out and touching others. But, like a pond, it was also still and deep, with corners unknown to the outside world as well as to other corners of the pond.

She wasn't the only one that carried secrets in her heart. Agnes, Maggie, their father, their mother, their grandmother. Could anyone reach old age without secrets? Secrets that had been carried for a lifetime, deep in the dark corners of one's soul.

Gram was right, all those years back when she said Molly was the family chronicler. And as chronicler, she had a duty to fulfill. A promise of silence that she couldn't break, not even to clear herself in Jeff's eyes. She couldn't have her happiness at the expense of others, but she could give Jeff his child.

The reunion dinner was finally winding down. Someone was showing ancient home movies in the activity room, while some others were across the street in the schoolyard playing basketball.

"You need to take a break," Molly's mother told her as they wrapped leftovers. "You've done nothing but work all day."

Molly just shrugged. "Maybe I'll take a walk when we're done here."

"You're already done here," the older woman said and took the box of plastic wrap from Molly's hand. "Now go."

Molly obeyed, not joyfully but more like someone hurrying to the dentist to get it over with. She had something she needed to do, something she wanted to get over with. She walked along Broadway and onto the bridge, stopping to look out over the river, seeking wisdom from the waters that had flowed for millennia.

Her father was accepting her and it was obvious he loved his granddaughter. Molly had accomplished what she'd come here for. It was time to go.

Pushing away from the side of the bridge, she looked upriver, down south toward Indiana. There was a figure sitting on the rocks.

It could be anybody but there was something about the individual's bearing that told Molly it had to be Jeff.

She went back the way she'd come and turned down the hobo path behind the police station, the same one she'd always used when ditching school. Only this time she wasn't skipping out on a lark. This time she had the truth to tell. Well, a little bit of the truth.

The twisted, brush-hidden path soon brought her out to River Park. Jeff was the only one there, looking forlorn, pitching pebbles into the river.

"Hi," Molly said.

"Hi," he replied.

Jeff didn't turn around. Obviously recognizing her voice, or maybe just sensing it was her. Whatever it was, he continued pitching his pebbles. His anger seemed to have faded.

"You know how many of these stones I've thrown into this damn river?" he asked.

Molly didn't reply.

"Millions."

Jeff pitched another one halfway across the river.

"And yet the pile never gets smaller," he said, still looking out over the river. "There must be some kind of fungus that grows pebbles."

She moved over to his right side and sat down a couple rocks away. "I have to talk to you," she said, but he stayed stiff and rigid, like one of these old oak trees on the river bank. "Dad sang your praises to the investigator from the foundation."

"He's just a wonderful human being."

The sarcasm in his voice was almost thick enough to see. Certainly thick enough to feel. How would he react when she told him the rest? Maybe she should just sneak away.

"You were right yesterday," Molly said, pushing the words out before she had a chance to run away. "That wasn't Maggie you had sex with. It was me. You're Lilly's father."

One bit of truth to give Jeff what he should have and one lie to keep everyone else happy. Everyone but her. No matter what Agnes said, there were some things best left hidden.

Molly turned away, looking toward the Broadway Street bridge. "We'll need to set up visits and that kind of thing." She paused a moment. "If you want."

"I sure do," he said, nodding slowly.

"Lilly will like that."

"So will I."

They waited and watched the river. "Well." She stood up and brushed off the back of her shorts. "I best be getting back. People will start wondering if I got lost."

"Molly."

She stopped and turned back slowly.

"Does Lilly know yet?"

She shook her head. "I'll tell her sometime this weekend when there's enough time to do it right."

He nodded and she walked back to the path. The steady plop-plop told her that Jeff was throwing pebbles again. Maybe someday he'd have made a bridge to the other side. Except she wouldn't be there. She'd wrecked her half of the bridge and there was no rebuilding it.

Jeff continued tossing his pebbles at the slow-moving ripples of water, going north, wending their way toward Lake Michigan. He continued tossing long after the light patter of sandaled feet had died away. Long after the silence had totally wrapped itself around him and filled his ears.

His father was right. The gods had an interesting sense of humor.

After all his years of wandering and being alone, he'd finally found the woman of his dreams. A woman whom he thought he could trust.

And, wonder of wonders, he'd also found a child that he hadn't even known he had. A child, man's hope of immortality. But, the gods, while giving him one joy, took away the other.

What did they really care about a mere mortal like himself? His hopes, his dreams. They were all insignificant. As insignifcant as—

He looked down at the water surface rippling at his feet. As insignificant as tears in the river.

Chapter Thirteen

"Where the hell is your mind, boy?" his father asked. "I just told you the joint was on fire and all you do is nod your head like some kind of idiot."

"Sorry." Jeff pushed back the pizza he'd been pretending to eat. "I was thinking about some stuff at work."

"Right."

"Believe me if you want," Jeff snapped. "Don't if you don't want. I don't give a damn."

"My, aren't you in a charming mood," Paul said. "What are you doing, practicing for a run at governor?"

"I didn't ask you to sit by me," Jeff pointed out. "You're more than welcome to go find some more amiable company." He glared at his father, using anger to put out the lights of concern he saw shining in the old man's eyes. "As I remember, you never had any trouble with that."

His father looked for a moment longer, then dropped his eyes to examine the cup of coffee before him. Jeff felt a twinge of guilt and buried himself in his thoughts again. Why had he come to O'Day's anyway? He should have gone back to his apartment after Molly'd gone. All he was doing was moping and brooding, an activity best done alone.

Jeff snuck a look at his father. Those brown eyes, so much like his own, were watching him.

"You look like you're carrying a heavy load," his father said. "Want any help with it?"

Jeff shook his head.

A crooked smile formed on his father's face. "You always were a stiff-necked little punk," he said. "I was hoping you'd mellow in your old age, but looks like I'll have to wait another ten years, or longer."

Jeff tried to stoke the fires of anger in his belly. He piled on old wrongs and blew the oxygen of past misunderstandings onto the embers, but none of it did any good. He felt beaten and busted. No energy left to rant and rave.

"Well, you want to talk about anything, just give a whistle."

What was there to talk about? Just the same old stuff. Like, Dad, you have a grandchild.

His eyes started stinging again. In a lot of ways, he'd be happy to tell his father about his new status. The old man helped out with the kids at the Y once in a while and seemed glad to do it. Probably would be glad to have a grandchild of his own. Spoil the darn kid rotten.

It was the next question Jeff was really afraid of. *When's the wedding?*

Or maybe it wouldn't be a question at all. More like a statement. *You two have certainly been cozying up to each other lately. Looks like it's time to tie the knot and be honest about it.*

Jeff took a deep breath. All he had to do was form the words and spit them out. There was nothing complicated about them. *Lilly is my daughter. You are now a grandfather, have been for about nine years. Congratulations.*

"Hello, boys."

Agnes's throaty barroom voice cut through the fog of his indecision. Jeff looked up in time to see his father's eyes light up as he stood and pulled out a chair. Jeff felt a flicker of sunshine in his own world. The old devil. Looked like a man was never too old. At least a Spencer man.

"What's up?" Agnes asked as she sat down.

"Nothing much," his father replied as he signaled the waitress. "Just watching junior here mope and grump."

Agnes looked at Jeff with her hard, sharp eyes. "Anything wrong?" she asked.

Jeff shook his head.

"Everything's ginger peachy dandy," Paul said. "He just enjoys playing Oscar the Grouch."

"Oscar the Grouch!" Jeff forced a laugh through his throat. "I didn't know you were a 'Sesame Street' fan."

His father paused as the waitress gave Agnes a beer. "Hey, I got to keep in touch with the real world," he said. "Never know when you might quit playing the jolly young bachelor and settle down."

I already have, Dad. But no, he couldn't tell him, not with Agnes here. Jeff's spirits grew more and more depressed. He should just get the hell out of here. Leave the old man and Agnes room for their games.

"Did you know this place is for sale?" Agnes asked Paul, poking into the veil of silence that wanted to settle on their shoulders.

His father nodded. "I heard some rumors to the effect," he replied.

Agnes took a long pull on her beer. "Want to go partners?" she asked.

His father's eyes grew wide and Jeff suddenly saw the growth of a dream. The old man had been a heavy drinker in Jeff's youth and had never held good jobs for long. Now he supported himself as a jack-of-all-trades, doing light construction work. Jeff had never thought about it, but being the owner of his own business had to be a dream of his father's.

"How much are they asking?" his father asked.

"Don't worry about the money," Agnes replied. "I've got a good offer on my place in Denver."

"I'm too big for anyone to carry me," his father said.

"I don't want to carry you, big boy." Agnes laughed and patted his father's hand. "I need a man to help me manage this place. Usually there's no trouble, but when it comes, you need someone who can move heavy freight, someone one who can settle things down."

"Isn't your partner from Denver going in with you?" his father asked Agnes.

Jeff felt his stomach tighten up, twisting like a wet towel somebody was wringing out.

Agnes's face grew serious. "No." She shook her head. "I have a feeling she's going back to Denver."

Agnes looked Jeff straight in the eyes but he looked away. He had no control over Molly. He didn't want any.

"Do you guys have any family in Denver?" his father asked. "Close friends?"

"No."

Jeff stared hard at the table before him.

"When Molly gets back there, she and Lilly will be all alone."

He wouldn't look up. It wasn't his fault. He wasn't the one who'd started this damn lie.

The floorboards creaked over by the door. A quick glance out of the corner of Molly's eye was enough to tell her it was Agnes. She folded a pair of slacks and threw them on top of the pile of clothes in her suitcase.

"I want to leave early in the morning," Molly said softly as she picked up a blouse. The reunion was over. Most of the relatives had gone; the ones remaining would be gone by dinnertime.

"Yeah, I know." Agnes walked into the bedroom and sat on the edge of the bed. "Gram's in her room crying."

Molly's own lips quivered and she had to turn toward the wall, biting at her lower lip to bring it under control. She just nodded.

"She was really hoping that you would move into this old house," Agnes said.

"I know," Molly whispered. Her back was still toward Agnes and she wiped at her eyes with the back of her hands. "I should never have come back. It was like Pandora opening up her box."

"She wanted to keep this old place in the family."

"Damn it." Molly spun on her heels and faced Agnes. "I know it. I know all about it. Don't you think I've listened to all her hints?"

They exchanged glares but her aunt's hard old eyes were too much for Molly. She turned her attention back to packing.

"Lilly know about this?" Agnes asked.

Molly couldn't hold the tears back any longer. They'd been building for hours now, slopping over the edges here and there, but now they came. Huge tears, pouring down her cheeks like a summertime gully washer. Molly turned away, wiping at the hot rivulets with her hand.

"I—" Molly choked on a sob and tried again. "Lilly's been busy. Playing with her cousins. I hadn't had a chance to talk to her." Her words sputtered and dribbled away, like the dying flame of a burned-out candle.

"Where is she now?"

"The Dinklers took her to Bonnie Doon's in South Bend. The one down on U.S.31."

"Paul and I went there the other day." Agnes laughed softly. "That place hasn't changed a bit. It's still just like it was back when I was going there on my dates."

Suddenly everything came crashing down around Molly's head, causing her to grow faint. She sank to the floor, leaned against the bed and cried, really cried. She released gut-racking sobs, until her heart was near to breaking.

Why was everything so hard? All she wanted was to give her daughter a sense of family. After nine years of being scared, she'd thought it was safe to come home. Then she'd found Jeff and lost him because of her secrets. Why couldn't life be easier?

It seemed like hours later that, too exhausted to cry anymore, she sat on the floor, quietly sniffling. Agnes was still sitting on the bed looking down at her, with eyes as hard as steel.

"Did you talk to Jeff?" Agnes asked.

"Yes." Molly looked up at the ceiling as her fingers dug into her thighs. "Yes, I did."

She could feel her aunt's eyes on her, that famous Agnes stare, the one that would bring a roomful of brawling cowboys to sitting in their chairs like little choirboys, but Molly was too beaten to care.

"What did you tell him?"

The voice was tough, uncompromising. Molly wanted to tell Agnes to get the hell out and mind her own damn business but she couldn't. She was too tired, too weak. And when she needed it most, this woman had given her more than a helping hand.

"That he was Lilly's father."

"And?"

Molly didn't even try to not answer. "That he was right. It was me he had sex with back in high school, not Maggie. That I was pretending to be her."

Agnes just sighed. "Why?"

Molly shrugged. "Because the truth isn't mine to tell. It would cause too much damage if it was known."

"So you sacrificed your relationship with him."

"I was going back soon anyway."

"Uh-huh."

Molly got up and found a tissue to wipe her eyes. It was over. No dissecting would resurrect a relationship that was doomed from the beginning. She refolded a pair of slacks, carefully lining up the creases as if her life depended on the job being perfect.

"I'm sorry I didn't talk to you earlier," she told Agnes. "But I really want to get back. If you want to come along, fine. Otherwise, you can grab a flight back when you're ready. Probably be easier than that long drive."

Agnes looked away and Molly felt a flutter in the pit of her stomach. She fought it with words.

"We'll get the old homestead back in shape for you," Molly said.

"I'm not going back."

A ton of ice filled Molly's chest, surrounding her heart. Agnes turned back to look at her.

"I thought—"

Her aunt stopped and licked her lips. "I'm going to sell the bar. I don't know what the new owners'll want, but I made sure you and Lilly can stay in the apartment. At least, for a couple more months."

More ice poured into Molly's chest, making it hard for her to breathe.

"I'm just an old woman who wants to come back home." The words were gentle, and her aunt's eyes pleaded for understanding.

Molly could only nod. She was going to be alone. She and Lilly were going to be alone in the big city.

"What's wrong with Aunt Agnes?" Lilly asked, as she bounced into the bedroom. "Doesn't she feel good?"

Molly closed the dresser drawer as her daughter threw herself on the bed. Lilly's face was pink, radiating good health and joy.

"She's okay, honey. Just a little tired."

Lilly rolled back on her shoulders, putting her feet straight up in the air. "Where's Gram?" she asked.

"In her room," Molly replied.

Lilly rolled back into a sitting position. "She tired, too?"

Molly nodded.

"I guess stuff like reunions tire old people out, huh?"

Her daughter's young face was so full of concern, so full of love. Molly hoped that she would be able to get through their talk without crying.

"Did you have a nice time with the Dinklers?" Molly asked.

"Yep."

Lilly bounced on the bed. "Bobbie was eating a banana split and he had these two straws in his nose and his mother got really mad at him."

"Lilly, I—"

"And she grabbed him by the arm and he started laughing and spit ice cream and stuff all over the front of his shirt."

Molly sighed as Lilly laughed.

"I mean it was really funny, Mom."

"Lilly."

"I guess you had to be there." Suddenly Lilly noticed the suitcases. A frown creased her forehead. "Why are you packing?"

"We're going—" Molly clenched her teeth and spit out the word. "Home."

The word left a sour taste in her mouth and, from the look on Lilly's face, it didn't go down any better for her daughter.

"But we are home, Mom. I mean, like everybody lives around here."

"We live in Denver, honey," Molly tried to explain, fighting the nausea that wanted to overcome her. "That's where my job is. We were only visiting here."

"But you can get a job here." A whiny edge of panic was creeping into Lilly's voice. "And Gram's getting old. She needs us here."

Molly just looked at her daughter, fighting her own emotions for control.

"Can't Aunt Agnes buy a bar here?" Lilly asked.

But Molly just felt more and more pain. "Aunt Agnes isn't going back," Molly said. "She's staying here."

Pain was filling Lilly's eyes and they were getting near to overflowing. Oh, Lord, Molly thought. Why had she ever come back home?

"Bobbie Dinkler said I can stay with them when he goes to the cherry pit-spitting contest."

"Honey, please—"

"And what if my father comes looking for me?" Lilly's voice was approaching a wail.

"He's already found you," Molly said quietly.

Momentary confusion clouded Lilly's eyes, then they sparkled with an angry light. "It's Jeff," Lilly said. "Isn't it?"

"Yes."

"You don't like Jeff." Lilly was now shouting.

"Honey, baby." Molly needed to calm her daughter. Gram didn't need anything more to be upset about. "Please."

Molly reached for her, but Lilly pulled away, standing on the bed. "You've never liked Jeff. And he's so nice. Always doing things for you."

Molly felt so tired. "Lilly—"

Lilly jumped off the bed, tears now streaming down her face. "I'm not going to Denver. I'm staying here with my father."

Molly reached out for Lilly again, but she pushed away. Anger twisted her normally beautiful features into something ugly.

"I'm staying here with my father and my grandfather and everybody. My whole family is here and I'm not going back to Denver."

Molly grabbed her daughter by both arms. "Lilly, calm down, please."

"Leave me alone." Lilly fought against Molly's grasp. "I don't want to go with you. I hate you."

She turned and ran from the room.

Molly felt so sick and hurt. Why couldn't some merciful god just strike her dead?

Chapter Fourteen

Molly peered into the darkened hallways of the YMCA office building. No lights anywhere. She tried the door again, but knew it would be locked. The place was closed on Sundays and Jeff was elsewhere. She walked back to her car and drove the few blocks to his apartment.

This wasn't a meeting that she had really wanted, but she had lots of notes about the special-ed program that he would need. And if she was going to be adult about all this, she would see it through. Sometimes being an adult was a pain in the butt.

Molly pulled into the small lot by his apartment building and saw Jeff. He was working on an old Mustang in the carport. She walked over, her heart threatening to jump ship.

"Hello," she said.

He had some grimy-looking piece of engine in his hands and put it aside when he saw her. His eyes were a wall of ice. "Hi."

She wanted to tell him it was all a mistake and ask him to love her, but she couldn't go back. She held out the manila folder of her notes. "These are some recommendations for you about the special-ed program. Whoever you get to run it might have some other ideas, but this should help you get started."

"Thanks." He started to reach for it, but then looked at his grease-covered hand.

"I'll just leave it here," she said and put it in the front seat of the car.

"Okay."

They stared at each other for a long moment. Time lost all meaning. How she loved him! She'd never meant to hurt him; she wished there was some way to convince him of that. But his eyes were shutting her out too completely and she turned away. She couldn't leave yet, though; she needed just a few more minutes with him.

"Nice car," she said, running her hand over the leather seats of the convertible. "You restoring it?"

"Trying to."

"Been at it long?"

He shrugged as if he knew how empty this conversation was. "A couple of years."

"Should be quite a showpiece when it's done."

"Should be."

And that ended that. He picked up the engine part along with a wire brush. It was time to go.

"I told Lilly," she said.

He looked at her, not with love or anything close to it, but at least she still had a piece of him. "How'd she take it?"

"Okay." Molly conveniently forgot all about the screaming, but then that had been over leaving, not Jeff. "I thought you might want to take her out for dinner tonight. We're going to be leaving tomorrow."

"Yeah, I'd like that."

"I'll tell her. About six?"

He looked at his hands as if gauging the time it would take to clean them. "Yeah. That'll be great." He had managed an iota of enthusiasm for Lilly at least.

Molly tried to go then, but her feet wouldn't move. Once she got them to turn around, they wouldn't walk back to her car. She gave up and looked back at Jeff.

"I'm sorry," she told him.

He looked away, seeming to hear voices in the waves of heat that covered the town. "Sure," he said, then sighed. His whole body seemed to sag with weariness as he turned to face her. "Look, I'd like to say it doesn't matter, but I can't. I guess I'm not the stuff that real heroes are made of. I'm flesh and blood and have a flesh-and-blood daughter that I never knew existed until a few days ago. And then it was your father who had to tell me the truth!"

He turned away, staring into the depth of his toolbox for the longest time. He finally looked back at her. "Why couldn't you at least have told me?" he asked. "All right, so I had left senior year and you didn't know where I was and didn't think to ask my father. But we were close, so close, these past two weeks. You could have told me anytime, yet you didn't."

"I was wrong," she said. About so much.

He just laughed, a bitter sound that hurt her ears and her heart. "Well, at least you admit that. What a victory!" He stared at the engine piece in his hand. "If you'll excuse me, I want to get this back in before I take my daughter out to dinner."

Molly nodded, and raced back to her car. She wasn't sure how she managed to pull away, the world was all a blur, but she did.

Just give me the strength to get back to Denver, she prayed.

Jeff settled himself in the driver's seat, fastened his seat belt, adjusted the rearview mirror and forced a smile to his face.

"All set?" he asked his daughter. His daughter. Boy, that was going to take some getting used to.

He turned to look down at Lilly. She hadn't answered his question, just sat staring straight ahead through the windshield.

Poor kid. All her fantasies and now she finds out that dear old dad is just a plain ordinary Joe.

"Got a taste for anything special?" Jeff asked.

Lilly shrugged.

"Like some fried chicken?"

Another shrug.

"How about some boiled yak livers?"

She didn't give even the faintest glimmer of a smile. Just another run-of-the-mill shrug.

"I think I'd like a hamburger," Jeff said, starting the car. "And I know a good place. Okay by you?"

"Yeah, okay. Any place you want."

The voice was unusually soft but Jeff was most disturbed by the slump in her shoulders. He sighed and put the car in gear.

They drove in silence over to Main Street and then took a left across the street from HI's.

"Need any help with the seat belt?" he asked.

Lilly shook her head as she released the belt, opening her door and springing out. He walked around the car and was about to take her hand, but the rigid little body was all posted with No Trespassing signs.

"It's across the street," he said, pointing at the restaurant. "I think you'll really like it."

Lilly looked at the rambling two-story building, then started to walk toward the street. Jeff stopped at the curb and looked both ways. He was about to step into the street when he felt a tug at his pant leg.

Looking down, he first saw Lilly's solemn little face and then her partially upraised hand. "Oh, sorry," he mumbled as he grabbed her hand.

Damn. How was a guy supposed to know when it was right? Maybe when you cross the street. That had to be it. She was a little kid and had most likely been taught to take an adult's hand when she crossed a thoroughfare.

Would he ever catch on? It certainly wouldn't help, her living in Denver. By the time he'd learn the proper way, she'd be going back to Mommy. Then when he saw her again, he would have forgotten all he'd learned. Being a distant parent wasn't going to be a cup of tea. They went into the restaurant.

"How many tonight?" the hostess asked.

"Two." The words seemed rather soft so he gave himself more volume. "Just the two of us."

The dining room was fairly full. All people he knew, from growing up here to working with their kids these past few years. Faces turned toward him, all carrying broad smiles.

"Yep," Jeff said loudly. "Just me and my daughter."

Then his eyes swept the room. That's right, folks. This is my daughter Lilly. She's the prettiest little girl in the whole world and smart as a whip.

His eyes slowly swept the room one more time, ready for a fight. Maybe even spoiling for one. But everyone turned back to their own table and their own food, easy smiles still in place.

Hell, probably most of them already knew about it. He was the last one to find out.

The hostess led the way to a table in the corner and he and Lilly followed, still holding hands. Their waitress brought water almost immediately.

"We have a kiddie special tonight," the woman said. "A burger with French fries and a chocolate shake."

"How does that sound?" Jeff asked.

Lilly shrugged.

"That sounds good to me," Jeff said, forcing an enthusiastic bravado into his voice. "I'll have one, too."

The waitress raised an eyebrow.

"Hey, you know," Jeff said, forcing a laugh. "I'm just a big kid."

"Okay."

They were left in silence. A silence full of people talking, children laughing, and a baby crying. The noisy silence of other people's happiness. Lilly stared at the table in front of her.

"Did you see the train?" Jeff pointed to the little train that ran on a ledge all the way around the restaurant. It was just passing over their heads. "It goes all the way around the place. Around and around."

Lilly stared at the train for a long moment.

Yessir, Jeff thought. Around and around, going nowhere. Just like any conversation that he tried to start.

"This is a nice place," Jeff said.

Lilly nodded.

"You probably have a lot of nice places in Denver."

She shook her head. "We ain't got nothing in Denver."

Neither of them said anything more until the food arrived, and then all he did was ask for catsup for the French fries. Lilly stared a long moment at her food.

He took a tiny bite of his hamburger. "Good burger," he said, chewing vigorously.

Lilly nodded as she pushed a French fry around in the glob of catsup on her plate.

Actually the damn thing tasted like cardboard but Jeff knew that it was no fault of the cook's. He couldn't imagine anything that would taste good right now. Oh, Lord. He'd give his right arm to be able to bring a smile to his daughter's face.

He glanced at Lilly, then looked again. She hadn't made a sound but they'd started, silent tears flowing down her cheeks, falling off the end of her chin into the plate of food before her. His own food soured in his mouth.

"Do you want to go, honey?"

Lilly wouldn't look at him, but she nodded her head.

Jeff stood up, throwing a twenty on the table, then grabbed Lilly by her hand and hurried toward the door. The faces of the other patrons swam before him.

"Anything wrong, Jeff?" the hostess asked.

"She just has a little headache," Jeff snapped as they hurried past.

By the time they were out the door, Lilly was sobbing. Painful wails and torrents of tears.

"Honey, honey." Jeff clutched her to himself but she wouldn't stop.

"Is something wrong, sir?"

Two couples stood staring at them. He hadn't even heard them come up. Suddenly it dawned on him that he and Lilly were blocking the door.

"She doesn't feel good," Jeff said, picking Lilly up. "Headache." He hurried across the street toward the car.

Lilly was still crying and his own vision was too blurred to drive, so Jeff walked past the car to the edge of the parking lot. He sat on a bench, looking down at the river, while he held his daughter on his lap and let her sobs roll. He felt more useless than he had ever felt before.

After a couple of millennia, Lilly tired and her sobs tapered off.

"I'm sorry, honey," Jeff whispered into the hair on top of her head.

"What for?" Lilly asked.

What for? Lord, where should he start?

I'm sorry for doing something stupid ten years ago. No, that was selfish. I'm sorry for giving you pain, honey. A pain that I can't do a damn thing about.

"I'm sorry that I was never a secret agent," Jeff said.

Lilly sniffled and shrugged.

"I mean I was in the army, but I was never a secret agent."

"That's okay," she murmured.

"I always try my best," he said. "But I don't always do that great."

"I'm not that great, either," Lilly said.

"Oh, honey." Another tear ripped through his heart. "Don't ever say that. You're the greatest."

She shook her head resolutely. "I'm sort of short."

"Nothing wrong with that." Jeff protested. "I mean the best things come in small packages."

Again, she shook her head. "I'll never be able to dunk like Michael Jordan."

"No one else can, honey."

He hugged her tighter, experiencing an exquisite sense of pain and joy when she didn't resist, when she just cuddled deeper into his embrace.

"He's special in basketball. And you're special too."

"In what?"

"We don't know yet," Jeff replied. "You're just a kid."

Lilly quivered as a little sniffle escaped her nose.

"Hey, you have time. Even Michael Jordan didn't become a superstar overnight."

She didn't reply.

"He was cut from his high school basketball team."

His daughter looked up at him, disbelief heavy in her eyes.

"Scout's honor," Jeff said, holding up his right hand. "He was cut in his sophomore year."

She shrugged, then leaned back against him, staring at the river below them. Jeff wished he'd had an in with one of the gods. He would have asked that he and Lilly be turned to stone so that they could remain together forever.

"I gotta go back to Denver tomorrow." The words were whispered but they boomed and echoed all through his head.

"I know, babe."

"But why?" She was looking at him again.

Jeff pulled his eyes away and stared at the river. "That's where your mother lives and that's where her job is."

"We don't have a place to live anymore," Lilly said. "And she's a teacher. She can get a job anyplace."

Jeff gritted his teeth against the pain.

"Why can't we stay here?" Lilly said. "Then we could all live together like a regular family."

He still couldn't look her in the eye. How could he explain to his daughter that her mother had lied to him, cheated him in the most intimate way possible? That he wasn't strong enough to forgive that kind of hurt.

"Aunt Agnes is staying here." The pain was overflowing Molly's voice. "We're going to be all alone in Denver."

He looked down into her eyes and wanted nothing else but to extinguish the fires of her pain. "I'll move to Denver, honey. I'll be there with you."

"You'll live with us?"

"No." He had to look away again. "I can't do that, but I'll be right there if you need me."

Her body grew stiff and Jeff knew that the tears were coming again. He looked down, feeling defeat. Lilly was shaking her head. The tears were rolling.

"I have to stay here," she said.

"Honey, please."

"Grammy's getting old and I promised I'd take care of her."

"She'll be taken care of, honey. Honest."

"And Cousin Emma said that I could help take care of the baby horse."

"They'll take care of her."

"And Rufus doesn't want to go to Denver." The tears continued rolling and now the sobs were coming back.

"Honey," he said, trying to soothe her. "Honey."

"He doesn't have a yard in Denver."

"I'll get him one," Jeff promised. Anything to still her pain.

"He hates Denver. He gets sick there. He'll get sick and die."

The tears were really flowing now, punctuated by painful gut-racking sobs that he could feel. Jeff clutched at Lilly and rocked her, praying silently to every god in creation for his daughter to stop. He'd give his own life to stop her pain.

Why couldn't he just forgive Molly and be done with it?

Chapter Fifteen

Molly stared at the black liquid in her cup. She'd wanted to get an early start, but the best-laid plans of mice and—

She shook her head and rubbed her eyes. Nothing was going right. She should never have come back to this damn little burg here on the bluffs of the St. Joseph River. She had a life in Denver. Lilly had known little about her family and certainly nothing about her father, but they had been happy in their ignorance.

But Molly had released the truth and released pain and misery. On Lilly, on herself, on anyone in the family who was near and dear to her. Finding her father hadn't been all that great for Lilly. The child would have been better off with her fantasies. The pain in her daughter's eyes last night had been proof of that.

It had seemed like a good idea for Lilly to have a good-bye dinner with Jeff. Get to know each other. Set up plans for writing and telephoning. Plan trips and vacations together. But it obviously hadn't worked out that way.

Lilly's eyes had been all red when Jeff brought her home last night and she had run right up to her room, refusing to talk to anyone. Jeff had looked like the walking dead and hurried home himself.

Everyone else had just gone to bed after that. Gram, red-eyed and teary, and Agnes, hard-eyed like a gambler down to his last dime waiting for his hole card.

Good job. She wasn't Molly the Moron anymore. Anyone who could screw up as many lives as she had, had to be talented. Extremely talented.

The coffee in her cup was turning cold. Molly got up and spilled the remains in the sink. She hadn't slept at all last night, but she really had to get started. Put some miles between herself and Niles, then she could pull into a motel and catch a few Zs.

Leaning back against the countertop, she let her eyes roam around the pleasant old kitchen. She almost wished that this could be hers. That they could live here and Lilly could grow up surrounded by family. That she herself could grow old with—

Angrily, Molly pushed herself away. She looked up at the clock, clenching her teeth. She really had to go. The longer she hung around here, the harder it would be on everybody, especially Lilly.

She made her way up the stairs. She would get Lilly some breakfast, then they would go through their farewells. She tapped on Lilly's door before pushing it open.

"Honey, get up. Time to—"

She stared stupidly at Lilly's bed. It was all neat and made up. That was certainly unusual for little Miss Messy. Hadn't she slept in it?

Molly fought down feelings of panic. Lilly was just in the bathroom.

But the bathroom door was open and no one was in there. Lilly's toothbrush was dry. Molly wanted to scream for her daughter, but bit back the cry. Agnes and Gram were still asleep.

Rufus. That was it. Lilly had taken the dog outside. Molly hurried over to the window. There was no one in the yard. Molly was starting to panic now. She rushed back to Lilly's room.

"Lilly," she called quietly, a hoarse edge to her voice.

No answer. Was she hiding? Molly looked under the bed and in the closet. Nobody.

Oh, Lord. She knew that Lilly was upset about going to Denver. Had she run away? Molly's feet stopped at the bed. The door to the tower was closed. Maybe Lilly was up there?

Molly tried the door. Locked.

It was an old-fashioned lock, the kind that was locked with a skeleton key. She bent down and looked in the key hole. It was dark. The key was stuck in from the other side.

Molly rapped lightly on the door. "Lilly?"

"What?"

It was just one word and the tone was surly, but Molly felt a huge weight slip off her shoulder. "Honey, please open the door."

"No."

"Lilly, please."

"We're not going," Lilly said. "Me and Rufus are staying in Niles. And we're going to stay here forever."

"This isn't our home, dear."

"We ain't got no home in Denver, either," Lilly snapped. "Aunt Agnes is selling everything. We'll go back there and live out on the street. And people will just holler at us. And Rufus will get sick and die."

"Honey, we'll find another home."

"Rufus doesn't want to go back. He hates Denver."

"Lilly." Although she was weary, Molly put a strong measure of firm into her voice. "Open the door, please. And let's talk about this."

"No. You'll just tie us up and drag us away."

"Lilly! I'd never do that."

"I'll never see Gram or Aunt Agnes or Grandma and Grandpa again. And I'll never see my father."

Molly closed her eyes and leaned against the wall. A few weeks ago she was just an average single mother, keeping on top of the bills and making sure that Lilly was enjoying school. She'd never imagined a drama like this, not in her wildest dreams.

"What's wrong, dear?"

Her eyes popped open. Gram was standing in the doorway, Agnes just behind her.

"Nothing." Molly shook her head. "Nothing really. Lilly and I are just having a discussion."

"Has she locked herself in the tower?" Gram asked.

"Yes. Yes, she has." Molly put a hand to her forehead. "But I'm taking care of it."

Gram walked up to the door and knocked. "Are you all right, dear?"

"I'm never coming out," Lilly shouted back.

"I have it under control, Gram," Molly insisted.

"Would you like some milk and cookies, dear?" Gram shouted through the door.

"You're not going to trick me," Lilly replied. "I'm not going to Denver. I'm going to live with you the rest of my life."

"I'll enjoy having you, dear," Gram said. "But you'll have to eat, brush your teeth and go to the bathroom."

"I'm never coming out," Lilly insisted. "I don't care if you call the police or the SWAT team or the army."

"You can't stay up there forever," Molly said.

"Now, Molly dear," Gram soothed. "She knows that. It's time for some understanding."

Molly could only roll her eyes, immediately feeling like a teenager. She was losing it. Things were getting out of control. Certainly out of her control.

Gram turned to the door again.

"Lilly," she said. "Why don't you come out? I'll make sure that you're not taken any place against your will."

"You won't be able to stop her," Lilly insisted. "She'll put me in the trunk and take me to Denver."

"Your Jeep doesn't have a trunk," Gram reminded her.

Agnes came back to the door. Molly hadn't even realized she'd gone. "I tried to call Jeff," she said. "He wasn't at his apartment and there was no answer at the Y."

"Maybe he could talk some sense into her, dear," Gram agreed.

Molly sighed, feeling beaten. "I'll go see if I can find him."

She left Gram and Agnes with the locked door and trudged down to her room, slipping on some shoes and getting her purse before going downstairs. She would drive by the Y and see if his car was there. If it wasn't, she'd try his apartment and then River Park. She grabbed her car keys from the kitchen counter and pushed open the back door. Why did this have to happen—

Molly's feet skidded to a stop. There was Jeff, half-lying in the porch swing. His eyes were open and he was struggling to sit up, looking as if he'd spent the night there.

"What are you doing here?" she asked. She wasn't going to let her foolish heart jump to conclusions, but the morning took on new freshness.

"I came to see you." He ran his fingers through his hair, looking as if his circuits weren't all connected yet.

"And fell asleep?"

"I came about one o'clock. I wanted to catch you before you left."

"Oh."

He swallowed hard, looked away, then looked at her. "I don't want you to go."

Her heart leaped for joy, but she forced common sense back in. "Because you don't want to lose Lilly?"

"I've got Lilly," he said, taking a step closer. "She'll always be my daughter, no matter where you go. I don't want to lose you."

It took her by surprise. She said nothing, didn't know what to say. His words ought to thrill her, but instead they brought fear to her heart. As much as she loved him, as much as she wanted to spend the rest of her life in his arms, it was impossible. Not without telling him everything.

He came closer, close enough to take her hand. She clung to him, knowing it could be for the last time.

"I did a lot of thinking after I brought Lilly home," he said. "And no matter how I looked at it, it boiled down to me being an absolute jerk."

She tried to protest, but he stopped her, putting his hand gently over her lips. "No, I was. All I talked about was how you betrayed my trust, but I realized last night that I had done nothing to earn that trust. Lilly is a precious gift. Why would you entrust her to someone who hadn't proved himself?"

"It wasn't like that at all."

"Sure it was. Look at me back in high school. I wasn't ready to be in charge of a doorknob, let alone a child. Then, when you came back, you didn't know me from Adam. Why should I expect you'd rush over to tell me I had a child?"

"You had a right to know," Molly said.

"You had a right to protect your child." He put his hands on her upper arms, holding her, but not in an embrace. "Molly, I love you. Can you forgive me?"

Forgive him when she had been the one who lied? "Only if you forgive me," she said.

He pulled her into his arms and it was like being in heaven, like winning the race. She closed her eyes and dreamed the impossible. Why couldn't she have love and Lilly too? Why couldn't she grab hold of happiness and keep it in her heart?

She looked up into his eyes and saw herself, saw it was her distrust that kept her distant. She'd always been afraid to trust the truth to anyone else, but was it really because of Lilly or had that been an excuse her heart used to stay safe? Was she just plain afraid to let someone love her?

Suddenly, here in Jeff's arms, she wanted to take the risk. Their love was worth fighting for. She needed to take the risk for Lilly, for them all. None of them was complete without the others, none was fully alive alone.

Molly pulled away, looking up into his eyes. "It wasn't you. It was me," she said. "It wasn't that you hadn't earned my trust, it was that I wouldn't give it."

"Can you give it now?"

She took his hands, holding them so tightly that she couldn't fall, couldn't fail. She could do it. It was time to trust someone else.

"I didn't tell you Lilly was your daughter because I didn't know," she said. "I always thought it was Tim McGinn."

Jeff frowned. Anger and pain racing across his face. "Now, wait a minute." His voice was uncertain. "I have a hard enough time accepting that it was you, not Maggie, I made love to in senior year. Now, you're telling me that I wasn't the only one."

"I don't know if you were or not," she said.

He seemed not to hear her. The hurt and anger in his eyes changed to confusion. "Wasn't he that jerk with the baseball cap? I thought he went with Maggie."

"Yeah. He was her date the night of the Christmas formal, the night Lilly was conceived." Molly wished Jeff could read her mind, that the words would not have to be said aloud where the echoes in the wind could play with them, but he just stared at her. She took a deep breath. "I didn't know until a few days ago that you were Lilly's father, not Tim. I lied when I said you had been with me. You were with Maggie."

He continued to stare, obviously lost in the mire of lies and pretense that she had lived with for the past ten years.

"Maggie and I switched identities when we went out to Denver," Molly said. She searched his face for some sign of understanding, some hint that all would be well, but he just looked dazed. "She pretended to be me and gave birth under my name."

"So she was the one—" he said slowly, then frowned. "Why'd you agree to such a thing?"

She just shrugged. "I owed her."

"And your reputation was payment? God, Molly, why do you let people use you like that?"

"She needed my help."

"But to let people think— Did your parents know the truth?"

"No one knew but Maggie and me. And Agnes figured it out. But I just learned that yesterday."

"And now?"

"You know, too." She held his hands to her heart, as if with contact she could make him understand. "You see, once I saw Lilly, she was mine. It didn't matter who gave birth to her. I couldn't let her go. But then when I brought her home from the hospital, I was afraid that someone would find out that I hadn't given birth to her and I'd lose her. The more I grew to love her, the more afraid I was. I know it was irrational. Who was going to take her away? But I grew afraid of her learning the truth more than anybody else. That's why I never really got close to anyone. Loving someone means trusting them and I never met anybody I trusted enough to keep my secret until you."

"Oh, Molly." He pulled her into his arms, holding her as if he'd never let her go. "Why didn't I see the truth right away? I knew you weren't the way you made yourself out to be."

"At least, we found each other now."

His arms tightened around her. "I'm not letting you go," he said. "I hope you realize that."

She just laughed and let her lips brush his in the tenderest of promises. "You and your daughter. I think we'd better go up and rescue Rufus. He and Lilly are locked up in the tower, refusing to come out."

Jeff started to laugh. "Something tells me that I'm in for it now."

"And if you laugh in front of her, I promise to make it worse."

She took him by the hand and led him upstairs. Gram and Agnes were still talking to Lilly through the door. They backed away when Jeff and Molly entered.

"Lilly, your father's here," Molly told her.

"I'm not falling for that," Lilly called back.

"Lilly, I think it's time to come out," Jeff said.

"Don't let her kidnap me," Lilly pleaded.

"I won't." Jeff's lips twitched as he glanced Molly's way.

She frowned a warning at him not to laugh, though she'd never felt more like laughing herself. "What can I say? You're finding out the truth about me in time."

He took her hand in his. "I think it's too late."

Suddenly, they heard the sound of footsteps coming down the stairs behind the door. After what seemed like ages, a key rattled and the door swung open. Lilly and Rufus stood in the doorway. Lilly was unwrapping wet towels from their faces.

"What are those for?" Molly asked.

"We didn't have any gas masks," her daughter replied.

Molly looked from Lilly to Gram and Agnes to Jeff.

"Tear gas," he said. "If you don't have a gas mask, then a wet towel is the next best protection against tear gas."

"This is unreal," Molly said, frowning first at Jeff, then at Lilly. "You're as bad as she is. There'll be no more cop shows on late-night TV for either of you."

"Oh, yeah?" Jeff said with a broad wink at Lilly. "How you gonna stop us?"

"Early bedtimes and regular bed checks."

"Sounds tough. Think we can get around her?" he asked Lilly.

"I think Rufus wants to go outside," Agnes said and took the dog's collar. "Gram and I'll put on the coffee and get breakfast started."

Lilly frowned at Jeff, then her mother, catching sight of their hands intertwined. "Are we staying?" she asked suspiciously.

"Yes," Molly said. "We're staying."

Jeff let go of Molly's hand to put his arm around her shoulder. The weariness of the night made her sag slightly, but he was there to lean on. What a thrill to have someone to share with.

"Yes!" Lilly cried, pumping her arm. "Wait till I tell Rufus!" She ran toward the door.

"Lilly," Jeff called her back. "I think maybe we'll take that key."

She grinned and pulled it from her pocket, giving it to him before racing out. They heard her feet clattering down the steps, then a shout for Rufus.

Molly just turned to Jeff. He folded her in his arms. "What a daughter we have," he said with a laugh.

She looked up into his eyes, seeking the reassurance that she needed. "She is ours, isn't she?"

"Totally. Now and forever." He brushed the top of her hair with his lips. "Trust me. Just trust me."

She did.

Epilogue

December 25
Dear Diary:

We got this tradition in our family. The grandmother gives the granddaughter a diary and the granddaughter is supposed to write stuff in it.

I don't know what to write.

Gram says to just write a letter to yourself, like you were your own best friend. That's really dumb because I already know me, so why should I write stuff to myself? But one of the bad things about tradition is that you got to follow it all the time. So here goes.

I got a horse of my own now. It's that little horse I saw get born. She's a little girl horse and my two grandfathers bought her for me. I named her Starlight. She has to stay on the farm with her mother, but I get to visit her a lot. And when she gets bigger I'm going to ride her and we're going all over the world. We'll be some kind of rangers and go to South America to make them stop burning the rain forests and stuff like that.

Oh, I got a new grandpa. Aunt Agnes married her friend Paul, and now I got two sets of grandparents. I still call Aunt Agnes Aunt Agnes.

Aunt Agnes and Grandpa Paul got this really neat bar in town. It's not as big as the one Aunt Agnes had in Denver and there aren't as many fights, but it's all dark and neat. I get to go there and eat hamburgers and play on the bowling machine.

Aunt Agnes says when I'm old enough I can drink beer and bet on the ball games. Grandpa Paul laughs a lot when she says that, but Mom gets this really dinky look on her face, like she's drinking something sour.

Gram has an apartment in a place where old people live, and I got my grandma's old room. Grandpa Chuckie says Gram's getting older and needs special care. I said we could take care of her but she said that she didn't want to be a burden on her children and grandchildren. She always talks like that. We go to see her a lot and she visits us a whole lot.

Oh, yeah. Aunt Maggie had a baby. I went to see it. It's small and all wrinkled up. Mom started crying and called it Wrinkles No. 2. I don't why she had to cry. I mean, it isn't the kid's fault she's so ugly, and we can always hope she'll grow out of it.

Uh-oh. He's knocking on my door. He always does that when he thinks it's past my bedtime.

Oh, I forgot. My father Jeff lives with us now. He married Mom and lives with us in Gram's old house. That's the trouble with writing a letter to yourself and telling yourself stuff you already know. It's easy to forget that kind of stuff.

Anyway, Grandpa Chuckie married Mom and Jeff and we never went to Denver, which we couldn't do anyway because Aunt Agnes, who's now my grandmother, didn't have the bar no more.

Oh, boy. Dad's knocking on my door again. That means he wants to come in soon and kiss me good-night and turn off my light so I can't sit up all night.

Mom and Dad have been acting really strange lately. I mean, they sneak around the house and whisper a lot. They should just come out and tell me that I have a baby brother or sister coming. I mean, it's not like I don't know about things like that. I did see Starlight being born.

I hope Mom has twins. It'll give Dad something to do. I mean, he's on my case all the time, asking how is school and how are my grades and how come it took me so long to walk to the store. All kinds of stuff like that and I'm almost grown-up. You'd think since he got that big prize for the Y, he'd be busy doing new stuff there instead of bugging me.

There's the third knock on my door. That means, count to a hundred and ready or not, he's coming in to turn out the lights.

Well, I don't really need lights. Because when Mom and Dad go downstairs, Rufus and I sneak up into the tower. Gram says Broadway used to be the Great Sauk Trail in the real old days and if I watch real good, some night I'll see Indians and French trappers and colonial soldiers walking down toward the river. I guess this is another one of those family traditions. Maybe somebody ought to tell those other people because I haven't seen anybody yet. Rufus hasn't seen them yet either, but we'll keep looking. It's tradition.

*   *   *   *   *

THE DONOVAN LEGACY
from Nora Roberts

Meet the Donovans—Morgana, Sebastian and Anastasia. Each one is unique. Each one is...special.

In September you will be *Captivated* by Morgana Donovan. In Special Edition #768, horror-film writer Nash Kirkland doesn't know what to do when he meets an actual witch!

Be *Entranced* in October by Sebastian Donovan in Special Edition #774. Private investigator Mary Ellen Sutherland doesn't believe in psychic phenomena. But she discovers Sebastian has strange powers...over her.

In November's Special Edition #780, you'll be *Charmed* by Anastasia Donovan, along with Boone Sawyer and his little girl. Anastasia was a healer, but for her it was Boone's touch that cast a spell.

Enjoy the magic of Nora Roberts. Don't miss *Captivated, Entranced* or *Charmed*. Only from Silhouette Special Edition....

Take 4 bestselling love stories FREE

Plus get a FREE surprise gift!

In the spirit of Christmas, Silhouette invites
you to share the joy of the holiday season.

Silhouette

CHRISTMAS

Stories
1992

Experience the beauty of Yuletide romance with Silhouette
Christmas Stories 1992—a collection of heartwarming stories by
favorite Silhouette authors.

JONI'S MAGIC by Mary Lynn Baxter
HEARTS OF HOPE by Sondra Stanford
THE NIGHT SANTA CLAUS RETURNED by Marie Ferrarella
BASKET OF LOVE by Jeanne Stephens

This Christmas you can also receive a FREE keepsake Christmas
ornament. Look for details in all November and December
Silhouette books.

Also available this year are three popular early editions of
Silhouette Christmas Stories—1986, 1987 and 1988. Look for these
and you'll be well on your way to a complete collection of the
best in holiday romance.

Share in the celebration—with Silhouette's
Christmas gift of love.

SX92

TAKE A WALK ON THE DARK SIDE OF LOVE

October is the shivery season, when chill winds blow and shadows walk the night. Come along with us into a haunting world where love and danger go hand in hand, where passions will thrill you and dangers will chill you. Come with us to

In this newest short story collection from Silhouette Books, three of your favorite authors tell tales just perfect for a spooky autumn night. Let Anne Stuart introduce you to "The Monster in the Closet," Helen R. Myers bewitch you with "Seawitch," and Heather Graham Pozzessere entice you with "Wilde Imaginings."

Silhouette Shadows™
Haunting a store near you this October.